SECRETS IN THE NIGHT

D1593180

Books by Amanda Ashley

"Born of the Night" in Stroke of Midnight
"Midnight Pleasures" in Darkfest
"Music of the Night" in Mammoth Book of Vampire Romance
A Darker Dream
A Fire in the Blood
A Whisper of Eternity
After Sundown
As Twilight Falls
Beauty's Beast
Beneath a Midnight Moon
Bound by Blood
Bound by Night
Dark of the Moon
Dead Perfect
Dead Sexy
Deeper Than the Night
Desire After Dark
Desire the Night
Donovan's Woman
Embrace the Night
Everlasting Collection *(coming soon: the three Everlasting stories)*
Everlasting Desire
Everlasting Embrace
Everlasting Kiss
His Dark Embrace
Immortal Sins

Books by Madeline Baker

A Whisper in the Wind
Apache Flame
Apache Runaway
Beneath a Midnight Moon
Callie's Cowboy
Chase the Lightning
Chase The Wind
Cheyenne Surrender
Comanche Flame
Dakota Dreams
Dude Ranch Bride
Every Inch a Cowboy
Feather in the Wind
First Love, Wild Love
Forbidden Fires
Hawk's Woman
Kade
Lacey's Way
Lakota Love Song
Lakota Renegade
Love Forevermore
Love in the Wind
Midnight Fire
Prairie Heat
Reckless Desire
Reckless Destiny
Reckless Embrace

Reckless Embrace
Reckless Heart
Reckless Love
Reckless Series *(coming soon: the five Reckless stories)*
Renegade Heart
Shadows Through Time
Spirit's Song
The Angel and the Outlaw
The Spirit Path
Under a Prairie Moon
Under Apache Skies
Unforgettable
Warrior's Lady
West Texas Bride
Wolf Shadow

SECRETS IN THE NIGHT

AMANDA ASHLEY

Secrets in the Night

Copyright © 2022, Amanda Ashley

All rights reserved.
This edition published 2022

Cover by Cynthia Lucas

ISBN: 978-1-68068-321-9

The characters and events portrayed in this book are fictitious. Any similarity to real persons, living or dead, is coincidental and not intended by the author.

No part of this book may be reproduced or stored in a retrieval system, or transmitted in any form or by any means, electronic, mechanical, photocopying, recording or otherwise, without express written permission of the publisher.

This book is published on behalf of the author by the Ethan Ellenberg Literary Agency.

You can reach the author at:
Email: darkwritr@aol.com
Websites: www.amandaashley.net and www.madelinebaker.net

DEDICATION

To Will and Heather
With love
May you find your own
happily-ever-after
now and forever more

TABLE OF CONTENTS

CHAPTER ONE

Los Angeles, California
Present day

Skye had dreamed of him again last night, a tall, dark man clad in a long, black leather coat. Hair the color of ebony fell to his waist, the perfect compliment to his copper-hued skin and deep blue eyes. His features were strong and beautifully masculine, from his fine straight brows to his high cheekbones and hawk-like nose.

It was the same dream she'd had every night since she had gone to the Natural History Museum to photograph their Indians of North America exhibit three weeks ago.

Skye didn't know why she continued to dream about a warrior who had lived over a hundred and fifty years ago, or why, in her dreams, he wore faded blue jeans and a black tee shirt instead of the breechclout and feathers he wore in the museum's life-sized cut-out. A placard stated that his name was Wolf Who Walks on the Wild Wind, and that he had been a man of some importance in his tribe.

Skye blew out a sigh. Perhaps she was dreaming of him simply because his image had captured her imagination, so much so that she had returned to the museum again this afternoon. She had spent the last thirty minutes staring at his image, thinking it was a shame that men like Wolf Who Walks on the Wild Wind didn't exist anymore. Of course, it was probably just as well. Most of today's women wouldn't know what to do with a strong, independent, alpha male. They wanted men who were caring and sensitive, men who were willing to help with the dishes and change the baby's diaper. Today's women didn't want to be taken care of. They wanted to go out into the world and earn a living and be treated as equals. They didn't want to stay at home and raise children like their great grandmothers had. They wanted to prove they could do everything a man could do, and do it better.

Kick-ass heroines, that was what the women of the world wanted to be these days. A part of her wanted to be a woman like that, too—strong-willed and confident, able to fight her own battles, dependent on no one, and yet another part of her couldn't help thinking it might be exciting to live with the kind of man who took what he wanted, a man strong enough to defend her honor, or her life, if need be. A man who would climb the highest mountains, swim the deepest rivers, or slay a fire-breathing dragon to save her. Not that there was much call for that kind of thing these days, she thought with a wry grin. Still, it would be nice to have a man like that, a combination of Superman and Mick St. John, with a dash of Jason Momoa, and a smidgen of a young Clark Gable added for good measure.

Skye sighed as she gazed at the Indian's face again.

And had the oddest sensation that he was looking back at her.

CHAPTER TWO

South Dakota
1878

Wolf rested his foot on the brass bar rail in the Ten Spot saloon, one hand curled around a glass of rye whiskey. Standing there, he found himself again thinking of the woman he had seen in the museum. She had been much in his mind since he had first seen her in modern-day Los Angeles some three weeks earlier—a petite, slender woman with an abundance of wavy red-gold hair and beautiful, honey-brown eyes. She had been standing in front of a life-sized cardboard out-out that been blown up from a picture some Western photographer had taken of him back in the late 1800s.

Keeping out of sight, Wolf had watched her as she studied the cardboard figure from every possible angle. It was an amazingly realistic likeness, even if he did say so himself.

Curious to know more about the woman, he had followed her out of the museum. She had gone shopping at Nordstrom's, taken in a movie, had dinner with a tall, blond, young man who had driven her home and kissed her goodnight at her door step. Wolf had been surprised by the sharp stab of jealousy he had experienced when he watched the two of them embrace.

He had lingered in the shadows outside her house long after she had gone inside, bemused by his jealousy over a woman he didn't know. Later, after he had dined on a succulent brunette, he had returned to the past, safe from the hunters and the bleeders in Los Angeles, but determined to see the woman again.

Wolf glanced around the Old West saloon. The occupants were a rough lot—uneducated cowhands in stovepipe chaps and cowhide vests; ruthless gamblers wearing white linen shirts and fancy cravats; drummers clad in striped suits and bowler hats; blue-clad troopers from the nearby fort. And flitting among them like colorful butterflies were the soiled doves, cooing and wooing, enticing the men to the cribs upstairs. The air was rank with the acrid stink of cigar smoke, cheap perfume, and unwashed bodies. The painting behind the long mahogany bar featured a buxom, red-haired nude reclining on a bearskin rug.

Wolf blew out a sigh. He much preferred the more refined haunts of the twenty-first century, although these days it was dangerous to linger there for too long. Vampyres, once accepted by humankind, were now hunted relentlessly by the Hunter-Slayers who had sworn to wipe the Undead from the face of the earth. He had to admit, they were doing a damn fine job. He knew of only a handful of vampyres still living in modern-day Los Angeles where there had once been a hundred or more. Then there were the Bleeders—humans who hunted vampyres for their blood and sold it on the black market for its alleged aphrodisiac powers.

And so Wolf traveled back and forth from the past to the future, feeding in the future where he had been turned, hiding in the past where he'd been born. Although, with his obvious Lakota heritage, it wasn't always safe in the past, either.

He grinned ruefully. It seemed that no matter what century he resided in, someone was out to kill him. Still, he spent the majority of his time in the future, not only because he preferred it, but because, in the past he was human, weak and vulnerable, subject to death like any other mortal.

He had to admit, it was a strange life. But, whether in the past or the present, he was always aware of his vampyre nature and, as the decades passed, he had come to prefer being a vampyre.

Skye returned to the museum late the following afternoon, drawn, as always, to the life-sized cardboard figure of Wolf Who Walks on the Wild Wind. She had spent the last three weeks scouring the Internet and searching the library, learning everything she could about him. Although he hadn't been a chief, he had been a warrior of great renown. He had fought against Custer at the Battle of the Little Big Horn, he had been at Fort Robinson the day Crazy Horse had been killed by a soldier. She had found Wolf's name and a grainy black-and-white photo in an old book on North American Indians. What she couldn't seem to find was information on how he had spent his later years and when or where he had passed away.

She tilted her head to the side. Why was she so obsessed with his past? she wondered. It was easy to see why she was so captivated by his image. If the life-size cut-out was accurate, he stood over six feet tall, had long black hair, tawny skin, broad shoulders, a flat belly, and eyes so dark a blue they were almost black.

Sighing, Skye left the museum. At home, she ate dinner, took a leisurely bubble bath, then went to bed, hoping she would dream of him again.

As she closed her eyes, she whispered his name.

Standing outside the woman's house, Wolf smiled as the sound of her voice whispering his name was carried to him by an errant breeze.

Perhaps it was time for them to meet.

A thought took him to her bedside and into her dreams...

She was walking at the edge of a clear, blue lake. Lakota lodges rose in the distance. The air was fragrant with the scent of sweet grass and sage. Painted ponies grazed on the lush grass near the village.

She paused and he knew she was looking for someone.

Looking for him.

In her dream, he stepped out from behind a cottonwood tree and drew her into his arms. Startled, she stared up at him, her eyes wide with fear until she recognized him.

"It's you," she murmured.

"You were looking for me."

She nodded, her gaze searching his. "How can this be? You feel so real, yet I know I'm dreaming."

"I am as real as you want me to be, Skye."

"How do you know my name?"

"Does it matter?"

"No." A faint smile teased her lips. "Since this is only a dream..." Cupping his face in her hands, she went up on her tiptoes, drew his head down, and kissed him.

She was unprepared for the wave of sensual heat that spiraled through her as their lips met. She told herself it was only a dream, but it was unlike any dream she had ever known.

She was breathless when he lifted his head. His gaze burned into hers, hotter than a thousand suns.

And then he was gone.

Skye woke with a start. Bolting upright, she switched on the bedside lamp, her gaze searching the shadows, but there was no one else in the room.

"Just a dream," she whispered as she slipped back under the covers and turned off the light.

"Just a dream." Skye murmured the words again when she woke in the morning.

But how to explain the long, black hair she found on her pillow?

Skye had just left the museum the following evening when she saw a man striding toward her on the sidewalk. A tall, broad-shouldered man clad in blue jeans, a long, black leather coat over a navy blue tee shirt, and boots. She blinked and blinked again, certain she was seeing things, but he was real. Solid.

She came to an abrupt halt, felt her eyes grow wide when she saw his face. It couldn't be.

But it was.

The man from her dreams. Her cardboard obsession come to life. Wolf Who Walks on the Wild Wind.

A slow smile spread over his face when he drew closer.

She heard him say, "Good evening, miss," just before she fainted dead away.

Eyes closed, Skye turned onto her side, wishing she could remember more of her bizarre dream, but the only thing she could recall was fainting after seeing a man who looked exactly like the cardboard cut-out of Wolf Who Walks on the Wild Wind.

Opening her eyes, she sat up, and decided she must still be dreaming, because she was lying on a sofa in a house she had never seen before, and he was standing beside her.

"Feeling better?" His voice was deep, smooth and yet rough, like velvet brushed the wrong way.

"Who are you?" she demanded. There was no need to be polite. He had kidnapped her, after all.

"Jason Wolf. And you're Skye Somers."

Skye stared up at him, a sudden chill skating down her spine. "How do you know my name?" She gained her feet, thinking she had asked that same question in her dream last night. She stood there, confused and ill-at-ease at being face-to-face with a man who so closely resembled one who was long dead. He was watching her intently.

"I looked in your wallet, of course, in case you needed medical care." The lie rolled easily off his tongue.

"I'd like to go now."

He nodded, then jerked a thumb over his shoulder. "Door's that way."

Was he going to let her go, just like that? "Why did you bring me here?"

"You fainted. Would you rather I had left you lying unconscious on the sidewalk?"

She crossed her arms under her breasts, regarding him through suspicious eyes. "No, of course not."

"Is something wrong?"

"No. It's just that you look so much like...like someone else."

"A friend of yours?"

She shook her head. "You'd laugh if I told you."

"Try me."

"Well, you look just like the life-sized cutout of an Indian at the Natural History Museum." She could easily imagine him wearing a breechclout and moccasins, an eagle feather tied in his long black hair, his handsome face painted for war.

"That's easily explained. We're related somewhere in the distant past."

"Really?" Skye stared at him in disbelief. What were the chances that she would run into one of Wolf Who Walks on the Wild Wind's descendants? "Can you tell me anything about him? When he lived and where...?"

"Like I said, we're only distantly related."

Disappointed, Skye shook her head to clear it. Maybe she was still dreaming, because none of this seemed real. Murmuring, "Well, good night, Mr. Wolf. Thank you for your help," she moved toward the door, only then remembering that her car was still at the museum.

"I could drive you home."

She paused, her thoughts racing. Getting into a car with a total stranger didn't seem like a good idea, but then, she was alone in his house. If he had meant her any harm, he'd had ample time and opportunity to do it. "I don't know..."

"At least let me call you a cab."

9

She turned to look at him. "Thank you."

He gestured at the sofa. "You might as well sit down while you wait. Can I get you something to drink? Water? A glass of wine?"

"Water, please." She sank down on the sofa, stomach fluttering, while he called for a cab. He was incredibly handsome, thoughtful, polite. And he scared her half to death, although she couldn't say why. He didn't look the least bit ominous, hadn't said or done anything to alarm her. But there was something about him … something that had all her instincts for self-preservation on edge.

Her thoughts scattered when he handed her a glass of water.

"Thank you." She took it from his hand, felt a jolt of electricity race up her arm as her fingers brushed his.

Perhaps sensing her unease, he sat on the love seat across from the sofa. Pulling a phone from his back pocket, he called for a cab.

Skye bit down on her lower lip as she glanced around. The room was large, the walls white, the carpet a deep shade of green. A fireplace took up most of one wall to the right of the matching black leather sofa and love seat. A wrought-iron candelabra hung on the wall over the mantel, flanked by two desert landscapes.

Conscious of his gaze, Skye sipped her drink, then cleared her throat, wishing she could think of some clever remark to break the taut silence between them.

"Do you go to the museum often?" he asked.

"Yes. No. Well.…" She shrugged. "I'm fascinated by the current exhibit."

"Let me guess. You love the romance of the Old West. Stories of cowboys and Indians and the like?"

"I always wished I'd been born back then," she confessed. "It seemed like such a wonderfully exciting time to live."

He grunted softly. "Believe me, it wasn't all that great."

"Oh? And how would you know that?"

"I'm related to Wolf Who Walks on the Wild Wind, remember?"

"Of course." She stared into the glass. Perhaps his grandparents and great-grandparents had told him stories about the old days. His parents might have recorded stories that had been passed down from family to family through the ages, first-hand accounts of battles won and lost, passed orally from father to son until someone had written them down. Authors in the past had often interviewed prominent characters in the Old West. Scores of books had been written about Butch Cassidy, Wyatt Earp, and Doc Holiday, Red Cloud and Sitting Bull, Cochise and Geronimo.

She had a dozen questions she wanted to ask, but he hadn't seemed inclined to answer them before and she was reluctant to try again.

"Are you married?" Wolf asked.

"Not anymore." She glanced over her shoulder when a horn honked. "My cab must be here."

"I'll see you out."

Rising, she placed her glass on the end table, picked up her handbag, and walked toward the door, acutely aware of the tall man striding beside her.

He leaned forward and opened the door for her. "It was nice meeting you, Miss Somers."

"Thank you for your hospitality."

"My pleasure." He smiled as he watched her walk toward the cab, and then, remembering her sweetness, he licked his lips. Meeting her had, indeed, been his pleasure.

11

Near dawn, Wolf left his house. Using a bit of vampyre magic, he transported himself to the cave hidden high in the sacred Black Hills of South Dakota. The location was known to only a chosen few of his tribe. It had been long ago when curiosity had sent him into the future. He had planned to stay only a night and a day, but Fate had had other plans. He had met a mysterious woman that night and she had changed his life forever.

He stood outside the cavern's entrance for a moment, enjoying the view of the Plains below. An uncomfortable tingle along his spine told him dawn was only moments away.

Taking a deep breath, he ducked inside the cave. After changing into a pair of buckskin pants and a long-sleeved shirt, he strapped on his holster and settled his Stetson on his head.

He stood there a moment, his eyes closed, and then he began to chant softly, the ancient words echoing off the walls, until the words faded away and with them, his preternatural power.

When he stepped out of the cave, it was 1878.

His favorite horse awaited him.

CHAPTER THREE

W olf swung into the saddle, then lifted his face to the sky. He sat there for a long moment, adjusting to the sense of weakness that came with the loss of his vampiric powers even as he relished the warmth of the mid-day sun on his face.

The air in the past smelled of sage and pine, of earth and sweet grass. There was a sense of freedom in the past, a sense of adventure, that was lacking in the future. There were no brick-and-glass buildings here to block one's view of the forests and mountains, no discordant horns or squealing tires to mar the reverent stillness of the sacred Black Hills.

People longed for the old days and in many ways, it was a great place to live, but they rarely took into account the down side, like the absence of modern plumbing and medicine, the high death rate among pregnant women and newborns, the amount of time it took to travel from one end of the country to the other. He had seen men and women in the Old West die long, drawn-out deaths from cuts, infections, and viruses that were easily cured in the twenty-first century.

And then there were the inventions that modern people took for granted, like cell phones and computers, washers and dryers, cars and planes, iPods and eReaders and the myriad other innovations that were so commonplace in the future, but would have been viewed as miraculous in this time.

He touched his heels to the pinto mare's flanks and she moved out at a brisk walk.

Time-traveling was an interesting phenomena. No matter how long he stayed in the future, it was always the next day when he returned to the past. Equally strange was the fact that time in the future moved as it should. It was always night when he returned to the future, and always mid-day when he revisited the past.

He had inherited the ability to travel through time from his grandfather, who had inherited it from his grandfather, and so on. Wolf thought it odd that the ability to move through time and space skipped a generation. As far as he could tell, there was no rhyme or reason for why it worked that way, but it did.

He rode all that day, and reached the dusty little town of Tumbleweed Springs at sundown – a town that no longer existed in the future. It was his usual haunt when he was in the past since it was only a day's ride from the cave.

Dismounting in front of the Ten Spot saloon, he tossed the pinto's reins over the hitch rail and then pushed his way through the batwing doors.

The usual Saturday night crowd was gathered along the bar, shooting the bull and telling tall tales. One of the doves sat beside the piano player, belting out a sad song about a love gone wrong. Wolf grunted softly. Was there any other kind?

The men at the bar made way for him as he approached, some out of fear of his reputation as a fast-gun, some out of respect, some because they just hated half-breeds. If his mind hadn't been preoccupied with Miss Skye Somers, it might have bothered him. Now, he scarcely noticed. What was there about her that intrigued him so? Sure, she was beautiful, but there were a lot of beautiful women in the world, past and present. Hell, he had bedded more than his share of them. He knew on some deep inner level that making love to Skye would be as different from sleeping with any other woman as this life was from his other one.

He ordered a whiskey, downed it in a single swallow, and ordered another.

He had come here intending to stay awhile, maybe even go visit his mother's people for a month or two, but suddenly that didn't seem like such a good idea. A lot could happen in two months' time. Skye could marry the man he had seen her with, move to another town, get hit by a truck. Mortals came and went all too quickly. He couldn't take a chance on anything happening to her. Right or wrong, he wanted to get to know her better.

And he couldn't do that from here.

"Hi, Wolf."

He turned at the sound of a familiar voice. Hattie was the youngest whore in the place. Still pretty, with rosy cheeks and eyes that still held a glimmer of hope, unlike her older sisters in the trade.

"How you doing, kid?" he asked.

"Business is slow." She trailed her fingertips down his arm. "I could use a drink."

"Sure." Motioning for the bartender, Wolf ordered her a glass of beer.

"I have some time." Lowering her voice, she whispered, "No charge."

"Not tonight, darlin'."

"You always say no," she said, pouting. "Don't you like me?"

"I like you fine." Hattie was a sweet kid, and he might have taken her up on her offer if she hadn't been so damn young.

And if he hadn't been so intrigued by the lovely Miss Somers. "Maybe another time, darlin'."

"I'll get you upstairs one of these days, Jason Wolf. You just see if I don't."

Grinning, he brushed a kiss across her cheek. Then, whistling softly, he left the saloon.

The faint scuff of a boot heel was his only warning. He dropped into a crouch, his hand reaching for his gun as his would-be assassin fired. Wolf returned fire while the echo of the first gunshot still hung in the air.

He didn't wait to see who it was. In a single fluid movement, he holstered his Colt, grabbed the pinto's reins and vaulted into the saddle. It had been awhile since anyone had taken a shot at him, but there was always a risk that someone would recognize him. It would be considered quite a coup for the man who took him down.

In moments, the town was behind him.

Riding hard, he returned to the cave. Dismounting, he stepped inside and chanted the ancient words that carried him from the past to the future.

Clad once more in the clothes he'd left behind, Wolf stepped out of the cave into the twenty-first century. A thought took him to Los Angeles. Although the cave was located in the hills of South Dakota, it took only moments to will himself wherever he wished to go. The world was a big place and he had seen most of it at one time or another. Although he loved the Old West, there was something about this century that he found exciting. And he had to admit, he loved being a vampyre. He loved the supernatural strength, the unbelievable power, his enhanced senses.

And the blood.

As always, his first order of business was to satisfy his hunger. Traveling through time always weakened his preternatural powers and spiked his thirst.

Day or night, prey was no problem in the greater Los Angeles area. Wealthy businessmen, wanna-be actors, streets lined with the homeless, the down-trodden, the forgotten. He traveled to La Brea Avenue, perhaps the oldest and longest street in the city, one that ran through a variety of neighborhoods, good, bad, and ugly.

He found a suitable donor stepping out of a high-end dress shop. He eased up beside the tall, middle-aged woman, mesmerized her with a glance, and walked her into the shadows between two buildings. He quickly took what he needed, escorted her back to the front of the store, and wiped the memory of what had happened from her mind.

Whistling softly, Wolf transported himself to his house, changed into a pair of black slacks, a dark-gray shirt, and his favorite pair of dress boots before willing himself to the museum, since it was the most logical place to find the woman he sought.

He wasn't disappointed.

"I was hoping you'd be here," he said, as he came up beside her.

"Were you?"

"Didn't you come here looking for me?"

A faint flush stained her cheeks. "Maybe."

"Maybe?"

"All right, I admit it. Are you happy now?"

"Yes, ma'am. Can I buy you a drink? There's a quiet little nightclub just around the corner."

Skye nodded, thinking there was no point in playing hard to get. Side by side, they left the museum and strolled down the sidewalk. Once again, she found it impossible to think of anything to say. She had never had trouble making small talk with other men. Why this one?

He held the door for her, followed her inside. It was a lovely room, the lighting and the music low and intimate. Booths lined one side of a small dance floor, tables the other.

"Over there," Wolf said, gesturing toward an empty booth.

He sat across from her, thinking she was even more beautiful than he remembered. Her hair fell over her shoulders in gentle waves, her honey-brown eyes were open and honest and curious. His gaze moved to her throat, to the pulse throbbing there, as he listened to the seductive beat of her heart, now pounding faster than usual, due, no doubt, to her innate sense of self-preservation. She seemed to be one of the few mortals who, on some deep, inner level, recognized when they were in danger.

When a waiter came to take their order, Wolf asked for a glass of red wine. Skye opted for a strawberry daiquiri.

"Why were you looking for me?" she asked, as the waiter moved away from their table.

He lifted one brow. "You're a beautiful woman interested in my heritage. I thought I'd like to know you better." He grinned at her, displaying remarkably white teeth. "Why were *you* looking for *me*?"

She laughed as her cheeks grew hotter. "I think you know."

SECRETS IN THE NIGHT

"Because I'm beautiful and you're interested in my Lakota background?"

"Something like that. Was that your house I woke up in the night we met?"

"Did you like it?" he asked as the waiter delivered their drinks.

"It's lovely."

"You said you were married but not now."

"My husband was killed by a drunk driver."

"I'm sorry, Skye."

"It was a long time ago."

"Do you have kids?"

A shadow passed behind her eyes. "No." She had miscarried the baby a few days after Joe was killed.

Seeing the hurt in her eyes, he let the subject drop, though he did wonder how she had acquired that enormous house. With prices being what they were, few people starting out could afford such a place on a single salary. But it was none of his business.

"What do you do for a living?" she asked in an obvious attempt to change the subject.

"What do you think I do?"

She took a sip of her drink, studying him over the rim of her glass. "Hmm. I don't know. Doctor? Lawyer? Indian chief?"

He chuckled. "Sorry, no."

"So? What *do* you do?"

"I own an interest in a casino in South Dakota."

"Really? Are you in L.A. on vacation?"

"No. I travel back and forth between California and the Dakotas from time to time."

"How long will you be here?"

His gaze moved over her. "Longer than I planned."

The look in his eyes made her heart skip a beat. There was no mistaking his meaning, Skye thought, as she took another sip of her drink.

Wolf lifted his glass. "To getting to know you better." He drained his glass and set it aside. "Would you care to dance?"

The thought of being in his arms sent a shiver of anticipation down her spine. At her nod, he stood and took her hand.

Excitement thrummed through her as he slipped his arm around her waist and drew her close. The lighting was dim, the music soft and slow, and the man ... he was tall and sexy and incredibly light on his feet. Everything female within her came to attention as they swayed to the music. There was something about him, some latent, inner strength, that called to her. This was a man who never backed down, one who would always fight for those he cared for. A man who would protect her with his life. She didn't know how or why she felt that way, only that she did.

His gaze locked with hers when she looked up at him. His eyes were a dark, dark blue. Clear and mesmerizing. Filled with an emotion she didn't understand. Skye felt suddenly adrift when he lowered his head and rained kisses along the length of her neck.

Wolf swore softly as he lifted his head and ran his tongue over the tiny bite marks in her throat. Almost, he had taken too much. Holding her arm to steady her, he led her back to their table, eased her onto her chair.

Skye blinked several times, and then frowned. When had they returned to their table? She looked up as the waiter brought them another round of drinks. Why did she feel so strange?. Why didn't she remember leaving the dance floor?

"What shall we drink to?" Wolf asked.

"What?"

He lifted his glass. "What shall we drink to?"

"I don't know." She massaged her forehead with her fingertips. "I feel kinda dizzy."

His mind brushed her, wiping away her confusion. "I guess I twirled you around a little too fast on that last dance."

"Yes. Yes, that must have been it. I feel fine now."

They danced one more time before leaving the night club and walking back to the museum parking lot where she had left her car. She unlocked the door and when she turned to say goodnight, Wolf took her in his arms.

"Can I see you again tomorrow night?"

Skye nodded. She had a date with Ken, but that was easily broken.

"Shall I pick you up?"

She hesitated. She had just met the man, knew little about him. Yet his heritage and the possibility of getting to learn more about his people was irresistible, as was the man himself. He had been a perfect gentleman thus far. Besides, if she had second thoughts between now and tomorrow night, she could always plead a headache.

Deciding to take the risk, she gave him her address and cell number. "What time?"

"Six-thirty okay?"

"Perfect."

Leaning down, he brushed his lips lightly across hers. "Good night, Skye."

"'Night, Jason."

Hands shoved in his back pockets, Wolf watched her pull out of the parking lot. He had a feeling it would be a long time before he returned to the past, because everything he wanted was right here, right now.

CHAPTER FOUR

Skye woke with the sun in her face. For a moment, she simply lay there while her mind replayed last night's date with Jason Wolf. He was the most incredibly handsome man she had ever met, and she had photographed quite a few in her day – including some of Hollywood's sexiest hunks— for one magazine or another. Sadly, with the popularity of the Internet, many magazines had either gone out of business or gone digital and as a result, her work load and her income had suffered. She had shot a few models for book covers in the past and she couldn't help thinking that Jason Wolf would be the perfect model for the historical western romances that had once been so popular.

Jason. What was there about him that intrigued her so? Yes, he was handsome, but it was more than that. She had a met a lot of hunky guys in Los Angeles, even dated a few. Perhaps it was his eyes – those deep blue eyes that seemed to see right through her. Perhaps it was his voice, as smooth as double bonded bourbon and almost as intoxicating as being in his arms. She blew out a sigh as she threw the covers aside and slipped out of bed. Whatever it was, she was helpless to resist.

Humming softly, Skye headed for the shower. No need to go to the museum today and drool over the cardboard figure of Wolf Who Walks on the Wild Wind, not when she had a date with his very sexy descendent tonight.

But first, she had to call Ken and cancel their date, not that it would be much of a problem. They had only gone out a couple of times and while he was nice and not bad looking, there was no chemistry between them, she thought. Nothing like the undeniable attraction that sparked between her and Jason Wolf.

Warren Gray drove slowly past the woman's home. By a lucky twist of Fate, he had been at the nightclub when she walked in last night – in the company of the very vampyre he had been hunting for over four years. Jason Wolf, the monster who had ripped out his younger brother's heart. Last night, it had been all he could do not to launch himself at the blood-sucker and drive a stake through his black heart. Instead, he had slipped out of the club before the vampyre caught his scent. They would meet again, but at a time and place of Warren's choosing.

He swore a pithy oath. Hunters were sworn to stay under the radar if possible, so as not to alarm the public. Vampyres had been accepted in society some seventy years ago, until one of them went berserk and wiped out a prominent Congressman and his entire family in a single night.

Since then, the government had put a bounty on their heads and they had been hunted almost to extinction. But almost wasn't good enough. As long as one of the monsters existed, mankind was in danger – not only of being killed, but of being turned into one of them.

Last night, Warren had followed the vampyre and the woman to the parking lot where he'd overheard the woman make a date with the blood-sucker for this evening. Earlier today, Warren had spoken to Jeff Moran, a friend of his who worked for the DMV. After some coaxing, Jeff had found the woman's name and address by looking up her license plate number.

All he had to do now was sit back and wait.

Skye found herself smiling all through the day as she looked through the numerous photographs she had taken at the museum – pictures of warbonnets and peace pipes, bows and arrows and war clubs, as well as cradleboards, moccasins, native dress and dance regalia, drums and flutes. She had no idea if there would ever be a market for the photos, but it didn't matter. She was happy with each and every one of them. Maybe she would try to write an article about the Indian exhibit to showcase her photos. Some of the museum pieces were rare and quite valuable. Probably a dumb idea, she thought, as she went upstairs to get ready for her date with Jason. Writing had never been her strong suit. Still, it was something to think about.

Wolf arrived at Skye's house a little before six-thirty. As always, he was aware of his surroundings – a few cars parked at the curb, an old man idling on the porch across the street, a couple of teenage boys shooting hoops in the driveway a few doors down.

Wolf's gaze rested on the black Dodge Charger parked on the other side of the street. A man sat behind the wheel looking at a cell phone. Wolf imprinted the man's image in his mind before ringing the doorbell.

He heard the sound of hurrying footsteps, the snick of a lock being turned, and then Skye was standing there, brown eyes sparkling, luscious lips curved in a smile of welcome.

"Hello."

"Hey, beautiful." And she *was* beautiful. The short-sleeved white sweater she wore, though modest, hugged her breasts, leaving little to the imagination, as did the jeans that hugged her slender legs.

"I'm almost ready," she said. "Come on in."

Stepping inside, he closed the door behind him. "Damn, girl, you look good enough to eat."

"Want a bite?" she teased.

Oh, lordy, did he ever! But he was pretty sure she wasn't thinking the same thing he was. "Maybe a nibble," he murmured. His gaze moved over her, lingering on the pulse throbbing in the hollow of her throat. Restraining his urge to take the bite she had innocently offered, he said, "What would you like to do tonight?"

"I don't care." She stared at him, thinking it was uncanny that he looked so much like Wolf Who Walks on the Wild Wind. Surely no two people, even twins, could look so identical, she thought. And then she grinned. Maybe he'd been cloned. These days, anything was possible.

When Wolf looked up, he found her watching him intently. A deep breath filled his senses with the seductive fragrance of her perfume—and the unmistakable scent of feminine desire. "This is going to get out of hand really quick, you know that, don't you?"

Skye didn't pretend she didn't understand what he meant. She had never felt this way before, never fallen so hard or so fast for a man she had just met. But there was something between them, something intangible that she feared wouldn't be long denied.

"I think we'd better get out of here and go someplace crowded," Wolf said, his voice husky with the need burning through him.

"I think you're right."

Skye grabbed a jacket and followed Jason outside. "Nice car," she remarked as he handed her into a black Ferrari convertible. "I have one, too, only mine is light blue and an older model."

"What can I say? You've got good taste." He slid behind the wheel and hit the ignition. The motor hummed to life, purring like a kitten.

Pulling away from the curb, he headed for the freeway.

"Where are we going?" she asked as she fastened her seatbelt.

"Anywhere you want."

"Surprise me." It was a lovely night, Skye thought, the air warm, the sky the same midnight blue as Jason's eyes. Traffic on the freeway was unusually light. Leaning forward, she turned on the radio and found a station that played Fifties hits.

She smiled when *You Are My Special Angel* came on. "I love this song."

"Into the Oldies, are you?"

"My grandmother loved it. She said it was the song that was playing when she met my grandfather. They were married for sixty-five years."

"That has to be some kind of record," Wolf remarked. "Over fifty percent of marriages end in divorce these days."

"I know. It's sad. Are your parents still together?"

"They're both gone."

"I'm sorry."

He shrugged. "It happened a few years back." A few hundred years back. "One right after the other. But my maternal grandfather is still alive. He lives in South Dakota."

Skye touched his arm. "I'm glad you have someone." She smiled when the ocean came into view.

"What about you?" he asked. "Your parents still around?"

"They're living in Germany. My father is a professor at one of the colleges there. I haven't seen either one of them in quite some time."

Wolf pulled off the freeway and turned into a parking lot near the beach. When he opened the door for Skye, she unfastened her seatbelt, kicked off her sandals, and tossed them into the backseat. Grinning, he pulled off his boots and socks and they walked hand-in-hand down to the shore.

It was Sunday night and there were only a few other couples in evidence. Overhead, millions of stars sparkled against a blanket of indigo blue. The silver light of the moon danced over the white caps.

"I love the beach," Skye said. "The sound of the waves. The smell of the sea. It's so peaceful. So beautiful."

"*You're* beautiful," he murmured, and drew her into his arms.

She didn't resist.

"Would you object if I kissed you?"

Skye stared up at him. She hardly knew the man. And even though she was wildly attracted to him, he was moving way too fast. But she couldn't deny that it was what she wanted, partly out of curiosity, and partly because of the almost overwhelming electricity that sparked between them whenever they touched.

"Skye?"

She licked lips gone suddenly dry. "We just met."

"I know. It's crazy as hell," he agreed, "and I know this is going to sound like a line, but I've never felt this way before."

Her gaze slid away from his as she murmured, "Me, either."

Wolf went still as he felt the faint vibration of footsteps drawing closer. Turning slowly, he put Skye behind him.

A man jogged toward them.

The same man he had seen behind the wheel of the black Dodge.

Clad in jeans, a tan shirt, dress shoes, and a long black coat, the stranger wasn't dressed for the beach. Not even close.

The man slowed as he drew closer and then stopped as one hand delved inside his coat.

Wolf swore under his breath. The man was a slayer, of that there was no doubt. But surely he didn't intend to launch an attack in front of Skye?

Or did he?

Wolf swore again as he weighed his options. He could transport himself and Skye to safety. He could mesmerize the hunter. Or he could kill him. None of which would be easy to explain.

Skye tugged on his arm. "What's going on?"

"I'm not sure. I think this guy is armed."

Her fingers tightened. "What are we going to do?"

"It's up to him." When the hunter took a step forward, Wolf summoned his preternatural power, then caught and held the man's gaze. *Go home.*

The hunter stopped in mid-stride. For a moment, he looked confused, then he turned and jogged back the way he'd come.

"Well, that was weird," Skye remarked.

"Yeah." Turning toward her, Wolf took Skye in his arms again. "I guess he lost his nerve. Now, where were we?"

Skye stared at her reflection in the bathroom mirror later than night as she got ready for bed. There was a sparkle in her eyes, her cheeks were flushed, her lips bruised from Jason's kisses. Never in all her life had she spent an evening kissing and cuddling with a man who was, for all intents and purposes, a complete stranger. She knew nothing about him except his name, that he could afford to drive an expensive car, he was half-Indian, and his grandfather lived in South Dakota. Yet she had sat with him on the sand and lost herself in his kisses. Lost herself, she thought. That was the understatement of the century. She was surprised she hadn't gone up in flames, the fire between them had burned so hot.

It had been after midnight when he drove her home and kissed her goodnight at her door, and it had been all she could do not to invite him inside to spend the night.

She sighed as she slipped her nightgown over her head and slid under the covers. She was twenty-seven years old and she had never felt this way before, never acted this way before, not even with Joe.

But then, she had never met a man like Jason Wolf before. And likely never would again.

He was dark and dangerous and a little mysterious. A throwback to an earlier time, she thought, an Alpha in a world that was trying its best to geld the male of the species. A little voice in the back of her mind warned her in no uncertain terms that it would be unwise to see him again.

After dropping Skye off at her house, Wolf returned to the beach where he picked up the scent of the hunter who drove the Dodge. He followed the man's scent to a white single-story house located in the middle of a cul-de-sac about five miles from Skye's place. He sat in front of the driveway for several moments before pulling away from the curb.

It was always a good idea to know where your enemies lived.

Wolf sat at one of the tables in the Ten Spot, a glass of whiskey cradled in his hands, his thoughts on the woman. Skye. There was no denying the instantaneous attraction between them. In all his life, he had never known anything like it. It wasn't just her blood that called to him. It was...hell, he didn't know what it was. Yes, she was beautiful and sexy and desirable, but it was more than that. More than her blood, although that was sweet, indeed.

He had never believed in soul-mates or people being destined to be together, never believed in love at first sight. Lust, sure, and yet what he felt for her was stronger, deeper, than that.

Sitting back in his chair, he pondered his existence. The vampyre part of him lived only in the future, where he had been turned over three hundred years ago. When he came here, he was twenty-nine and mortal again. He could walk in the sun. He could consume human food. In the future, the sun scorched his flesh, food was abhorrent, and he hungered only for blood.

With a shake of his head, he drained his glass and left the saloon, unable to resist his need to see Skye and hold her in his arms once more.

Skye wandered through the house the next morning, thinking how empty it felt. It was far too big for one person and she often thought of selling it. Her grandmother had bequeathed it to her – along with a sizeable fortune – shortly after Joe's death. Somehow, it felt wrong to sell it. The old house held many wonderful memories for her, days and nights spent with her grandmother, making Halloween cookies, decorating the Christmas tree, sitting in front of the fireplace eating s'mores while her grandmother read to her. There were other memories, as well, like the too few days she had spent here with Joe.

Needing to do something to pass the time, she went up to her grandmother's bedroom, unchanged since Nanny Marie had passed away five years ago. Opening the closet door, she ran her hand over her grandmother's dresses. Nanny had shopped only in the most exclusive shops for clothes and shoes, handbags and jewelry. There was a small fortune in dresses alone. Nanny had always said you can't take it with you. But, try as she might, Nanny Marie hadn't been able to spend the sizeable fortune her husband had left her. Skye had inherited what was left.

She grinned as she imagined donating the dresses to the local Goodwill. Gowns by Oscar De La Renta, Chanel, Dolce&Gabbana, and shoes by Louie Vuitton and Manolo Blahnik would certainly add a touch of class to the racks and shelves.

Well, there was no time like the present to get started, she thought. And it would be a good way to think of something besides Jason Wolf. He'd made no mention of seeing her tonight and she chided herself for taking it for granted that he would want to see her every night. He had a life of his own, after all. Still, after the hot make-out session they'd had at the beach, she had at least expected a call.

With a shake of her head, she sorted through her grandmother's dresses. They were all lovely and she decided to keep several of them. After all, some classic styles never went out of vogue. She studied a blue gingham dress with short, puffy sleeves and a pleated skirt that Nanny had bought to wear to a square dance years ago. She was about to put it on the giveaway pile when she changed her mind. It might come in handy as a costume for the annual church Halloween party later in the year.

Each dress held a memory and her eyes were damp by the time she folded the ones she had decided to give away and stacked them on the bed. She would have to find some boxes tomorrow for those she was giving away, she thought, as she hung the ones she had decided to keep back in the closet. And she'd need more boxes for the dozens of pairs of shoes, none of which would fit her.

It was after five when she finished sorting and stacking. Closing the bedroom door behind her, Skye headed downstairs to cook up something for dinner, only to find that the cupboard was bare. She hated cooking for one and, more often than not, she ordered pizza, or picked up take-out of one kind or another.

Locating her cell phone, she called the nearest pizza place and ordered a small pepperoni, hot wings, and a green salad.

While waiting, she went into the living turn and switched
on the TV. Five minutes later, the doorbell rang.

"Wow, that was fast," she muttered as she opened the
door.

Only it wasn't the pizza delivery man.

"I hope you don't mind my stopping by without calling
first," Wolf said.

"No. No, not at all," she murmured, wondering why she
was so flustered. "Come in. I just ordered a pizza."

Wolf followed her into the living room. He hadn't
paid much attention to the furnishings before, but now he
noticed that the glass-fronted cabinets and tables were all
antiques. The carpets were plush, the sofas luxurious, the
paintings exquisite. The mantel held a number of photographs of historical sites – Custer's Last Stand, Bodie Ghost
Town, Deadwood, Silverton, and Durango.

He gestured at the photos. "Did you take these?"

"Yes."

He wondered what she would say if he told her he could
take her back to those places as they had been in the eigh-
teen-hundreds. "They're very good."

"Thank you. It's what I do for a living."

"Take pictures of the Old West?"

"Not always. I freelance for an outdoor magazine,
among others."

"I've never known a photographer before," he remarked,
as she indicated he should take a seat.

"I don't think I've ever met anyone of Native American
heritage before," she said, settling into the chair across from
the sofa. "Have you ever thought about modeling?"

"Modeling? Are you kidding?"

"My friend, Cindi, creates covers for romance novels. I'll
bet she'd love to use you."

He thought of the romance books he'd seen, usually with beautiful, buxom woman and shirtless men on the covers. He grinned inwardly. "I don't think so. Have you lived here very long?"

"About five years. My grandmother left the place to me in her will."

Must be good money in taking photographs, he mused, if she could afford the taxes and the upkeep on a place like this. He tensed when the doorbell rang, relaxed when his preternatural senses told him it was just a kid delivering pizza.

Murmuring, "Excuse me," Skye went to pay for the pie. Carrying the boxes into the living room, she set them on the coffee table. "Would you like some?" she asked.

"I've already eaten," Wolf said. "I was hoping to take you out for drinks and dancing."

"Sounds better than pizza," Skye said. "Just let me put this stuff in the fridge and change my clothes."

They went to the nightclub where they had gone before.

Skye grinned when Wolf bought her a personal-sized pepperoni pizza, which was the only food the nightclub served.

"You wanted pizza, you get pizza," he said with a roguish grin. "I don't want you to miss your dinner on my account."

"Do you want a slice?"

He shook his head. "It's hardly big enough for one."

They made small talk while she ate, and all the while butterflies fluttered in the pit of her stomach at the thought of dancing with him again, feeling his arms around her.

He asked her to dance as soon as she finished eating.

Skye rested her cheek on his chest. The music was soft, the lights were low, the man was oh, so gorgeous. She inhaled his scent, which defied description. It wasn't cologne, she thought, but the scent of the man himself, sexy and beguiling. He held her close, plying feather-light kisses along the side of her neck, until the nightclub seemed to fade away and there was just the two of them, his arms holding her close, his tongue like a flame against the side of her neck...

Wolf sealed the tiny wounds in her throat as he released her from his thrall. He had taken no more than a few sips. She was as sweet as he remembered, her blood pulsing with youth and life, warming him, strengthening him.

She looked up, a dreamy expression on her face. His bite had that effect on women, he thought, and wondered how she would look at him if she knew what he had done. What he was. He shook the thought aside. There was no reason why she should ever find out.

Skye hummed softly as she got ready for bed that night. Funny how life could surprise you. She had been feeling somewhat lonely of late, wondering if she would ever find love again, and then one afternoon she'd gone to the museum on a whim and seen that life-sized figure of Wolf Who Walks on the Wild Wind. And then she had met a man who looked enough like him to be his twin, and suddenly the future seemed bright again, full of possibilities. Silly, maybe, since she hardly knew the man, and yet, he filled something inside her that had been empty for a long, long time.

Smiling, she put on her nightgown, turned out the light, and slipped under the covers, hoping she would dream of him again tonight.

CHAPTER FIVE

W arren Gray smiled with satisfaction as he watched the vampyre drive away from the woman's house. He had been watching her place for over a week now, keeping track of the time the bloodsucker showed up and the time he left.

Tonight, he decided to follow the vampyre. Pulling away from the curb, he trailed him for several blocks, nodded when he realized the creature was going to Night's End, a Goth club located on the outskirts of the city and often frequented by the Undead. He had discovered more than one bloodsucker in the place, caught them unawares when they stepped outside, and collected the rewards for their heads. Of course, they had all been young ones, unlike the monster he was tailing now.

He felt a rush of adrenaline as he pulled into the parking lot behind the vampyre and watched him go inside.

Getting out of the car, Warren checked his pockets – two small bottles of holy water, a silver-bladed dagger, a couple of sharp wooden stakes made of hickory. The machete he used to take their heads was in the trunk, along with a box black garbage bags to carry them in. Claiming a kill wasn't enough. The government wanted physical proof.

Warren started toward the door, only to pause when he recalled how the vampyre had worked some sort of mind-control over him when they had come face-to-face on the beach. Reaching into the glove compartment, he pulled out a heavy silver collar and fastened it around his neck. Damn thing weighed a ton, but he'd bought it from a store that specialized in items guaranteed to repel vampyre magic. He sure as hell hoped it worked against the old ones. If not...

He muttered an oath as he walked briskly toward the entrance. If the collar didn't work, he wouldn't live long enough to demand a refund.

Wolf smelled the hunter before he entered the nightclub, shook his head when he recognized the man as the one who had confronted him at the beach. Damn fool, he thought irritably. He frowned when he saw the silver collar at the man's throat. Supernatural power radiated from the damn thing.

Wolf snorted with disdain. It might prevent him from being able to control the hunter's mind, but he could break the man in half with little more than a thought. Once, a century or so ago, he would have done that very thing. But he had mellowed some since then.

Turning toward the bartender, he ordered a glass of red wine. And waited.

Warren felt his courage slip away as he approached the vampyre. What the hell was he doing, going up alone against one as ancient as this one? Sure, he made his living collecting bounties on vampyres, but he had never gone after one more than fifty years old. What good was a ten-thousand dollar reward if you weren't alive to collect it? He could feel the vampyre's supernatural power moving over him, a tangible thing. It felt like tiny pinpricks dancing over his skin.

Wolf met the hunter's gaze head on. The man was scared to death. He flashed his fangs. "Can I buy you a drink?"

The hunter stared at him as if he'd spoken in a foreign language. And then gasped, "Whiskey."

Wolf signaled for the bartender. "Pour some Jack for my friend."

The bartender pulled a bottle of Jack Daniels from under the bar and splashed a healthy amount into a glass.

Stifling the urge to laugh, Wolf watched the hunter reach for the glass with a shaky hand and down it in a single swallow.

"Are you ... gonna ... kill me?" he croaked.

Wolf shrugged. "That all depends on what you do next. But if you want my head, this is the best chance you'll ever have."

A sudden stillness fell over the room as the tension grew between hunter and vampyre. There were only a few people in the club. All were human save for Wolf and one other vampyre.

The hunter glanced around. When no one made a move to help him, he swallowed hard. Slowly and deliberately, he set his empty glass on the bar.

Wolf watched the hunter gather all the courage he possessed as he turned his back toward him, squared his shoulders, and headed for the door.

Wolf stared after him. If the hunter had truly lost his nerve, it would be one less slayer to worry about.

If.

Skye woke with a smile, thinking how much she had looked forward to each new day since meeting Jason Wolf. After

Joe's passing, she had vowed never to marry again. Since then, she had dated only rarely. And then she'd met Jason and her whole world had turned upside down.

She showered and dressed, ate a leisurely breakfast, and then looked through all the photographs she had taken at the museum again, sorting them into stacks – clothing, weapons, drums, etc. There were several shots of Wolf Who Walks on the Wild Wind's cut-out, of course, but who could blame her? She was also pleased with the ones of the Native American village display, as well. With some creative murals depicting tree-covered hills in the background, the museum had presented the village so that it appeared as if the lodges were actually set up in the Old West rather than inside a museum.

Sitting back, she found herself thinking of Jason. What was he doing today? She was tempted to drive over to his house and surprise him, only she wasn't sure where it was. She hadn't looked at the address when the cab picked her up that first night, and had only a dim memory of the area.

Still, she had nothing else to do today. Occasional boredom was the curse and the blessing of not having to work for a living.

Skye glanced out the window. It was a beautiful day for a drive, she mused, as she grabbed her handbag and her keys and headed out the door.

It took the better part of an hour before she found a neighborhood that looked familiar. It was an older part of town. Most of the houses, though no longer new or fashionable, were still well-maintained, the paint reasonably new, the yards clean and uncluttered, the lawns routinely mowed.

She drove slowly down the street. It wasn't until she turned down a cul-de-sac that she found the house she thought was his. The lawn was green. Large trees grew on either side of the house. There were no flowers or plants. The curtains were drawn. It looked unlived in, she thought, as she pulled into the driveway.

Shutting off the engine, she climbed the three steps to the covered front porch and rang the bell. She heard it echo inside the house. When there was no answer after a few moments, she rang it again.

Disappointed, she muttered, "I guess he isn't here."

Driving home, she wondered where he'd gone. He had never mentioned having a nine-to-five job, or any other kind. He seemed awfully young to be retired but maybe he didn't need to work. Perhaps he received an adequate income from the casino in South Dakota. Whatever, it was doubtful he sat home all day twiddling his thumbs. After all, she didn't keep regular working hours either, but she managed to keep busy.

She frowned as a new thought crossed her mind. Maybe he was out with another woman...

She banished that thought immediately, but it immediately crept back in. He was a handsome, single, virile male. No doubt he had a string of beautiful women waiting in the wings who were just dying to go out with him.

She had to remember that.

Wolf roused with the setting of the sun. He knew immediately that Skye had been at the house. He caught her scent with his first breath.

41

Rising, he showered and dressed, curious to know what had brought her here. Eager to see her again

Hold her again.

Taste her again.

It would have been faster to will himself to her house, but he grabbed his keys instead, in case she wanted to go out.

Whistling softly, he left the house.

Skye's heart skipped a beat when the doorbell rang. Thinking, *Let it be him, let it be him,* she took a deep breath and opened the door, felt her stomach curl with pleasure when he smiled at her. "Hi."

"Hi, yourself."

She stepped back to let him in. "How was your day?"

"Uneventful."

She led the way into the living room, took a seat on the sofa, felt her heart skip a beat when he sat beside her.

"How was *your* day?" He wanted to ask why she had come to his house, but could hardly explain how he knew she'd been there.

Skye felt her cheeks grow warm. Should she tell him she'd gone to his place? Would he think her too forward? After all, they had only known each other a few days.

"Skye?"

"I . . . I drove to your house."

He took her hand in his and gave it a squeeze. "I'm sorry I missed you."

She smiled uncertainly, hoping he would tell her where he'd been. But he didn't, and she didn't have the nerve to ask. Or maybe she just didn't want to know.

"What would you like to do tonight?" he asked, his thumb lightly stroking her palm.

"I don't know. I wasn't sure you'd come by."

"I'll be here every night, unless you tell to stay away." He slid his arm around her shoulders and drew her closer. "I think I'm getting addicted to you."

His voice washed over her, deep and sexy and laced with desire.

"Are you?"

"Do you mind?"

"What do you think?"

"You probably don't want to know," he said with a grin, and claimed her lips with his.

His lips were firm and cool, laced with an intensity and a passion she had never known. She wrapped her arms around him, wanting to be closer, closer, as he deepened the kiss, his tongue like a flame stroking hers, igniting a fire deep inside of her. She moaned a soft protest when he lifted his head. His eyes were dark with a heat of their own as he lowered his head to her neck, his tongue hot against her skin.

He murmured to her in a language she didn't understand, felt herself falling, drifting, all thought lost in the red wave of pleasure that engulfed her...

And then reality returned and he was kissing her again and nothing else mattered but his mouth on hers, his arms tight around her.

She sighed when he ended the kiss, content to be held in his embrace.

"Why did you come to see me today?" he asked.

"I was missing you, that's all," she admitted.

"I'm rarely home during the day," he said. "I have casino business that often takes me out of town."

"Oh."

His knuckles caressed her cheek. "I missed you, too, sweetness."

His words, the endearment, warmed her through and through. Resting her head on his shoulder, she closed her eyes, filled with a languid sense of well-being.

Wolf sifted his fingers through Skye's hair as her breathing and heartbeat slowed and she fell asleep wrapped in his arms. She was incredibly sweet, he thought, as he ran his tongue along the side of her neck. He'd taken only a little while he kissed her. It was getting harder and harder to stop when she was so near, so trusting. Her blood was intoxicating. It called to him, sustained him, like no other. And then there was the woman herself, warm and sweet and desirable. It was a dangerous combination, he mused, the desire for the woman, the hunger for her blood.

Dangerous in more ways than one.

Warren Gray paced the living room floor, his stomach churning with shame and self-disgust as he remembered how he'd slunk out of the nightclub like some spineless coward. He'd been a slayer for five years, destroyed more than two dozen vampyres, and yet he had turned tail and fled. He had tried to rationalize his gutless behavior. After all, the vampyre was one of the old ones, infinitely more powerful than any he had ever faced before, but his excuses fell flat.

He poured himself another shot of bourbon and downed it in a single swallow, hoping to find his courage in the bottom of the glass. The bloodsucker was so damn powerful, maybe no single hunter could take him down ... But there were other hunters in the city. He was acquainted with most of them, knew where they congregated when they were together.

The club was small, a hidden haven for the Hunter-Slayers and the Bleeders. A place to exchange confidential information – like which vampyres were currently in town, which had moved on, which had been destroyed, which unfortunate humans had been turned. A vast network of information that was exchanged locally and through the Dark Web to all parts of the world.

Warren had contacted three of the slayers he knew were in town and invited them to meet him at the club at midnight. They had readily agreed. At the appointed hour, they met in a private room.

As succinctly as possible, Warren told them about the vampyre he had recently tangled with.

"I don't know where he takes his rest, but he's involved with a mortal woman and I know where she lives. He's gone there every night for the last several weeks. All we have to do is wait for him to show up again." Warren glanced around the table. "Are you with me?"

Neal Maxwell nodded. "Count me in. I haven't taken a head in over a week."

"I guess I'm in," Rod Kimball said, dragging a hand across his jaw. "But it's a hell of a risk. Wolf's taken out a lot of hunters."

"We've taken out a lot of vampyres," George Miller reminded them. "I say let's go for it."

"Might as well," Kimball said. "What have we got to lose?"

"Our heads," Miller and Maxwell replied in unison.

Warren grinned. It was an old joke, though not really very funny.

They agreed to split the reward four ways.

"So, Gray, when were you planning this assault?"

"Tomorrow night." He glanced at his companions, who each nodded in turn. They spent the next hour planning their strategy.

"Hot damn!" Warren crowed as he drove home. "Tomorrow night, there will be one less monster in the city."

CHAPTER SIX

Skye woke in her bed, fully clothed except for her shoes. Frowning, she threw back the covers and sat up. And then she smiled. Last night she had fallen asleep in Wolf's arms. He must have carried her up to bed. She sat there a moment, remembering the night past, the magic of his kisses, the husky sound of his voice. Just thinking of him made her heart swell with excitement and...and what? Infatuation? Affection? Love? It couldn't be love. She had known him for such a short time, and yet in some ways, it seemed as if she had been waiting for him her whole life. He was all she could think about. His voice, his touch, the way he looked at her, whatever it was she felt for him, she didn't want it to end.

Too excited to sit still, she ate a quick breakfast and then, on a whim, decided to rearrange the furniture in the living room. She managed to move the sofa and the chairs without much trouble, but there was no way she could possibly move the glass-fronted curio cabinet. Made of solid mahogany, it weighed more than she did. As she emptied the contents, she wondered if Wolf would move it for her.

When everything else was in place, and all the pictures rearranged, she stood in the middle of the living room floor and surveyed the results. "I like it," she decided.

Feeling weary, Skye went into the kitchen for a bottle of water, then sank down on the sofa and switched on the TV. She smiled when *The Last of the Mohicans* came on. She had always loved that movie, had seen it in the theaters more than once, watched it on cable numerous times. Her favorite scene had naturally been the love scene. Sensual and romantic without being graphic, with no dialogue, it had captured her imagination. She sighed as she pictured Wolf as Hawkeye and herself as Cora. She had always wondered if two people who had so little in common, who had come from vastly different worlds, could have lived happily-ever-after, or if the differences between them would eventually have driven them apart. Was love enough to bridge a gap so wide?

If she continued to see Wolf, would they discover that the things they had in common were strong enough to overcome their cultural differences?

Sighing, she closed her eyes, chiding herself for looking for trouble when things were going so well...

She felt herself slipping into a dream state and Wolf was there, clad in a buckskin shirt, pants, and moccasins. Her eyelids fluttered down as he took her in his arms, his mouth covering hers in a long, heated kiss that made her toes curl inside her shoes. She gasped his name as his hands boldly caressed her, awakening sensations that she thought had died with Joe. She trembled with desire as he rained kisses on her brow, her eyelids, her cheeks, along the side of her neck...gasped when he bit her. Startled, she opened her eyes, let out a strangled cry when she looked into his eyes – eyes burning red. His buckskins were gone and in their place he wore a black silk shirt, slacks, and a long black cape that swirled around him like the devil's own breath. With a cry, she twisted out of his arms and began to run, only to let out a terrified shriek when his hand closed over her shoulder...

Skye woke to the sound of her own frightened cries. Sitting up, she glanced wildly around the room.

There was no one else there.

She blew out a sigh. "Just a bad dream." Rising, she went to close the curtains even though it was broad daylight. "Just a bad dream," she chanted, as she went through the house, drawing the drapes, locking all the doors and the windows.

But it hadn't felt like a dream. Suddenly chilled to the bone, she went into the bathroom and stood in front of the mirror. She turned her head from side to side, afraid of what she might find. But there were no tiny bite marks in her throat.

Weak with relief, she sank down on the bathroom floor and buried her face in her hands. "Only a dream."

Wolf woke as soon as the sun slid behind the horizon. No sooner had he done so than he sensed Skye's distress. Wondering what had caused it, he let his mind brush hers. He unleashed a string of oaths as the reason for her fright unfolded. What on earth had made her imagine him as a vampyre? He searched his memory. Had he inadvertently said something? Done something? He shook his head. He had never even mentioned the word vampyre. They had never discussed their existence. And yet she had conjured both of his images – past and present, mortal and Nosferatu.

It was uncanny.

It was impossible.

Uncertain of what it might mean, he dressed and went out to feed.

❧ ❧ ❧

Skye glanced at the clock on the mantel as she paced the floor. Wolf would be here any minute. All day, she had been haunted by the memory of her dream. Dream, hah! It had been the most vivid, realistic nightmare she'd ever had. She had told herself over and over again that it was nothing to worry about, that it was just a figment of her overactive imagination. Vampyres didn't exist. They were just a myth, like werewolves and zombies, scary tales to frighten children. But the nightmare images remained.

Feeling foolish, she had gone to her computer earlier in the day and done a search for vampyres – only to discover that there were two spellings of the word – vampyre and vampyre. She wondered if there was a difference and if so, what it was.

Link after link appeared, some for books and comics, some for movies and TV shows, some detailing the history of vampyres, how to recognize them, how to destroy them, phone numbers for hunter-slayers, as well as links for additional web sites where you could buy vampyre blood on line...

She had grimaced when she clicked on that one, surprised that people paid hundreds of dollars for a small vial of vampyre blood which was touted for its aphrodisiac powers. She shook her head, wondering how anyone could be foolish enough to fall for such an obvious con game. Vampyre blood, indeed. Anyone could sell a bottle of blood and claim it came from a vampyre. Some silly actress was supposedly selling her farts in bottles.

Skye had been about to sign out when curiosity sent her back to the page on how to recognize a vampyre. They tended to wear black, didn't eat, couldn't walk in the sun, were "dead" by day, had pale skin, were incredibly strong, and able to move faster than the human eye could follow. They never aged, were never sick, and had the power to heal with remarkably speed.

Now, sitting in the living room, it occurred to her that she had never seen Wolf eat. He wore a lot of black. She only saw him at night.

She had a vague memory of her grandpa Earl teasing her on Halloween when she was five or six, telling her to "beware of the vampyres." Her grandmother had been furious. Taking Skye into her arms, Nanny Marie had assured her that vampyres no longer existed.

Skye frowned. She had forgotten all about that, never given it a moment's thought. Until now. Nanny Marie hadn't said they *didn't* exist, only that they no longer existed…

Her heart skipped a beat when the doorbell rang. Wolf was taking her to the movies tonight. She took a deep breath when the bell rang again, sent a quick glance in the mirror before she opened the door. "Hi."

"Are you ready?"

She stared at him. "I … um …"

She was afraid of him. The scent of the fear rising from her skin was stronger than the flowery fragrance of her perfume. "Have you changed your mind?"

"I don't know." He was wearing black again – shirt, shoes, slacks.

"What's wrong, Skye?" It was a foolish question. He knew exactly what was bothering her.

"I'm not feeling very well." She pressed her fingertips to her temple. "Headache, you know? I think I'm coming down with something. I … I think I'd better stay home tonight."

He nodded. "Whatever you want."

She felt suddenly foolish. What was wrong with her? For the first time in forever she had met a gorgeous, sexy guy who was interested in her. Was she going to let a silly nightmare that made no sense keep her from going out with him?

"I hope you feel better." Leaning forward, he kissed her lightly on the cheek, then turned and descended the stairs.

Skye closed the door. She wanted to call him back, but what could she say? *I'm sorry, I had a moment of temporary insanity. I thought you were a vampyre.*

She was about to turn off the porch light when she heard the sound of scuffling. Pulling back the curtain beside the door, she peered into the darkness, let out a gasp when she saw four men attacking Wolf in the driveway.

Throwing open the door, she hollered, "Hey! Stop that!"

Three of the four men turned and bolted down the sidewalk.

The fourth man lay unmoving on the ground.

Wolf stood over him, panting heavily. He looked up as she hurried down the steps toward him.

Skye slowed as she drew near. He looked awful. His shirtfront was wet with what she feared was blood. It was splattered all over him. His shirt was ripped in several places, revealing long gashes on his arms and chest, and what looked like a nasty burn on one cheek.

She laid a tentative hand on his shoulder. "Are you all right?"

He closed his eyes and took a deep breath. "No."

"Come inside."

"That's not a good idea."

"I don't care." She tugged on his arm. "What do you want to do? Stay out here and bleed to death? Come inside."

In too much pain to argue, Wolf let her pull him into the house, and into the bathroom where she removed his shirt and tossed it into the waste basket.

"Who were those guys?" she asked as she pulled a clean wash cloth and a towel from a shelf.

"I don't know." It was a lie, but he could hardly tell her the truth. His cheek burned like hellfire from the holy water they'd thrown at him. The cuts on his arms and chest, made with silver-bladed knives, stung like the devil. One of the hunters had driven a stake into his back, missing his heart by inches. Yanking it from his flesh had been almost as painful as being stabbed with the damn thing.

He sat on the edge of the bathtub while she wet the washcloth, muttering under her breath as she washed the cuts and then smeared some kind of thick yellow ointment over the cuts in his arms and chest and on the burn on his cheek.

She gasped when he stood and she saw the wound in his back. "We should call the police. And a doctor."

"No. No cops."

"Why did those men attack you?"

"I don't know." Another lie. He had recognized Warren. The others wouldn't be hard to find.

She bandaged his arms, covered the wounds in his back and chest as best she could with gauze pads, then wound a thick strip around his middle to hold everything in place.

He could have told her it was a waste of time. His injuries might hurt like hell now, but they would be gone by tomorrow night. Of course, he couldn't tell her that, either.

"Well, I've done all I can," Skye said, her hands fisted on her hips. "Can I get you anything?"

His gaze moved to the hollow of her throat, to the slender curve of her neck. Tempting. So very tempting. But he feared one taste would not be enough. Not tonight, when his whole body was throbbing with pain. "Wine, if you've got it."

With a nod, she picked up the bloody towel and the wash cloth and dropped them into the tub.

He followed her into the kitchen, took a seat at the table.

Skye was aware of his gaze following her every move. Why didn't he want to notify the police? Or go to the hospital? Or at least see a doctor? He could have been killed. She splashed a healthy amount of red wine into a glass and handed it to him, watched as he drained it in a single swallow. "More?"

"No, thanks. I should go." He had fed earlier but he needed to feed again. Needed warm, fresh blood to ease the pain and heal his injuries.

"Will you call me later?"

"If you like."

"I'm sorry about tonight," she said. "I hope you feel better soon."

He smiled faintly. "Not to worry." Rising, he caressed her cheek with his knuckles. "Good night, sweetness. Thanks for patching me up."

She followed him to the front door, stood there while he walked to his car. Moonlight washed over him, highlighting the coppery hue of his skin, casting silver highlights in his inky black hair.

When he looked at her over the roof of the car, she could have sworn his eyes glowed red.

CHAPTER SEVEN

Wolf drove to the cul-de-sac where Warren Gray lived. Every light in the house was on. There were bars on the windows, a security screen door with a solid lock on the front door. The lot was fenced. A large German shepherd barked at him as he vaulted the fence. One look in the dog's eyes and it tucked its tail between its legs and ran into the back yard.

Grinning inwardly, Wolf padded quietly up to the door and rang the bell.

After a long moment, the front door opened an inch or so and Gray peered out. All the color drained from his face when he saw Wolf.

"What do you want?" he asked gruffly, though Wolf didn't miss the faint tremor in his voice.

Baring his fangs, Wolf let his eyes go red. "The next time you come after me, I'll kill you. If I ever sense you've been prowling around the woman's house again, I'll kill you. Got it?"

Gray swallowed hard, licked his lips, and then nodded.

"That goes for your friends, too," Wolf said, a growl in his voice.

Gray nodded again.

With a last warning glance in the hunter's direction, Wolf vanished from the man's sight, wondering if he had made a mistake. In years past, he would have killed the hunter and his buddies without a qualm. But times had changed and, for better or worse, so had he.

CHAPTER EIGHT

When Skye woke in the morning, her first thought was for Jason. He had been badly hurt last night. None of his injuries had looked life-threatening, save for the dreadful wound in his back. Another inch or so to the left and it would have pierced his heart. She couldn't help thinking it odd that he had refused to call the police and report the incident. He could have been killed. And why had he so adamantly refused to see a doctor or go to the emergency room? She knew he'd been in pain. A doctor could have prescribed something for it, and done a far better job of bandaging his cuts. Men! She thought. They could be so stubborn.

She frowned as a new thought crossed her mind. Was he wanted by the law? Was that why he'd been so adamant about not calling the police? She considered it a moment and dismissed it. Surely, if he was wanted by the cops, he wouldn't be taking her out dining and dancing.

She disposed of the bloody towel and washcloth, then took a quick shower, dressed in a pair of jeans and a tee shirt, and enjoyed a leisurely breakfast.

In her office, she thumbed through her photographs again. Maybe she really should try her hand at writing a book about the exhibit at the library. Or maybe a blog post, she mused. It would take less time, be less expensive, and wouldn't have to be as long. Plus, she could post her photos on the blog with a short comment on each one, which would certainly be easier and cheaper than having them printed in a book. And who knew, maybe a publisher would see her blog post and ask for a real book. Stranger things had happened. And if not...well, at least it would give her something to do until one of the magazines she typically worked for called with a new assignment.

She booted up her computer and uploaded the photos to a new file. In addition to her other photos, she had pictures of a rattle made from a tortoise shell, a feathered lance, a buffalo hide and a deerskin, several trade blankets, a hide lodge, a beaded headband, a rag doll, and, of course, the life-sized, cardboard cut-out of Wolf Who Walks on the Wild Wind taken from several angles.

Going to Google, she typed in his name, and spent the next two hours researching everything she could find about him. In addition to riding with Crazy Horse and Red Cloud, he had gone north to Canada with Sitting Bull. There was no mention of him on any of the Sioux reservation lists. No mention of his parents, or of his death.

While perusing old photos online, she thought she saw him standing next to Wild Bill Hickok in a grainy taken in Deadwood, South Dakota, in the 1800s. The caption under the photo read, "Wild Bill Hickok and friend outside Saloon #2."

She had never seen pictures of Wolf Who Walks on the Wild Wind attired in anything but a breechclout and moccasins, but in the old black-and-white photo, he wore a Western shirt, trousers, and a wide-brimmed black hat. A leather holster sat low on his right hip.

Frowning, she pulled a magnifying glass out of her desk drawer. It was the same man, she was sure of it. She didn't recall reading anything about Wolf Who Walks on the Wild Wind leaving the reservation. She shook her head, thinking it was amazing how much Jason looked like his ancestor.

She spent the next hour writing a short biography of the life and times of Wolf Who Walks on the Wild Wind for her blog.

It was after four when she leaned back in her chair and stretched her arms over her head. Pleased with the day's work, she saved everything, then shut down her computer and wandered into the kitchen. She really needed to go to the store, she thought, as she peered into the refrigerator looking for a snack. Like her cupboards, the refrigerator was bare save for a wilted head of lettuce, a quart of milk, a couple of apples, and the usual condiments. Since it was too late for lunch and too early for dinner, she grabbed an apple and closed the door.

Maybe she would read for a while, then go out to dinner. After her lie about being sick last night, Jason wasn't likely to come calling. Nor was he likely to feel up to going out after last night's vicious assault. His injuries, though not life-threatening, must still be painful. She wondered again why those men had attacked him. A mugging, perhaps? she thought, then shook her head. More like they had wanted to kill him. But why? Questions with no answers, at least none that made sense.

Putting them from her mind, she settled into her favorite easy chair and opened the novel she had started days ago, only to sit there, the book and the apple forgotten, as she stared out the window, wondering what Wolf was doing. How did he spend his days? What did he do for fun? When they went out, they usually went dancing or to a movie, sometimes for a drive. She wondered if he liked amusement parks like Disneyland and Magic Mountain. Did he enjoy going to football games, or ice skating, or bowling? She had bowled on a league with her parents one summer and though she hadn't been very good at it, she'd had a good time. Once, Wolf had taken her to the beach. Did he also like the mountains and the desert? This was California, after all. You could go to Malibu in the morning and be in the San Gabriel Mountains in the afternoon.

She frowned at the clock over the mantel when her stomach growled. Returning the apple to the fridge, she changed her clothes and grabbed her handbag. It was time she went grocery shopping.

She was about to go out the kitchen door into the garage when the doorbell rang.

Thinking it might be Wolf, she smiled as she turned around and hurried back into the living room.

Only it wasn't Wolf standing on the porch.

"Can I help you?" she asked.

"I'm here to help you," the man said, glancing nervously behind him.

Wonderful, she thought. No doubt he was a salesman of some kind. Why did they always show up at dinnertime?

"If you'll excuse me," she said politely, "I was just leaving."

"This will only take a minute. I'm here to warn you."

Not a salesman, she thought. Someone come to save her soul. "I really am in a hurry."

"That man you're seeing, Jason Wolf, isn't a man. He's a vampyre."

Skye stared at him, a sinking feeling in the pit of her stomach. And then she frowned. How did this man know she was seeing Wolf? "Who are you?"

"My name doesn't matter. I'm a hunter. And I'm risking my life to come here and warn you."

She stared at him, wide-eyed. "You were one of them!" she exclaimed. "One of the men who attacked him last night. And the beach...you were there, too."

"Yes. And if you value your life, you'll never see him again. He's old and he's dangerous." The hunter glanced over his shoulder. "If you're smart, you'll heed my warning." And so saying, he quickly returned to his car and peeled away from the curb.

Skye stood there, staring after him. It couldn't be true, she thought, even as vivid images from her nightmare flashed through her mind. It couldn't be true.

But what if it was?

She was about to close the door when Wolf pulled into the driveway.

Wolf caught the hunter's scent as soon as he stepped out of the car. A look at Skye's stricken expression told him everything he needed to know. The cat was out of the bag and unless he wiped Skye's memory, there was no putting it back in.

He walked around the car, then stood by the front fender, watching her. When she didn't run back inside and slam the door, he walked slowly to the edge of the porch stairs and stopped.

Arms folded, she took a deep breath. "Is it true?"

He nodded.

In the fading light of the sun, she noted there was no sign of the nasty red burn on his cheek, which seemed to have healed overnight. The tee shirt he wore revealed muscular arms devoid of cuts or scars. Had his other injuries also disappeared? How was that even possible? She had a million questions, but couldn't seem to put any of them into words. She could only stare at him, thinking of the nights she had spent in his arms, the thrill of his kisses, the touch of his hands. *Vampyre. Undead.*

"Do you want me to leave?"

She stared at him. Of course she wanted him gone. Didn't she? He was a vampyre! By not telling her the truth, he had lied to her, let her believe he was something he wasn't. How could she forgive him for that? How could she ever trust him again? How could she send him away when he was looking at her like a puppy that had just been kicked?

"I wanted to tell you," he said, his voice laced with regret. "But how could I?"

"How could you not!" She felt the sting of tears behind her eyes.

"Perhaps because I didn't want to see that look of revulsion on your face."

"You should have told me," she whispered.

"And lost you sooner?"

Her tears came then. She tried to blink them away but they only came faster.

"Skye..." He took a step forward and when she didn't object, he climbed the three stairs to the porch. "I'm sorry," he murmured. "So damn sorry." He clenched his hands at his sides to keep from reaching for her, wondering how he could ever make things right between them again. Wondering if it was even possible. "Skye?"

Sniffing back her tears, she looked up at him.

"I'll go if that's what you want."

She heard the pain in his voice, the aching loneliness, the sadness. She told herself to ignore it. He was a vampyre. A monster, according to what the hunter had said, and what she had read online. But he didn't look like a monster. He looked like the man she was falling in love with – a man who had been nothing but kind to her, who made her laugh. A man who made her toes curl with pleasure when he kissed her.

"Wolf…"

"It's all right, Skye. I understand. Have a good life."

She watched him turn away, knew if he left now, she would never see him again. Never hear his voice, feel his hands in her hair, on her skin. "Wolf, wait!"

He paused at the end of the porch but didn't face her.

"I … I don't want you to go."

He turned around, his gaze searching hers. "Are you sure?"

"I don't care what you are." She hadn't cared for anyone for so long, how could she let him go? He had filled a soul-deep emptiness inside her, made her look forward to each new day. Reaching for his hand, she pulled him into the house and shut the door.

Murmuring her name, Wolf wrapped her in his arms and held her close, unable to believe he hadn't lost her.

Resting her head on his chest, she said, "I'm still mad at you." But there was no anger in her voice.

"I know."

They stood that way for several moments. Wolf brushed a kiss across the top of her head and when she looked up, he kissed her, ever so gently.

Tugging on his hand, she led him into the living room and drew him down onto the sofa beside her. "Tell me," she said, her hand still clinging to his. "Tell me everything."

"I'm not sure where to start."

"The beginning seems like a good place."

"I was born in the Black Hills. My mother called me Chaske, but my warrior name was Wolf Who Walks on the Wild Wind."

For a moment, she stared at him, wide-eyed. "No wonder you look so much like that cardboard figure in the museum," she exclaimed. "But wait…how…"

He pressed a finger to her lips. "All in good time. My grandfather was a powerful medicine man. He could speak to the spirits, and see into the future, as could his grandfather before him. When he began to be old, he took me to a cave in the mountains. I was twenty-five or twenty-six by then. It was, he said, a sacred cave that allowed those of his blood to travel into the future and back again.

"I didn't believe him, of course, until he took me through and we came out in the future." Wolf shook his head with the memory. "It was like entering a foreign land. Everything looked alien – buildings, clothes, the people. We didn't stray far from the cave's entrance and my grandfather warned me that I should never go into the future alone.

"I should have listened to him, but I was intrigued by the little I'd seen. I waited a few days and then I went back. I hadn't gone far from the cave when a woman walked up to me. I had never seen anything like her in my life. She was tall and willowy and blonde and her eyes…damn, they were mesmerizing. She didn't say anything but I heard her voice in my mind, telling me not to be afraid, that she was going to give me a wonderful gift. When she told me to follow her, I did. I know now that I'd had no choice. She took me to her lair and she turned me. I was hovering between light and darkness when heard her voice in my mind again. She told me what she'd done, what I had become, what I needed to do to survive, and then she carried me back to where she'd found me and left me there.

"I crawled back to the cave, fell inside, and blacked out. When I woke up, it all seemed like a bad dream. When I went out of the cave on the other side, it was mid-afternoon.

My horse was waiting for me and I rode back to my grandfather's people. It was the next day, and nothing had changed."

"Wait a minute. I thought she turned you."

"She did, but when I woke up in the cave, I thought I must have dreamed it."

"I don't understand."

"Neither did I. I still don't." He lifted one brow when her stomach growled. "I think I'm keeping you from your dinner."

She shrugged. "I haven't eaten yet. I was about to go out when you showed up. Just give me a minute to order a pizza."

He watched her call for delivery. Never before had he told anyone of his past, or how he'd become a vampyre. It occurred to him that it would make a hell of a science-fiction movie. Maybe he could sell the rights to Hollywood.

"Go on," Skye said, resuming her place on the sofa.

"I went back to the cave again a few days later. The sun was up when I entered, but it was night when I stepped into the future. For a moment, I just stood there, bewildered by what I heard, what I saw. It was like I'd been blind and deaf all my life until that moment. Sounds were clearer, louder. I could see the tiniest details in everything around me. I was trying to figure out what was happening to me when my whole body spasmed. It was the worst pain I've ever felt. I thought I was dying. It was then that I remembered what the vampyre had done to me, what she'd told me about surviving. I staggered down the street, my insides on fire, the hunger burning through me. I thought I'd go mad with the pain, until I tripped over an old drunk sprawled face down in an alley."

Wolf stopped abruptly.

"Go on," Skye said, eager to hear the rest.

He never should have started this, Wolf thought bleakly. She had never seen him at his worst, had no idea what he was capable of, the atrocities he had committed before he learned to control the hunger that burned inside him, to feed without taking a life, to blend in with humanity.

"Wolf?"

"How much do you know about vampyres, Skye?"

She shrugged. "Not much. Just what I've seen in movies and read on the Internet." And what that hunter had told her. "Why?"

He blew out a sigh. "New vampyres have little control over the instinct to feed," he said, choosing his words with care. "It takes a while to master that urge."

. Did feeding mean drinking blood? Skye frowned. Of course it did. She had learned he was a vampyre and somehow she hadn't taken time to really think about what that actually meant. He didn't look or act like a monster. He looked like Jason Wolf, the man she could see herself falling in love with, because she had never seen him as anything else. But what did she really know about him? Did he have fangs? Sleep in a coffin? She grimaced. Kill others for their blood?

Wolf sensed the change in her, felt her withdrawal as keenly as if she had distanced herself from him physically.

She flinched when the doorbell bell. "Pizza's here," she said, and practically ran out of the room.

He should have lied to her, he thought glumly. Wiped the memory from her mind. Even now, it was tempting, but he couldn't do it. Couldn't go on living a lie.

Wolf heard her footsteps as she returned to the living room, the pizza box in her hands. "I guess I know now why I've never seen you eat," she murmured.

He nodded. "I won't bother you anymore," he said quietly. "I was a fool to think this could work."

"Wolf..."

But she was talking to an empty room.

Skye stared open-mouthed at the spot where Wolf had been sitting only seconds ago. Never in her life had she seen anyone just disappear. Where had he gone? And how on earth was it possible to just vanish into thin air like that?

Her appetite gone, Skye shoved the pizza box into the refrigerator. Returning to the living room, she dropped down onto the sofa and wrapped her arms around her waist. He was gone. Perhaps it was just as well. She had told him that what he was didn't matter. And she had believed it when she said it. She loved him. Or thought she did. But what kind of life could they have had together? Truth be told, she really didn't know him at all. Everything she thought she knew was a lie...

She bolted upright as a new thought occurred to her. If he was really Wolf Who Walks on the Wild Wind, if he had truly fought against Custer, associated with Wild Bill Hickock, then he must have been born sometime in the eighteen hundreds, which would make him over three hundred years old! She fell back against the sofa. He was much too old for her, she thought, and burst out laughing. But her laughter soon dissolved into tears. Curling up on the sofa, she cried herself to sleep.

Hidden in the shadows outside, Wolf stared into the darkness, the sound of her tears like a knife in his heart. He hadn't meant to cause her pain. Damn that hunter for interfering in his life and yet, he couldn't really fault the man.

Even though it had cost Wolf the thing he loved most, the man's intentions had been honorable, his only thought to save Skye from a monster. And he was a monster. Why fight it? He dressed like a mortal man, moved among them as if he was one of them, but he wasn't. And never would be, not here. Only in the past was he human. But Skye was here. And in spite of what had just happened, he wasn't ready to give her up.

Not just yet.

CHAPTER NINE

Skye tossed and turned all night long. In the morning, she told herself she was glad Wolf was gone. He wasn't a man. He was a vampyre and she was better off without him. How could they ever hope to find a life together? Better to end it now, she thought, before things went too far. She was already way too crazy about him. But, try as she might, she couldn't stop thinking about him, missing him. Wanting him so badly she ached with it.

Common sense told her she would be treading a dangerous path if she stayed with him, even as a little voice in the back of her mind made her wonder if Wolf was using some kind of vampyre magic to make her want him so.

Somehow, she made it through that day and the next, but no matter what she was doing, Wolf was rarely out of her thoughts for long. She had to see him again. She wasn't happy with the way they had parted.

Convinced that she needed closure, and wanting to look her best the last time he saw her, she dressed with care the following night, and drove to his house, making sure she arrived before the sun went down in hopes he would be home when she arrived.

❧ ❧ ❧

Wolf caught Skye's scent before she stepped out of the car. Barefooted and wearing only a pair of sweat pants, he cursed under his breath, wondering what the devil she was doing here, knocking on the monster's door when the sun was just going down. Did she have a death wish?

He muttered an oath when she rang the bell.

"Wolf? Wolf, it's me."

As if he didn't know that. As if the flowery scent of her hair, her skin, the warm red river flowing through her veins wasn't driving him out of his mind.

He raked his fingers through his hair, then flung open the door. "What the hell are you doing here?"

She took a step back, startled by his appearance and his rude greeting.

"I'm sorry," he said, his voice gruff. "What can I do for you?"

"Invite me inside?" she asked, hating the tremor in her voice.

"Sure," he said, taking a step back. "Welcome to my parlor, said the spider to the fly. Sorry," he muttered. "Please, come in."

Gathering her courage, she crossed the threshold.

He gestured for her to sit down, took the chair across from hers.

Skye tried not to stare at him, but she couldn't stop herself. His long, black hair was tousled, his feet and chest were bare, as if he had just gotten out of bed, which he likely had. She looked at his arms, corded with muscle, arms that had held her close.

Wolf took a deep breath, bemused by her nervousness, curious as to what had brought her here. "Skye? What's going on?"

"I…" What could she say? What little courage she had deserted her and she blurted, "I came to hear the rest of your story."

He lifted one incredulous brow.

"I…I have to know how it ends," she said, the words tripping over themselves. "Not knowing is keeping me awake nights."

He grunted softly. "Just let me go get dressed."

She nodded, thinking that was a great idea. It was impossible to think clearly when he was sitting there half-naked, looking so darn sexy. When she longed to throw herself into his arms and run her hands over his copper-hued flesh, sift her fingers through his hair.

She blew out a sigh when he left the room. It had been a mistake to come here. When she was in his arms, it didn't seem to matter what he was. But when she was home alone, she was tormented by doubts and fears. He was a vampyre, a man who lived in two worlds. A man who had lived for hundreds of years before she'd been born.

He returned a few minutes later wearing a pair of black jeans and a short-sleeved black tee shirt, as if to purposefully remind her of what he was.

"Are you sure you want to hear this?" he asked, sinking down on the chair again, his long legs stretched out in front of him, his feet still bare.

She nodded, though he thought she wasn't ready at all.

Wolf cursed under his breath. What the hell. "Where was I?" he asked, though he knew exactly where he had left off. And why.

71

"You … you said you tripped over an old drunk. In an alley."

"Yeah. Do you also remember what I told you about it being hard for new vampyres to control the urge to feed?"

She nodded. It was in this part of the story that things had fallen apart.

"Waiting is painful. Ignoring the need is excruciating for fledglings. You cannot imagine the agony. The man smelled of cheap whiskey and vomit and I didn't care." She had asked to hear it, he thought. He would tell her the whole, ugly truth. "I fed on him," he said, his gaze holding hers. "I drank him dry. He wasn't the first, and he wasn't the last."

He paused, waiting for her to tell him she'd heard enough. And although she looked as if she might faint, she didn't ask him to stop.

"It took close to a year before I learned to control the hunger that raged inside me. And another year before I learned that I didn't have to kill to satisfy the awful thirst that plagued me. After feeding that first time, I went back to the past. I stayed there for quite a while, but the future called to me. Every year or so, I traveled to the future."

"Anyway, when the tribes were conquered and sent to the reservation, I ran away. I stole some clothes from a white man and went to Deadwood. I can't tell you the number of times that miners and the like got together to beat the crap out of me. Until I started to fight back. I learned to speak English and then I found someone to teach me how to read and write. I found an old Colt and practiced with it until I could hit what I aimed at, and then I practiced some more. Pretty soon I had a reputation as a fast gun and with it a certain amount of grudging respect.

"I spent the next few years going back and forth from Deadwood to the reservation to see my grandfather. And then one day I decided to go through the cave again. This time, when I came out, it was the end of the twentieth century. It took a while to adjust to life here, to find a safe place to spend the day, to learn to adjust to being a vampyre."

"Wait a minute. Are you saying that in the past you're human and in the present, you're a vampyre?"

He nodded.

"But... that's impossible. How can you possibly be both?"

"The only explanation that makes sense is that I was turned in the future and when I go back to the past, it hasn't happened yet. But that's only a guess. I don't really understand it any more than I understand the difference in the way time passes. Days and nights pass normally here, in the present, but when I go into the past, it's always the day after I left, and the last time I left was sometime in 1880."

Skye shook her head. The whole story sounded like some other-worldly tale out of a sci-fi movie, or from the pages of some dystopian novel.

Wolf watched the play of emotions cross her face.

"It's so hard to believe," she murmured. "I can't imagine what you've been through."

He shrugged. "It is what it is."

"Which life do you prefer?"

He considered a lie and settled on the truth. "If I had to choose one or the other, I'd be a vampyre. The only reason I ever go back to the past these days is to visit my grandfather." The surprise in her eyes told him it wasn't the answer she had expected. Or wanted. But it was true. He liked the preternatural power being a vampyre gave him, the strength, the endurance. The blood.

"That man who warned me about you, he was one of the men who attacked you in my yard. And he was the man on the beach, too, wasn't he?"

"Yeah. He's braver than I gave him credit for. Anything else you'd like to know?"

"Do you sleep in a coffin?"

His laugh was short and without humor. "No."

"Can you turn into a bat, like Dracula?"

"No."

"But you still drink...?"

"Blood. Yes." And he loved it, the taste, the texture. The smell.

She contemplated that and then, eyes wide, she pressed a hand to her throat. "Did you ever drink from me?"

"Yes." He waited for her to run out of the house, but she only stared at him, face pale with shock. "When? How? And why don't I remember it?"

"Because I erased the memory from your mind."

"You can do that?"

"I'm a vampyre, my sweet. I can do almost anything. Read your mind. Manipulate your thoughts. Start a fire in the hearth with only a thought."

She flinched as a fire sprang to life before he finished speaking.

Hands clasped tightly in her lap, she stared at him, frightened and fascinated in equal measure.

Holding out his hand, he said, "Come, I'll walk you to the door."

But she continued to sit there, watching him.

"Skye?"

"You've never mentioned a single soul you care for, except your grandfather," she said, her voice quietly contemplative. "In all that time, you've never married?"

He shook his head.

"Never loved anyone?"

He shrugged. "I've *made* love to a lot of women. But I've never been *in* love with any of them." His gaze moved over her. "Until now."

His words, so softly spoken, brought tears to her eyes. How could she leave him when he was looking at her like that, as if waiting for her to tell him goodbye? How could she go when she wanted nothing more than to throw herself in his arms and tell him they would find a way to work it out? And even as the thought crossed her mind, she was standing, reaching for him.

"Skye?"

She heard the uncertainty in his voice as he pulled her close.

His gaze searched hers. "Do you know what you're doing?"

"I'm taking a chance," she said. "The first real chance I've ever taken in my whole life."

"It's a hell of a risk." For both of us, he thought.

"I know. I'm proposing that we see how it goes for a little while. Take things slow while we get to know each other better before we...you know." She blushed when his heated gaze moved over her, lingering on her lips, her breasts. Her throat. "So you know what I'm talking about."

Wolf nodded. "I hear what you're saying, but...." He shrugged. "You should know that my hunger increases my desire for...you know."

"That's why we're going to take it slow."

He closed his eyes. How long could he hold her without possessing her, kiss her without taking her? How long before his desire for her sweet flesh, his hunger for her blood, overcame his self-restraint?

As if reading his mind, she said, "You have to promise me that you won't drink from me again."

He swore softly. "I'm not sure I can make a promise like that, love."

"Then promise you won't do it without asking first."

"And if I asked, what would you say?"

"I don't know."

"What if I was asking now?"

She shuddered in his arms. Closed her eyes. Turned her head to the side.

Humbled by her willingness to let him do something he knew she found abhorrent touched him deeply. Cupping her face in his palms, he kissed her lightly. "I promise I won't drink from you in the future without asking, sweetness. Tonight, a kiss will do."

Skye hadn't realized how difficult 'taking it slow' would be. The next few weeks passed in a flurry of activity, as if by keeping busy they could ignore the attraction that sizzled between them whenever they were together. They spent most nights in crowded places – Disneyland, Knott's Berry Farm, Magic Mountain, dancing at popular night clubs, going to the movies, strolling through the mall, always surrounded by people.

But at the end of the night, when he drove her home, it was just the two of them.

Tonight was no different. He followed her inside, dropped down on the sofa while she removed her coat and kicked off her shoes, ran her fingers through her hair. When she shivered, he glanced at the hearth and a fire crackled to life.

"I don't think I'll ever get used to that," she remarked as he pulled her down beside him.

He shrugged. "You're cold." His gaze met hers. "I can think of a better way to warm you up."

"Yes," she said dryly. "I'm sure you can."

His arm slid around her shoulders as he leaned forward to nuzzle her neck. "You smell so good."

"Wolf, behave yourself."

"Skye, let me."

She tensed at his words. She had known that, sooner or later, he would ask again. She had just hoped it would be later. Much later. They sat together on her sofa every night, cuddling and kissing like a couple of teenagers. She didn't know about Wolf, but it took every ounce of self-control she possessed to keep from inviting him to her bed and surrendering to the need that burned brighter and hotter than the fire in the hearth when he held her close. Yet always, in the back of her mind, was the thought that he was a vampyre. It worked like being doused with ice water.

"Skye?"

"Will it hurt?"

"No, not at all. In fact, you'll like it."

She uttered a very unladylike snort. "I doubt that."

"You'll never know until you try." His fingers traced her lips. "Aren't you the least bit curious?"

"Not at all."

"Liar." His smile took the sting from the words.

"Do you, ah, drink from your ..."

"I think the term you're looking for is prey."

"Well, do you drink from one of them every night?"

"Yes."

"The same people?"

"No." Variety was the spice of life, he thought. Not all blood tasted the same, some was sweet, some was bland, some more satisfying, but it was all good.

"Do you like drinking it?"

"Honestly?"

She nodded.

"It's addictive. Like chocolate or potato chips," he said, with a grin.

"Do they like it when you feed on them?"

"They don't know it's happening."

Her eyes widened in disbelief. "How is that possible?"

"Mind control. I mesmerize them, then wipe the memory from their minds."

"You've done that to me, haven't you?"

"In a way. But I made sure it was pleasant for you."

Skye frowned. "You bit me while we were dancing, didn't you? I remember feeling so strange, like I was drifting on a crimson tide."

"You remember that?"

"Yes. Why?"

He grunted softly. There was no way she should have been able to recall what had happened. No way in hell. "You never answered my question," he reminded her.

Skye took a deep breath. She had to admit, all this talk had stirred her curiosity. "You'll only take a little?"

"I promise." He brushed her hair aside. "Relax, sweetness. I won't hurt you." He ran his tongue over her neck, tasted the fear on her skin as her heart beat increased. He bit her gently, felt her tense and then relax, her heart beat slowing as she relaxed in his embrace. He knew what she was feeling. He had felt the same sensual pleasure when he was turned so many decades ago.

Lifting his head, he licked the tiny wounds, sealing them. "Skye?"

She sighed. "Why did you stop?"

"I promised to take only a little."

"How can something that should be so gross feel so good?"

He stroked her cheek. "I would never cause you pain, love."

"Does the blood they sell on the Internet give people the same sensual high?"

"So I've heard." Cupping her face in his palms, he kissed her lightly. "Lucky you, getting it for free."

CHAPTER TEN

Wolf stalked the dark streets of the city in search of prey. Since being turned, he had fed almost every night. In the beginning, because he had needed it, craved it the way addicts craved their next fix. Later, as an older vampyre, he fed simply because he loved the taste. Now, he fed and fed well because, as he'd told Skye, being with her, wanting her, increased his desire not only for her sweet flesh, but for the sustaining warmth and strength of her life's blood.

Prey was scarce this night. He was about to go to another part of the city when he got the scents of blood and death.

And vampyre.

Turning down a dark alley behind a liquor store, he found the headless body of a vampyre lying between two dumpsters, the stake still lodged in its heart. A deep breath carried the scent of a vampyre that he knew. Jody Norcott had been in his early twenties, young in the life, having been turned only a few years ago. Wolf considered leaving the body where it was. The morning sun would disintegrate it, but he had liked the kid and leaving him lying in an alley with the trash seemed indecent somehow.

Lifting his head, Wolf took a deep breath, hoping to identify the hunters who had killed Norcott, but he didn't recognize their scents. New hunters, he thought, or new in town.

Either way, it didn't bode well for the other vampyres in the area.

Skye glanced at the clock for the tenth time in as many minutes. Where was Wolf? He had shown up at her house at the same time every night for the last month and a half. Had something happened to him? Had he suddenly tired of her?

Needing something to do, she hand-washed her dinner dishes and put them away, wiped down the stove and the refrigerator doors. And every few minutes, she glanced at the time. Where was he?

It was almost ten when Wolf materialized in the living room. "Sorry I'm so late."

"I was beginning to worry," she admitted as she moved into his arms and tilted her head back for his kiss. "Where have you been?"

"I found a dead body in an alley."

"Oh, Wolf, that's awful."

"It was a young vampyre."

She leaned back in his arms so she could see his face. "Was it someone you knew?"

"Yeah. He was just a kid. I carried him into the mountains and left him there."

"That seems..." She shrugged. "Wrong."

"The sun will incinerate his remains."

She looked at him in horror.

Wolf shrugged one shoulder. "It's the best way to dispose of the body. It leaves no trace behind."

"Will that...would that happen to you?"

"No. It doesn't work on older vampyres. Only the young ones. I went looking for his killers but I didn't have any luck."

He had searched all the places hunters were known to frequent but he'd struck out.

"I was worried," she said. "Call me the next time you you're going to be late, okay?"

"All right." Tugging on her hand, he led the way to the sofa, pulled her down beside him. Holding her close, he absently delved his fingers into her hair, but it was Norcott's body he saw in his mind, somehow more grotesque without his head, which was now in the possession of some hunter as proof of his kill.

Rage stirred deep inside him, fueled by the needless death. Norcott had never hurt a living soul. A pacifist in mortality, he had refused to prey on people. Instead, he'd fed on animal blood or on blood stolen from hospitals and blood banks. Dammit!

Skye felt the tension in him, grew suddenly apprehensive when she saw the faint red glow that burned in his eyes. Uncertain of what it meant, she muttered she had to check something in the kitchen and fled the room.

Wolf stared after her, then cursed under his breath as he realized what had sent her running from his presence.

Rising, he followed her to the kitchen and paused in the doorway. She stood at the sink, her hands braced on the counter. "Skye?"

"Wh..." She cleared a throat gone dry. "What?"

"I'm sorry."

"Sorry?"

"For scaring you."

She turned to face him. "What happened? Why did your eyes change like that?"

"It happens when I'm angry or when I've gone too long without feeding."

"Oh."

"I should have warned you."

She nodded. "I guess I still have a lot to learn."

Wolf shrugged. She had no idea. "Do you want me to go?"

"No."

Her denial held a world of doubt.

"Maybe it's for the best."

"Stay. It just surprised me, that's all," she said with a shaky smile. Walking toward him, she took his hand and led him back to the sofa. "Tell me more about vampyres."

Skye stood on the porch, watching Wolf get into his car and drive away. She lingered there long after he was out of sight, thinking of all the things he'd told her. A lot of the stuff she had read online had been myths and fairy tales, but some things – the scariest things – were true. Vampyres had the strength of twenty men. They grew stronger as they grew older. They could move faster than the human eye could follow, hypnotize mortals with nothing more than a glance, compel them to do their bidding. The Undead were immune to sickness and poison, and could only be destroyed by a wooden stake in the heart, by fire, or by beheading. She wondered, morbidly, how Wolf's friend had been killed, although she really didn't want to know.

Feeling suddenly vulnerable, she hurried inside, locked the door behind her, and engaged the dead bolt.

While getting ready for bed, she wondered how many other vampyres were in California, how many were here, in Los Angeles County.

After crawling under the covers, she stared up at the ceiling. How many of the unsolved murders she'd read about in the paper or heard about on the news through the years had been committed by vampyres? Like the deaths attributed to attacks by wild animals? Or the bodies drained

of blood that had been explained away as ritual killings by
a coven of witches?

Sleep was a long time coming.

Wolf sat at the bar in the Night's End, his thoughts turned
inward. Had it been a mistake to answer all of Skye's questions about his kind? He had been reluctant to tell her a
few things, yet she deserved to know the truth, deserved to
understand what she was getting into if they stayed together.
He wondered what her reaction would be when she saw him
at his worst, when he was badly hurt and angry, or when
he had gone without feeding for a few days, when all trace
of humanity was gone, his fangs bared, his eyes blood-red.
Hopefully, she would never see him like that.

He was about to seek his lair when Warren Gray entered
the club.

Wolf swore under his breath. Just what he needed, he
thought glumly, another encounter with the slayer.

Warren took a deep breath as he crossed the floor
toward the vampyre.

"What the hell are you doing here?" Wolf growled.

"I came to warn you."

Wolf arched one brow in surprise. "Is that right?"

The hunter nodded. "There are some new hunters in
town."

Wolf grunted. "Tell me something I don't know."

"They're here for you."

"Are you?"

"I admit, I've got good reason to want you dead."

"Yeah? What did I ever do to you?"

"You killed my brother three years ago."

Wolf grunted. "So, what do you want from me? My head, or an apology?"

"You don't even remember him, do you?"

"Can't say as I do. Was he a hunter, too?"

Gray nodded.

"What did you expect me to do? Just stand there and let him take my head without a fight?"

"I guess not."

"So, to what do I owe this warning?"

"Partly because you let me live when you could have killed me."

A faint smile twitched Wolf's lips. "I could kill you now."

"I've been tracking you for years," Gray said. "I don't think you kill without a reason."

"You said partly before. What's the rest?"

"The woman," Gray said. "Any human involved with you is in danger."

Wolf nodded. He couldn't argue with that. "So, why are these hunters after me, in particular?"

Warren shrugged. "All I know is that they're asking around for information on your whereabouts."

"Did they destroy a young vampyre and leave him in an alley?"

"Maybe, but I doubt it. They're after bigger fish."

Meaning me, Wolf thought. "Well, thanks for the warning."

With a nod, Gray turned and hurried out of the club.

Wolf stared after him, bemused by the hunter's visit. If it was true that he'd killed Gray's brother, why would the hunter warn Wolf that he was in danger? It didn't make a lick of sense.

Tossing back the last of his drink, he ordered another. These days, good sense was hard to find.

CHAPTER ELEVEN

In the morning, Skye rose early, ate a quick breakfast, packed the book she'd been reading, along with an apple, some chips, and a candy bar, grabbed a blanket and a towel, and headed for the beach. Lying on the sand, she listened to the gentle lapping of the waves as she watched a handful of sea gulls strut along the shore. With the sun shining brightly overhead, it was hard to imagine that vampyres were anything but ancient myths told to frighten children.

But Jason Wolf was very real. She knew she should be frightened of him, but the mere sight of him filled her with delight. His touch, his kisses, the rich dark velvet of his voice, the desire in his midnight-blue eyes, somehow chased away all her doubts and fears when they were together. Only now, in broad daylight when they were apart, did she wonder if she was making a terrible mistake – a mistake that could prove to be fatal.

Determined not to think about it, she went for a walk along the shore. Later, she took a swim and then a nap. On waking, she went searching for sea shells.

After returning to her blanket, she unwrapped the candy bar and reached for her book. For the next hour, she lost herself in the story of a gallant knight and a fairy princess who, in spite of numerous, seemingly insurmountable obstacles, found their way to a happy ending.

⚜   ⚜   ⚜

Wolf woke two hours before sunset. Rising, he opened his senses, searching for Skye. Ten minutes later, dressed in a black shirt and trousers, he transported himself to the beach.

Skye looked up when a shadow fell across her book. She let out a gasp of surprise when she saw Wolf standing there. "How did you know I was here?" she asked as he dropped down on the blanket beside her.

He shrugged. "I always know where you are."

Well, that was disconcerting, to say the least! "How is that possible?"

He cocked his head to the side, waiting for her to make the obvious connection.

"Ah, vampyre," she murmured. And then she frowned. "It's not even dark yet."

"The sun's not very strong right now. I thought I'd take you to dinner, unless you have other plans."

"You know I don't."

His gaze moved over her. The black, one-piece bathing suit she wore clearly outlined every delectable curve. It was a figure he longed to spend hours exploring. Shaking off his lustful thoughts, he said, "I guess you want to go home and change first."

"Good guess." Gaining her feet, she grabbed her bag and tucked the book inside, shook out the blanket, and draped it over her shoulder.

When they reached the parking lot, she looked around for his car, but there was no sign of it. Surely he hadn't taken a bus? "How did you get here?" she asked, tossing the bag and the blanket on the back seat.

"What's the difference? How about giving me a ride home?"

"Sure."

He closed her door when she slid behind the wheel, then walked around to the passenger side.

Frowning, Skye started the engine and pulled out of the lot. "Tell me how you got here," she said. "It isn't a secret, is it?"

"If you must know, I thought myself here."

She glanced at him to see if he was kidding, but he wasn't smiling. "You *thought* yourself here?"

"It's like teleporting," he explained. "I just think of where I want to go, and I'm there."

"Must save you a lot of money in gas."

"Indeed, it does."

She mulled that over as she pulled onto the freeway. That would be pretty neat, being able to just think yourself wherever you wanted to be. "How far can you go that way?"

He shrugged. "As far as I want."

"I guess you save a lot on air fare, too."

"Jealous?"

"Don't be silly." She slowed as she took the off-ramp, stopped at the signal. "Do you need to go home, or do you just want to come to my place?"

"Your place is fine, unless you think I need to change."

"You look fine." Better than fine, she thought. "You wear a lot of black."

"Goes with the territory."

"Makes it easier to sneak up on people, I guess."

"Believe me, honey, I don't have to sneak up on them."

She could believe that, she thought irritably, at least where women were concerned.

Wolf laughed softly, amused and pleased by her jealousy.

"Don't you ever drink from men?"

"Only in emergencies."

When they reached the house, she was out of the car before he could hold the door for her. Well, damn, he thought, as he followed her up the porch steps and into the house. He'd stepped in it this time.

He waited in the living room while she went upstairs to change. Standing at the window, he thought about what Warren Gray had told him and wondered again why the hunters were after him, in particular. To most slayers, a vampyre was a vampyre and the only good one was a dead one.

He turned at the sound of footsteps, whistled softly when he saw Skye coming down the stairs. She wore an ice-blue sheath that was modest in cut, but there was no disguising the luscious curves beneath.

"Are you sure you want to go out?" he asked, as his gaze moved over her. "I can think of lots of things to do, right here at home."

Batting her eye lashes at him, she purred, "Can you?"

"Oh, yeah."

"Like what?"

"Like peeling that dress off of you an inch at a time. Laying you down in front of the fire, and making love to you until the sun comes up."

Skye's heart skipped a beat as a vivid image of the two of them making love in front of the fire flashed through her mind.

Moving toward her, Wolf took her in his arms. "What do you say, sweetness? Want to skip dinner and take a walk on the wild side with me?"

"We're taking it slow, remember?" she said, breathlessly.

"Aren't you the least bit tempted? The least bit curious?"

She was. Oh, lordy, was she ever. Jason Wolf was temptation wrapped in danger and sex appeal. Closing her eyes, she murmured, "I need a little more time."

"I can wait," he said, his voice tight. But, heaven help him, he wasn't sure how much longer that would be true.

Leaving Skye's house later than night, Wolf paused on the front porch, his gaze darting left and right as he caught an unfamiliar scent in the air. Opening his preternatural senses, he took a deep breath, his gaze focusing on the low hedge that separated Skye's property from the place next door. There was a rustling in the brush, the sound of running feet.

Curious, Wolf pursued the prowler and managed to catch him at the corner. The man whirled around, the knife in his hand glinting in the bright light of the moon as it slashed toward Wolf's heart.

Wolf ducked under the blade. It sliced across his back, cutting through cloth and flesh. Cursing, he wrapped his hands around the man's head and with one, quick twist, broke his assailant's neck.

Ignoring the pain burning in his back, he searched the shadows, but detected no one else. Kneeling beside the body, he went through the man's pockets. The hunter carried no identification of any kind, only a thick wad of cash, a wooden stake, and a bottle of holy water. Was this one of the hunters Warren Gray had warned him about?

Shit!

A thought carried him back to Skye's house.

The front door was open.

The house was empty save for Warren Gray's body. It lay in the entry way in a widening pool of crimson. His throat had been cut from ear to ear.

A sheet of paper rested on his chest, held in place by the blood-stained blade of a butcher knife.

A chill ran through Wolf's body when he read the message, printed in block letters.

If you care about the woman,
meet us tomorrow night
at midnight at 22 Middleton Circle

A muscle throbbed in Wolf's jaw as he read the address a second time.

It was the address of the late Warren Gray.

CHAPTER TWELVE

Skye had never been more so scared in her life. She sat on a hard metal chair in the middle of a square room, her hands tightly bound behind her back with a strip of duct tape.

She stared at the five men huddled together in the corner of the room – a room unlike any she had ever seen. It had no windows. There were two doors. One led to a bathroom. The other was a narrow iron door with a heavy crossbar instead of a lock. It looked like something out of medieval castle.

A long table held an assortment of weapons – guns, knives, a long, double-edged blade reminiscent of a medieval sword. Several bottles of clear liquid looked out of place in the midst of so many instruments of death.

She swallowed hard when the men glanced her way, their eyes dark with speculation. They were all clad in black from head to foot.

They looked like ordinary men, clean-cut, clean-shaven. Just regular guys, but they were vampyre hunters, she thought, licking lips gone dry. And they were after Wolf. From what little she had overheard, there was some kind of contest between these men and another group of hunter/slayers to see which of them could take Wolf's head.

A cold chill slithered down her spine as she wondered how secure her own head was.

CHAPTER THIRTEEN

It took Wolf only moments to follow Skye's scent to an abandoned meat packing plant located in an unincorporated part of the city. Dissolving into mist, he drifted around the single-story building. Made of cinder block and cement, with doors that had been heavily reinforced, every crack and crevice repaired, so that all sound from within was muffled. The barred windows had been boarded up so that no light emanated from inside.

Wolf paused beside one of the windows, debating his next move. Would it be easier to take them here, or at Gray's house? He had no idea what—or who—waited inside. He had little doubt the hunters had planned for any contingency. But one thing was certain. Materializing into unknown territory was reckless and might well be fatal.

He opened the blood link between himself and Skye, knew the moment she felt it, though she wasn't sure what it was. He cursed himself for not explaining it to her.

Skye.

Wolf? I can't see you. Where are you?

I'm outside.

Her relief was palpable in spite of her confusion at being able to hear him when he wasn't in the room.

Are you all right? he asked. *Have they hurt you?*

No. They have a lot of weapons in here. There's a heavy net above the door. I've never seen anything like it. The ropes look like they've been dipped in silver.

Clever, Wolf thought. If they could trap him in a net threaded with silver, it would not only hurt like hell, it would render him nearly powerless. It occurred to him that they had been expecting him to come here. The Gray house must be their back-up plan.

Wolf? How can we be talking like this?

It's because I've tasted your blood. It formed a link between us. One that could only be broken by her death. Or his. But he didn't tell her that. *Sit tight, love. We'll be together again tomorrow night.*

Tomorrow? There was a tremor in her voice.

Don't be afraid. They won't hurt you. I'll be touch. I love you.

He had a lot to do before the sun came up.

Skye woke with a start. Her arms ached, her limbs were stiff from being in one position for so long. She was hungry. And thirsty. And she needed to go to the bathroom.

She glanced around the room. Of the five men who had been there the night before, only one remained. She reached out to Wolf, but nothing happened. Of course, she thought, he was at rest if the sun was up. At least she thought it was. Save for the overhead light, the room was as dark now as it had been the night before.

She tensed as the man strode toward her, breathed a sigh of relief when he cut the duct tape and released her hands.

"Bathroom's in there," he said, jerking his head toward the wooden door.

Skye rose unsteadily and made her way to the rest room. She grimaced as she stepped inside. The walls were grimy, the ugly green linoleum ripped and stained. The toilet seat was disgusting. The sink filthy. There were no windows.

Moving gingerly, she stood over the toilet and relieved herself. She decided to forego washing her hands, since she didn't want to touch the faucets.

When she returned to the main room, the man handed her a breakfast burrito and a paper cup of coffee. She saw no need to thank him.

Perching on the edge of the chair, she nibbled at the burrito, her gaze darting around the room. There was only one way out. She glanced at the table. If she could get hold of a weapon...

"Don't even think about it," the man said. "You about done there?"

Skye nodded, her heart racing as she handed him the remains of her burrito, then threw the hot coffee in his face and ran toward the table.

With a cry of pain, he darted after her.

With a cry of her own, Skye grabbed the long-bladed knife and turned to face her captor. She stared in horror as the man tried to stop his momentum, and failed. He let out a cry as he impaled himself on the blade, staggered back, and dropped to his knees, the knife embedded in his chest near his left shoulder.

Stricken, Skye stared at him. He was badly hurt. But she couldn't worry about that now. She ran toward the door, let out a wail of defeat as it opened and the other four men blocked her way.

Terrified by what their reaction would be when they saw their companion, she scuttled away to the far side of the room, her back pressed against the wall.

"What the hell happened here?" one of the men said, glancing from his downed companion to Skye and back again.

"She attacked me," the wounded man gasped as he pulled the blade from his shoulder and tossed it aside.

Two of the men grabbed Skye's arms, thrust her onto the chair, then quickly duct-taped her hands behind her back. One of them slapped her. "Try anything like that again and you're dead," he growled.

There was a scurry of activity as the men hovered over their injured comrade. One of them pulled a large first aid kit from under the table and they spent the next twenty minutes patching him up.

Head bowed, Skye closed her eyes. She had tried and failed. It was up to Wolf now.

Wolf rose with the setting of the sun. He dressed quickly, then went in search of prey. He fed on several women, knowing he would need the additional strength before the night was over.

When that was done, he opened the blood link between himself and Skye to ascertain that she was all right. When he was sure, he closed it again.

After returning to Skye's house, Wolf found a blanket, wrapped it around Gray's body, and transported the corpse to the morgue. He left Gray lying by the back door. If the hunter had kin, the police would notify them of his death.

Back at Skye's, he mopped up the blood, thinking she would probably want to replace the carpet, but that was a problem for another day.

When he'd cleaned it up the best he could, he left the house to prowl the dark street, as restless as a caged tiger as he waited for the hours until midnight to pass, his rage growing with every tick of the clock.

At eleven-thirty, he sensed that the hunters had moved out of the abandoned building and relocated at Warren Gray's place.

At eleven-fifty, he willed himself to the hunter's house. The front door was shut, the drapes drawn over all the windows With the owner dead, the threshold had no power to repel him... Dissolving into mist, he slipped under the door.

Skye was seated on a kitchen chair in the middle of the living room floor. One hunter stood behind her, a wicked-looking dagger at her throat.

A second hunter was positioned beside the door so that he would be behind Wolf when he entered the room. He held a sword in one hand and a large bottle of holy water in the other. The third hunter waited behind a Chinese screen in a corner of the living room. The fourth slayer stood to the right of the first, a rifle in his hands. Wolf could smell the silver bullets in the breech.

A clock on the mantel began to toll the hour. At 12:01, Wolf materialized beside Skye. He picked her up, chair and all, and vanished from the premises.

Two seconds later, Warren Gray's house exploded.

CHAPTER FOURTEEN

Wolf transported the two of them to Skye's living room. He freed her hands, then wrapped her in his embrace and sank down on the sofa, rocking her gently.

She burrowed into his arms as sobs and shivers wracked her body.

"That's it, love, let it all out."

"I was ... so ... so scared ... they would ... kill you."

He brushed a kiss across the top of her head. "Don't think about it. They'll never bother anyone else again."

Dashing the tears from her eyes, she looked up at him. There had been a note of finality in his voice. "Are you going to ...?" She couldn't say the words.

"It's already taken care of."

The finality in his voice, in his eyes, sent a chill down her spine.

Brow furrowed, she stared at him, wondering what he had done and when he'd had time to do it. She was about to ask when she decided she would rather not know, at least not right now, when it was all so fresh in her mind.

She wondered briefly about the man the hunters had killed. Had he had a wife, children? She didn't even know his name, yet she felt guilty for his death.

Resting her cheek against Wolf's broad chest, she closed her eyes. She couldn't go through anything like this again, she thought. Maybe she was a coward, but she hadn't been raised to fight off vampyre hunters. She loved Wolf. If only he was just a normal man ...

"Jason?"

"Yes, love?"

"You said you're just a regular guy in the Old West. Is that true?"

He nodded, eyes narrowed. He had a hunch he knew where this was going.

"Can anybody go through the cave?"

"Anyone who's with me."

"I think we should go into the past."

"You do, do you?"

"Yes," she said, warming to the idea. "I've always wanted to see the Old West, you know. We could be together there, just a man and a woman. No vampyres. No hunters." She looked up at him, her eyes suddenly sparkling with excitement.

"Are you sure about this?" He made a broad gesture that encompassed the house and everything in it. "Living in the Old West is nothing like this, you know? No hot running water, no flush toilets. No toilet paper. No cell phones. No Starbucks."

Skye glanced around the living room. She had never even been camping. Was she ready to live in a log house and go without all the modern conveniences that took the drudgery out of housework? Or cook over a wood burning stove, and give up social media, movies, iTunes, Instagram, health insurance?

Would she rather give up Wolf?

"I'm willing to try," she said, slowly. "Besides, it wouldn't be forever. Everything will still be here whenever we come back."

"All right, love, we'll go. If that's what you want."

She bit down on her lower lip. It would be rough, she thought, going without all the creature comforts she was used to. But it would also be the adventure of a lifetime. He could take her to all the places she had photographed, places she had only dreamed about, but with Wolf, she would see them as they had really been.

She had been fascinated by cowboys, Indians, and the Old West ever since she was five years old and saw her first cowboy movie. And now she had a chance to see it all up close and personal. She thought of the photographs she could take, the places she had only seen depicted in magazines and old movies. Instead of cardboard cutouts and museum exhibits, she would have a chance to experience the real thing up close and personal.

"I think we should go," she said resolutely. And then she frowned. "If I don't like it, if it's more than I can handle, you will bring me back here, right?"

Wolf grinned at her. Did she think he'd keep her there against her will? "Yes, love."

She worried her lower lip between her teeth, took a deep breath. "I'll need a day or two to get in touch with the utility companies and tell them I'm going on a long vacation. And I'll need to go to the post office and have them put a hold on my mail. And hire someone to come and look after the yard." She picked up her cell phone and checked the calendar. "How about this Wednesday? Does that work for you?"

"Whatever you want." Rising, he set her on her feet. "You need to get some sleep."

She yawned behind her hand. "I think you're right. Will you stay here tonight?"

He grunted softly. As if he would let her out of his sight after what had happened. His gaze searched hers and then, very slowly, he drew her into his arms. "I love you, Skye," he murmured.

"I know." She looked up at him, waiting for him to kiss her, felt her heart skip a beat when he lowered his head and claimed her lips with his.

"Sweet dreams, love." Settling on the sofa, Wolf watched her climb the stairs. He was afraid she was in for a rude awakening when she faced the reality of the Old West, but getting out of the city for a while seemed like a hell of a good idea.

He listened to her get ready for bed, heard the rustle of sheets as she slid under the covers. He waited until he heard the soft, regular sound of her breathing, then he materialized in her room and stretched out beside her, content to lie there and watch her sleep until the sun chased the moon from the sky.

Slipping quietly out of bed, he made his way to the guest room and stretched out on the floor of the walk-in closet. For the next two days, he intended to stick like glue to the beautiful and oh, so desirable Skye Somers.

Skye frowned when she woke alone in bed. Even in her sleep, she had been aware of Wolf lying beside her. No doubt he had gone to his lair to spend the daylight hours.

She showered and dressed, then went into the guest room where she kept her luggage.

She let out a yelp of surprise when she saw Wolf lying on his back on the floor.

He opened one eye. "Something wrong?"

"No. I ... I was just a bit startled to find you in here. I thought's you'd gone home."

"I don't want you to be alone."

She smiled uncertainly as she reached for her rolling suitcase, and then paused when she saw her grandmother's flowered valise. It seemed a more suitable choice for a trip to the past, she thought, as she lifted if from the shelf and quietly closed the closet door.

The next two days flew by. While Wolf rested in the guest-room closet, Skye stopped her mail, emptied the refrigerator and cupboards of everything perishable, and covered the furniture. She asked her neighbor next door to keep an eye on the house and hired one of the neighbor's teenage sons to water the yard.

She went shopping at a Country Western store, hoping to find something suitable for the Old West. She found just what she was looking for in a small section in the back of the store—two country-style dresses, one a dark pink, the other a yellow print. They both had long skirts. The yellow one had short, puffy sleeves and a wide, white sash, the pink had long sleeves. She picked out a couple of petticoats, a pair of low-heeled boots, and two bonnets, one white, one yellow, a pair of jeans, and a Western-style plaid shirt.

Back at home, she packed everything, along with a dozen changes of underwear, socks, and a pair of shoes that didn't look too modern. She also packed her make-up, two bars of soap, shampoo and conditioner, and anything else she figured she wouldn't be able to find in the past.

Rummaging through her closet, she located an old Canon PowerShot camera that ran on batteries and used an SD card. She found a case, stuffed it with extra batteries, and several memory cards. She picked up her cell phone, then put it down, thinking it wouldn't be much use without Internet or wi-fi or any way to recharge the battery.

That night, she curled up on the sofa with Wolf, listening while he told her of his life in the past, of card games and gunfights, of cattle rustlers and tinhorn gamblers. He had crossed paths with some famous people besides Red Cloud and Wild Bill Hickok, men like Butch Cassidy and Wyatt Earp.

By Wednesday afternoon, she was having second thoughts. What if Wolf took her into the past and something happened to him and she couldn't find her way back to the cave? What if she couldn't get back home without him? What if they got trapped in some kind of limbo between the past and the present? What if he refused to bring her back home? What if she got sick? Doctors in the past had limited knowledge and resources. What if she got a toothache? Cramps? A migraine?

She went through her medicine cabinet, made a hasty trip to the drug store to load up on aspirin, band-aids both large and small, a roll of adhesive tape and two rolls of gauze, antiseptic cream, suntan lotion, feminine sanitary needs, and three tubes of toothpaste. She bought a new toothbrush and also bought one for Wolf in case they didn't have them in the past.

Hoping she had thought of everything, she took a long, hot shower and washed her hair, stepped into her petticoat and donned her grandmother's blue gingham dress. Looking in the mirror, Skye grinned at her reflection. She looked like she had just stepped out of an episode of *Little House on the Prairie*. Or maybe *Seven Brides for Seven Brothers*.

Laughing, she went downstairs to wait for sundown.

✤ ✤ ✤

When Wolf rose that evening, he had to admit he was surprised to find Skye decked out in a blue gingham dress with short, puffy sleeves, and a pair of low-heeled cowboy boots. He had fully expected her to have changed her mind at the last minute.

"Are you ready?" he asked, noting the bulging valise waiting by the front door.

"I think so."

"If you change your mind once we get there, or you forgot something, we can always come back."

She nodded, excitement and trepidation building within her. "Let's go before I do change my mind. How long does it take to get there?"

"Not long." He picked up her valise bag and slid his free arm around her waist.

"What are you doing?"

"You'll see. Just relax."

Before she could question him further, he transported the two of them to South Dakota.

Skye let out a gasp and closed her eyes as the world fell away into blackness and abruptly righted itself. When she opened her eyes, they were in front of a cave cut into a stone mountain.

"Almost there." Taking her by the hand, Wolf led her inside.

The cavern was cool and totally dark.

"Don't go wandering off," Wolf said. "I need to change clothes."

Skye shivered. She heard the whisper of cloth against skin as he undressed and dressed again. What was she doing here, wherever here was? She was a city girl through and through. What made her think traipsing off to the Old West was a good idea? She breathed a sigh of relief when ?Wolf reached for her hand again, frowned when he began to chant. His voice was low, the words foreign, yet strangely beautiful and compelling, weaving a spell around her.

A moment later, he tugged on her hand and she followed him through the darkness. She felt a rush of excitement as the cave grew lighter, and then they were outside.

Skye blinked against the bright sunlight. As far as the eye could see, there was nothing but rolling prairie and trees. A black-and-white pinto stood tied to a nearby tree. It whinnied softly when Wolf emerged.

Her gaze ran over Wolf as he secured a pair of well-worn leather saddlebags behind his saddle. He wore a pair of black trousers, a dark green, long-sleeved shirt, a black leather vest, hat, and boots. She stared at the .44 Colt holstered on his right hip. It looked right at home, she thought. "I don't believe this," she murmured. "It isn't possible."

"I know," he agreed. "But here we are." He secured her valise behind the cantle, swung into the saddle, then reached down to lift her up, so that she sat sideways in front of him. It was a tight squeeze. "The town's not far."

Skye nodded. Unless she was dreaming, she was somewhere in the Old West.

Wolf took up the reins and clucked to the mare and she moved out at a brisk walk.

Skye stared wide-eyed at the countryside as they rode. The sky, so blue it almost hurt her eyes, seemed to stretch away forever, as did the prairie. They rode for hours and just when she thought they would never reach their destination, they crested a high hill. In the gathering dusk, she saw a town spread out below. It looked just like every cow town in every Western movie she had ever seen, she thought, as they descended the hill.

The streets were wide and dusty, lined with businesses on both sides – saloons, mainly, but also a restaurant, a gun shop, a blacksmith, a doctor's office, a barbershop, a general store, a millinery shop with wide-brimmed hats in the window. Men and women who looked as if they had just stepped out of a Hollywood western strolled along the boardwalk. A scantily clad woman leaned over the balcony of Maud's Pleasure Palace, a cigar in one hand. Her gown displayed a generous amount of cleavage.

Skye had seen movies and documentaries about life in the Old West, read books, but nothing had prepared her for the real thing – the dirt, the smells, some she didn't recognize, the noise.

A beer wagon pulled by a pair of draft horses rumbled down the street, stirring a cloud of dun-colored dust. Horses stood hitched to a long rack in front of the Ten Spot Saloon. She heard the sound of a tinny piano coming from inside, along with raucous male laughter and high-pitched feminine giggles. In the distance, she heard the ring of a blacksmith's hammer.

She was really here, in the Wild West.

Her heart beat with trepidation and excitement as Wolf drew rein in front of a two-story hotel. The Monarch was painted white with dark green trim. The door was the same shade of green. Four steps led to a raised entrance. A life-sized wooden Indian stood to the left of the door.

Wolf held Skye's arm as she slid from the saddle to the ground. Dismounting, he untied her valise and his saddlebags and slung them over his shoulder. "Here we are." He tethered the reins to the hitching post, and gave the mare an affectionate pat on the neck.

Looking around, Skye murmured, "This is amazing."

"If you say so."

She followed him up the stairs and into the hotel. The lobby was papered in a green-and-gold stripe, the floor was hardwood. A mahogany reception desk stood opposite the door. A pair of sofas faced each other in front of a fireplace to the left of the desk, a small table and two chairs took up space against the wall to the right.

The clerk behind the desk forced a smile when he saw Wolf striding toward him.

"I need the room adjoining mine," Wolf said.

"Yessir." The man reached behind him and plucked two keys from a peg board. "How long will you and your ... ah, guest, be staying, Mr. Wolf?"

"I'm not sure."

The man nodded again as he handed Wolf the keys. Skye thought it odd that he didn't ask Wolf to sign a register or request payment in advance.

"Do you stay here often?" she asked as she followed Wolf up a narrow staircase to the second floor.

"Whenever I'm in town. The hotel keeps a room for me. Like I told you, it's always the next day when I return to the past."

"The clerk doesn't seem to like you."

"I'm a half-breed," he said, as if that explained everything. He turned left at the top of the stairs, stopped in front of Room 207, and opened the door.

Skye stepped inside. The room, like the town, looked like part of a movie set. The walls were white-washed. There was a small, square table beside the brass bed, a ladder-back chair in one corner, a white porcelain pitcher and bowl atop a battered four-drawer chest. She spied a white chamber pot under the bed. Lace curtains fluttered at the open window that looked down on Main Street.

Wolf dropped her valise on the foot of the bed, then opened the door to the adjoining room, which looked exactly like the one they were in, save the dresser was made of oak instead of mahogany, and the cover on the bed was a patchwork quilt instead of a flowered bedspread.

They were here, Skye thought, suddenly apprehensive. Really here. She shivered as the reality of it suddenly hit her. A magical trip through a magical cave and she was in the Old West. Maybe she was dreaming, she thought, and pinched herself.

It didn't hurt in dreams.

Wolf grinned at her. "You always wanted to see the Wild West," he said. "This is it."

She nodded slowly. "What now?"

"I could use something to eat," he said. "How about you?"

"I am hungry, now that you mention it."

The Delta Restaurant was a long, narrow building located at the far end of Main Street. Skye glanced around as they stepped inside. Frilly white curtains hung at the windows. The walls were papered with a pretty, flowered print, the floor was polished wood. Lanterns hung from the ceiling. Red-and-white cloths covered the tables.

Wolf chose a small table away from the windows and sat with his back to the wall. It reminded her of the Westerns she'd read, where the notorious gunfighter always sat facing the door.

A petite brunette offered them one-sheet paper menus. She smiled broadly at Wolf. "Nice to see you again, Jason."

He nodded. "You, too, Anna."

Anna sent a curious glance at Skye. "Who's your friend?"

"This is Skye. Skye, Anna."

Skye looked up in time to see a flash of jealousy in the other woman's eyes. "Nice to meet you, Anna."

"You, too," the waitress replied. And then she smiled at Wolf again. "Do you want the usual?"

"That'll be fine."

Anna looked down at Skye. "And you?"

"I'd like chicken and dumplings, please," Skye replied, her voice cool.

The waitress jotted the orders on a pad, picked up the menus, and sashayed away from the table.

"She's pretty," Skye remarked.

"Reckon so."

"Do you know her very well?"

Wolf grinned. "Depends on what you mean by 'well.'"

"I think you know *exactly* what I mean."

"Well enough," he said. "You jealous?"

"Of course not!"

"Good. She doesn't mean anything to me."

"You obviously mean something to her."

"No reason for you to be jealous," Wolf said. "In spite of her flirting with me, we're just friends, nothing more. She's happily married." Leaning forward, he reached for her hand. "I wouldn't have brought you here if I was involved with anyone else."

"I'm sorry. It's really none of my business. I shouldn't have said anything."

"No worries, sweetheart." He sat back as Anna brought their dinner.

Skye stared at the slab of meat on Wolf's plate. It was the biggest steak she had ever seen.

She had ordered her meal on a whim, never having had chicken and dumplings before. The chicken was surprisingly good and tender, the dumplings soft, the broth delicious.

"So, what would you like to do tomorrow?" Wolf asked as he cut into his steak.

"Take some pictures of the town," she said. There was so much to see, she couldn't wait to get started. The buildings, the people, the horses, the wagons and the stagecoach, the land itself. She wished she could have brought her cell phone. It was newer than her camera and took great photos, but there was no way to recharge it. She didn't even know if the camera on the phone would work.

"That shouldn't be a problem, although you might get some odd looks when people see your camera. The ones in the 1880s are a lot bigger and bulkier. I guess you can tell anyone who asks that it's the latest model from back East."

Skye grinned at him. She planned to take some photographs of him, too, as many as she could.

Skye frowned when the waitress brought their check. Leaning forward, she whispered, "How are you going to pay for this? You can't use money from the future."

Reaching into his pants' pocket, he said, "I keep some bank notes and silver in my saddlebags for just such an occasion."

With dinner over, they decided to take a walk around the town. Skye peered in the windows of the millinery shop, enchanted by the quaint hats and bonnets with their plumes and fake flowers, the wide ribbons meant to tie under the chin.

When they reached the general store, she stepped inside. It was a large building, filled with counters and barrels, shelves, and glass-fronted cabinets, which held everything from guns and knives to baby rattles, shirts, pants, belts, Stetson hats, pots, pans, pillows and blankets, cans of vegetables, bags of flour and sugar, rounds of cheese.

She wandered up and down the aisles, wishing she had brought her camera with her, not only to record the amazing number of goods, but the prices. Twenty-five cents for a pound of bacon, forty cents for a pound of butter, thirty-five cents for a dozen eggs.

Wolf trailed behind her, amused by the expressions that played over her face as she held up a set of long underwear. He grinned when she looked at him, one brow raised, obviously wondering if he wore longjohns while in the Old West. He didn't.

They passed the Ten Spot Saloon on the way back to the hotel. Curious, she peered over the top of one of the swinging doors, then pushed it open.

"Hold on there," Wolf said, laying his hand on her arm. "Decent women don't frequent saloons."

Skye huffed her irritation, but didn't argue.

She was ready for bed by the time they reached the hotel. It was still early, but the stress of travelling through time had taken more of a toll on her than she'd thought.

Wolf followed her upstairs, waited while she unlocked her door. She looked up at him, wondering if he would kiss her goodnight. While she waited, it occurred to her that there was something different about him. And then she knew what it was. Always before, he had been surrounded by an aura of preternatural power that was now missing. She hadn't recognized it for what it was before and only noticed it now because it was gone. It occurred to her yet again that he was no longer invincible. He was human here, vulnerable without his supernatural abilities. It was a frightening thought, one she'd had briefly before they came here. But now the reality of it was staring her in the face. What would she do if something happened to Wolf?

"Good night, Skye."

"Night."

His gaze moved over her face and then, ever so gently, he drew her into his arms and kissed her. It was little more than the brush of his lips over hers, but it sent a rush of heat spiraling through her all the way to the soles of her feet. She grinned inwardly. *That* hadn't changed!

Lifting his head, Wolf smiled down at her, and then he kissed her again, longer, deeper, his tongue stroking the insides of her lower lip, all the while cursing his promise to take it slow.

She was breathless when he let her go.

"See you in the morning, sweetness."

Skye nodded, then stepped into the room and closed the door. She stood there a moment, her fingers pressed to her lips. Lordy, that man knew how to kiss!

In his room, Wolf blew out a sigh as he sat on the edge of the mattress and imagined what it would be like to spend the night with Skye in his bed, in his arms, to hold her close and slowly explore the lush hills and valleys of her slim figure, to make love to her all through the night and into the wee small hours of the morning.

His thoughts produced the expected results. For a moment, he thought of going to visit Delia to ease the desire

Skye had aroused in him. Once, he would have done so. But not now.

Muttering an oath, he stripped down to his briefs and crawled into his lonely bed. Like it or not, he feared the lovely Skye Somers had permanently killed his desire for any other woman.

CHAPTER FIFTEEN

Skye woke to the rumble of wagon wheels and the whinnying of a horse. Frowning, she sat up, momentarily confused. She glanced at the white-washed walls, the curtains fluttering at the open window. Where the heck was she?

She blinked and then bounded out of bed. She was in the past. With Wolf! Hurrying to the window, she peered down at the street below. The town lay beneath a bright blue sky. The wagon she had heard rumbled down the street, leaving a cloud of dust hanging in the air. Three ladies in long dresses and wide-brimmed hats gathered on the wooden boardwalk, their heads together. Horses stood at the hitchrack, tails idly swishing flies. A man wearing a long-sleeved shirt, pants, and chaps strolled across the street, spurs jangling.

She was really here. Where was Wolf?

Moving to the door that opened into his room, she knocked lightly. "Wolf? Are you awake?"

She stepped back as the door opened, felt her heart skip a beat when she saw him. He was clad in black from his hat to his boots. And even though the aura of supernatural power was gone, his presence was still commanding. She glanced at the Colt holstered at his side and knew instinctively that, human or vampyre, he was a man to be reckoned with.

"'Mornin', beautiful," he drawled. "How'd you sleep?"

She grinned at him. He seemed so different here. So...normal. "Fine."

"You ready for some breakfast?"

Skye looked down at her nightgown. "Not quite yet," she said. "Give me ten minutes."

They went to breakfast in the same restaurant where they'd had dinner the night before. A different waitress came to take their order. She seemed as friendly with Wolf as the previous one. Not that Skye could blame the woman. He was sexy as hell whether he was a cowboy or a vampyre.

She ordered scrambled eggs, bacon and coffee. He ordered steak and eggs. "I don't understand it," she said when the waitress left the table. "How can you be just a guy here, and a vampyre in my time?"

He shrugged. "Beats the hell out of me."

"So you remember what it's like to be a..." She lowered her voice. "A vampyre when you're here?"

"Yeah."

"Does it bother you, knowing you're a vampyre and that you...that you do what you do?"

"No. I only *do what I have to do* to survive, same as anyone else."

She frowned as she mulled that over. What a strange life he led. She leaned forward. "In my time, you're practically immortal. Is that true here, too?"

"I doubt it, although I don't know for sure."

"So, isn't it kind of risky for you to come here?"

He shrugged. "I've spent a lot of time here. Life is risky no matter where you are."

Well, that was true, Skye thought, as the waitress brought their order. She shook her head as she watched him eat, thinking he certainly had a hearty appetite. But then, he was a big man, she mused, with a lot of lusty appetites.

Looking up, he grinned at her bemused expression. "Guess I've got the best of both worlds," he remarked. "Blood in the future. Steak and eggs in the past."

Skye grimaced. Judging by his steak, he liked blood in the past, too, she thought. If the meat had been any more rare, it would still be walking.

After breakfast, they strolled through the town again. Skye paused now and then, unobtrusively snapping pictures of a Wells Fargo stage coach, the front of the National Bank, a pair of scantily clad women leaning over the balcony of Maud's Pleasure Palace. She wished she'd been able to bring her Sony with the telephoto lens, but it just wouldn't have been practical, and the telephoto lens might have drawn attention.

"Hey, Wolf!" one of the women called. "When are you gonna come up and see me again?"

He paused and looked up. "Delia, how's it going?"

She leaned a little further over the rail, allowing him a good view of her ample cleavage. "My bed's awful cold and lonely without you," she said with a pout.

Wolf laughed. "As you can see, darlin', I'm no long available."

Delia stared at Skye. "She don't look like much to me."

Wolf laughed again as he slipped his arm around Skye's waist. "She's more than enough for me." With a wave of his hand, he turned his back on the working girl. "Where do you want to go now, love?"

"I don't know. Is she a ... a lady of the evening?"

"She's not a lady any time of the day or night," he said, looking amused. "Where do you want to go now?"

Skye glanced around, then shrugged. There really weren't a lot of fun things to do as far as she could see. No movies, or museums. No beaches or amusement parks. No parks at all. Just a dozen or so businesses located on either side of a dusty street, a school, and a small, white-washed church with a bell tower at the far end of the town.

She paused to take a photo of the livery stable, the burly blacksmith across the street, the Sheriff's Office, the barber shop.

She supposed the women in this day and age didn't have a lot of spare time, what with housework, baking bread, and raising kids. A few basic things were available at the general store – canned goods and some clothing, a few staples brought in from the surrounding farms. But there were no fast food restaurants, no stores with packaged meat and meals. Everything had to be made from scratch. There were no microwave ovens, refrigerators, washing machines, or dishwashers. No dry cleaners or laundromats. She had read somewhere that in the old days, most people never ventured more than a few miles from where they were born, and that doing the laundry could be an all day job.

They turned around at the end of the town, crossed the street, and started back toward the hotel.

"We could go for a ride, if you're up to it," Wolf suggested. "Have you ever been on a horse?"

"Once, when I was a little girl."

They stopped at the livery, where Wolf arranged to rent a horse for Skye – a pretty red roan with one white stocking and a narrow blaze. Skye had brought a pair of jeans with her, but she hadn't seen any of the town ladies wearing pants. She glanced down at her dress. The skirt long and full enough to cover her legs. She tucked her camera into the small leather case and draped the shoulder strap over the saddle horn.

Wolf lifted her easily into the saddle, then swung onto the back of his pinto. "You ready?"

"I guess so," she said dubiously.

"We'll take it slow."

Skye bit down on her lower lip as they headed out of town. The horse she had ridden as a child had been a small pony. This one was considerably larger. The ground seemed to be a long way down.

Gradually, her fears eased and as she relaxed in the saddle, she began to enjoy the ride. The land spread out before them, untouched and untamed. The prairie was in bloom, the grass thick and green, dotted here and there with swaths of wildflowers and stands of tall timber. Jagged mountains rose in the distance, their tops still white with snow.

Wolf glanced at Skye, riding beside him. "You doing okay, cowgirl?"

"Yes. It's so beautiful out here. Everything smells so clean and fresh. It's like no one ever breathed the air before. And the sky's so big and blue."

Wolf nodded in agreement. The future smelled heavily of smog and smoke, gasoline and oil, perfume and scented shampoo, and a myriad other smells, some too faint for humans to detect. And the noise – his preternatural senses picked up every sound for miles around. It had taken him over a year to learn how to tune out most of it.

He blew out a sigh. He loved it here, but always, after a few weeks, he was drawn back to the future. Even though he wasn't a vampyre here in the past, sooner or later he began to miss the taste of blood. He had tried feeding here, no easy task, without fangs, but drinking blood – human or animal—had sickened him. But the need for blood, the hunger for it, was still alive deep within him. Eventually, he had learned that it was more than a remembered craving, it was a necessity he couldn't live without. Sooner or later, he had to return to the future to feed. He had never understood why. If he was human here, why did he still have a desire for blood? But, whatever the reason, the need was real and could not be denied.

Skye found herself constantly stealing glances at Wolf as the miles slipped by. He rode easily in the saddle, almost as if he was a part of the horse. He held the reins loosely in one hand, his other hand resting on his thigh. He had a strong profile. She never tired of looking at him. She blushed when he found her staring at him yet again. He smiled at her, but said nothing, for which she was grateful.

Another mile passed. They topped a small hill and Skye gasped with delight. A meadow spread out below them, and in the center was a lake that sparkled in the sunlight like a diamond in the middle of a blanket of emerald velvet.

"Feel like a swim?" Wolf asked.

Skye's eyes grew wide. "A swim?"

"Why not?"

Why not, she thought. Why not?

"You can swim in your underwear," he said, waggling his eyebrows like some burlesque comedian.

Skye sent him a withering glance.

"What's the matter? Chicken?"

"I prefer to think of it as modest."

"I won't look."

"Yeah, right."

"Don't you believe me?" he asked with a laugh.

"Not one bit." Still, the lake was beautiful. The air was warm, the water looked inviting. And it would give her a chance to see him, too...

Wolf grinned. He didn't have to be a vampyre to know what she was thinking. He touched his heels to the mare's sides and she trotted down the hill. He smiled when he heard Skye's horse following him down the gentle incline.

When they reached the bottom, Wolf dismounted. Lifting Skye from the saddle, he let her body slide seductively against his as he set her feet on the ground. He gestured at a couple of tall bushes a yard or so away. "You can undress over there."

Afraid she was making a terrible mistake, Skye ducked out of sight. She hesitated a moment, then shrugged. What the heck? There was no one else for miles around.

Wolf stared after Skye as he shucked his clothes down to his Jockey shorts and waded into the lake, wondering if she would join him.

A few minutes later, she called, "Turn around. And don't peek."

"Yes, ma'am."

Standing on her tiptoes, Skye peered over the top of the bushes. Wolf stood in waist-deep water, his back toward the shore. Sunlight caressed his broad back and shoulders, cast blue-black highlights in his hair.

Stepping out into the open, she ran into the water.

Wolf turned around, whistled when he saw her. The water covered her from the waist down. Her black bra was no more revealing than a bikini top.

She blushed under his admiring gaze. "Stop that."

"Stop what?"

"Looking at me like that."

"I can't help it. I'm a healthy male, you're a beautiful, desirable woman." His gaze moved over her. "I want you," he said, the humor gone from his voice. "I've wanted you since the day we met."

Her heart skipped a beat at his words, the heat in his eyes.

"I knew this wasn't a good idea," she murmured. Vampyre or man, she wanted him, too. And she was afraid he knew it.

"Come on," he said briskly. "I'll race you to the other side. I'll even give you a head start."

"You're on." She wasn't much of a rider, she thought, but she had spent hours swimming at the gym, been on the swim team in college. Filled with determination, she struck out for the opposite shore.

Wolf grunted softly as he watched the way she cut smoothly through the water. Maybe giving her a head start had been a mistake.

Sure enough, she beat him to the other side.

Skye laughed at the expression on his face when he dropped down on the grassy bank beside her.

"I won't make that mistake again," he muttered good-naturedly.

"It's beautiful out here," she remarked. "Everything is so...so pristine. The old photographs and paintings I've seen don't do it justice."

"It's hard to capture the wildness of the land, the freedom, on film or canvas," he agreed.

"True. You can't take pictures of the sighing of the wind, or the cry of a hawk."

"You should have been a poet," Wolf remarked with a smile. "Something else you can't capture," he murmured, drawing her into his arms, "is the taste of a woman's kisses."

Skye's heart skipped a beat as he claimed her lips with his in a long slow exploration. When his tongue dueled with hers, she felt it clear down to her toes. She was breathless, her body on fire, when he lifted his head. His gaze searched hers, a silent entreaty in their smoky depths.

He wanted her.

And she wanted him. But not now. It was too soon. Had he been a mere mortal, she might have said yes. But he was more than that and she feared that once he made her his, she would be bound to him forever, although where that thought had come from, she had no idea.

Sitting up, she ran her fingers through her damp hair. "We should head back," she said, suddenly flustered without knowing why. "I'm getting hungry. We missed lunch, you know. "

He rose to his feet in a single, fluid movement. Taking her hands in his, he lifted her to her feet. "Race you back," he said with a wink. "But you don't get a head start this time."

CHAPTER SIXTEEN

It was near dusk when they returned to town. Skye ran up to her room to freshen up before dinner while Wolf returned the horses to the livery.

It had been an exciting first day, she thought, as she washed her hands and face and brushed out her hair. What would they do tomorrow? How long before she got homesick for running water and flush toilets? And toilet paper? For pizza and French fries? For movies and Instagram? How long before anyone missed her?

She had called her parents before she left. While waiting for one of them to answer the phone, she had laughed as she imagined telling them she was going into the past with a man who was sometimes a vampyre, and that she would call them when she got back home. She couldn't tell them that, of course. Instead, she had just said she was going on am extended vacation and she would give them a call as soon as she got back.

If she got back...

A knock at the door scattered her thoughts. Smiling in anticipation, she opened the door. "Howdy, pardner."

"Howdy to you, Miss Somers. Are you ready to go?"

With a nod, she grabbed her camera case and followed him down the stairs.

❧ ❧ ❧

There were perhaps a dozen other people in the restaurant when they arrived, mostly couples or single men. Skye guessed the women in the Old West didn't often go out unaccompanied. Considering some of the rough-looking men she had seen on the streets, she didn't blame them.

Wolf ordered steak again, Skye asked for fried chicken and mashed potatoes.

"Do you always order steak?" she asked when the waitress went to turn in their order.

He shrugged. "Pretty much." He didn't tell her it was because of the blood, that even though he was human here, he still had a taste for it.

"Does eating seem strange?"

"It does if I haven't been here in a while."

"Do you always come to this town?"

"Usually. It's the closest one to the cave. I go visit my people now and then, but it depresses the hell out of me. The reservation is a miserable place. I tried to convince my grandfather to come with me into the future, but he won't. He said he was born here, and here he will die. He left the reservation a few months ago. A few of the people went with him."

"Do you have other family there?"

"A few distant cousins. A couple of friends."

Skye nodded, thinking how strange it would be to live two lives that were so vastly different.

Their dinner arrived a few minutes later. Lost in thought, Skye hardly tasted what she was eating. Wolf had told her of his past, of how he had become a vampyre, and yet she didn't think she would ever really know that side of him.

Glancing up, she found him watching her, a speculative look in his eyes. Vampyre or mortal, he was devastatingly gorgeous. She wondered what he was thinking, feeling. Was it hard, going from one world to the other? Did he feel like he belonged in both? Or that he didn't belong in either one?

Lowering her gaze, she took a bite of chicken, but she could still feel him watching her. "Is something wrong?"

"No. I just like looking at you."

Heat climbed up her neck and washed into her cheeks.

"You can't deny the attraction between us," he remarked.

She couldn't argue with that. Even now, sitting in a restaurant surrounded by people, there was no denying the sexual magnetism that hummed between them. What would it be like to let him make love to her? She had little doubt that, man or vampyre, he would be an amazing lover. Just thinking about it sent a quiver of desire thrumming through her. She had a feeling that if they made love once, she would be addicted. Like eating potato chips, one always led to more.

With a sigh, she pushed her plate away and wished she could do the same to her troubling thoughts.

Wolf signaled the waitress, paid the check, and they left the restaurant.

The town really came alive at night, Skye noticed. Bawdy music blared from Maud's Pleasure Place. Across the street, at the Ten Spot Saloon, someone was pounding out "Carry Me Back to Old Virginny" on a piano that was sadly out of tune. A moment later, two men came tumbling out the batwing doors, their faces bloody. Scrambling to their feet, they began punching one another. Three ladies of the evening hurried across the street to avoid the fight.

The Wild West really was wild, Skye thought, as Wolf reached for her hand. "Is it always like this?"

"Pretty much," he said. "Although it's worse on weekends when the cowboys get paid."

"Worse than this?"

"Oh, yeah. Fist fights, gun fights, cowboys shooting up the town. The ladies stay inside and lock their doors."

"Sounds like a good idea to me," she said when they reached the hotel.

Wolf held the door for her and followed her inside.

"How do I arrange for a bath?" she asked as they crossed the lobby.

"Go on up to your room. I'll take care of it."

"Thanks." She headed for the stairs, paused half-way up to glance over her shoulder to see Wolf talking to the desk clerk.

Smiling, she slid the key in the lock, but the door opened at her touch. Thinking she must have forgotten to lock it, she stepped inside. She was fumbling for a match when a large, calloused hand clamped over her mouth.

"Keep your mouth shut, hear?"

Heart pounding, Skye nodded as best she could.

She heard heavy footsteps as a second man emerged out of the darkness and closed the door. After lighting the lamp on the bedside table, he tossed her valise on the bed and began rummaging through it. "Nothing in here but a bunch of female duds," he complained.

Skye closed her eyes, afraid she might faint, when the door slammed open. She let out a gasp as the man by the bed turned, his hand reaching for his gun. But Wolf was moving, too. The two gunshots blended into one long report.

Feeling weak in the knees, Skye slumped forward, certain she was about to be killed.

She started at the sound of a third gunshot, but there was no pain. The man behind her reeled back and dropped to the floor, his pistol skittering across the room. She collapsed with him, surprised that she was still alive.

And then Wolf was beside her, lifting her to her feet and into his arms.

His gaze searched hers. "Are you all right?"

"I think so." She shuddered as she glanced at the two men sprawled on the floor, at the bright red blood pooling around them. The first had a neat round hole in his chest. The man who had been holding her had a bullet hole in his head.

She felt the bile rise in her throat as she glanced away. "You killed them." It was a foolish thing to say.

"Damn right."

Running footsteps sounded in the hallway and suddenly the room was filled with men, all talking and gesturing at once.

"Move aside."

The men in the room moved back as the sheriff stomped into the room. "What the hell's going on in here, Wolf?"

"I caught these men going through Miss Somers' things," Wolf said, one arm still around Skye. "The one by the bed turned and drew on me when I came in. The other one fired from behind Miss Somers."

"Uh-huh." The lawman turned his gaze on Skye. "Is that what happened?"

She nodded, shaking too hard to speak.

"I'll need you to come down to the jail in the morning and make a statement," the sheriff said. "Both of you."

"We'll be there," Wolf said. "Now, clear out, all of you."

Skye looked away as four men carried the two bodies out of the room.

In moments, she and Wolf were alone. "Does...does that...kind of thing...happen often?"

He shrugged. "Now and then."

"The one by the bed...he was...so young."

"Young and stupid," Wolf muttered. "Come on, let's go to my room."

Skye nodded.

Wolf had just unlocked his door when several teenage boys came down the hall, each carrying two buckets of steaming water. "Looks like your bath is here," he said. "Put the water in here, fellas."

"Could you get my bag, Wolf?"

"Sure."

Skye stood aside while the boys went into Wolf's room. They set the pails on the floor. Pulling an enamel bathtub from behind the screen in the corner, they quickly emptied the buckets.

Wolf returned with her valise as they were going out.

"Thank you."

"I'll wait in your room," he said, closing and locking the hallway door. He paused, his hand on the knob of the connecting door. "Are you gonna be all right?"

Skye nodded. As soon as Wolf went into her room and shut the door, she rummaged through the bag for her soap, then sank into the tub in hopes the hot water would drive away the numbness that had settled over her. She had never seen anyone die before, never seen anyone killed in front of her. Sure, she had seen the results of shootings on the nightly news, seen the covered bodies in the street, but this...She shivered in spite of the hot water around her. She would never forget the sight of those two dead men, the coppery smell of freshly spilled blood, or the acrid stink of gun powder.

She closed her eyes, wondering if she would ever feel safe again. Wondering what those men had thought they would find in her valise. Had they mistaken her for someone else? Or were they just common thieves hoping to get lucky? Not that it mattered now.

She lingered in the tub until the water cooled. After drying off, she pulled on the long, cotton nightgown she had bought, then knocked on the connecting door. "Wolf?"

It opened so fast, she was sure he'd been standing on the other side.

One look at her face and he pulled her into his arms. "Get some sleep, love. You'll feel better in the morning."

"Can I sleep in here?" She never wanted to go back into that room, or remember what had happened there.

"Sure. We'll change rooms tomorrow."

"Will you stay with me tonight?"

"If that's what you want."

"I don't want to be alone." She wasn't sure she ever wanted to be alone again.

"Get into bed, love, and I'll put out the lamp."

She did as he asked, then turned her back toward him. In the ensuing darkness, she heard the sound of his boots hitting the floor as he tugged them off, the whisper of cloth against skin as he undressed.

The mattress sagged as he slid in beside her. Good Lord, was he naked? She tensed when he placed his hand on her waist, wondering if he had taken her invitation the wrong way.

"Go to sleep, sweetness." His voice was quiet, soothing.

But it wasn't until she felt his jeans-clad leg brush against hers that the tension left her body. "Wolf? Can I ask you something?"

"Sure, honey."

"You killed two men tonight. I mean, I'm glad it was them and not you. Don't get me wrong. But... does it bother you?"

"The truth?"

"Of course."

"No. I'd kill anyone who put your life in danger."

CHAPTER SEVENTEEN

Skye woke beside Wolf, her head pillowed on his shoulder, one hand resting on his chest, his arm around her. She had been certain she would never be able to sleep after all that had happened the night before, feared that she would relive the blood and death in her dreams, but she had slept like a baby. Apparently, so had he.

She studied his profile, the arch of his brows, his strong jawline, a nose that had obviously been broken at least once. His hair was long and inky black, his skin the color of copper. Asleep, he looked younger, and she realized that when he was awake, he was always a little on edge, even here, where he belonged. Maybe, for a man like Wolf, it was to be expected.

She was about to slip out of his embrace when his arm tightened around her. "Don't go yet," he murmured, his voice still thick with sleep. "I like holding you like this."

With a sigh, she put her head back on his shoulder. She liked it, too. Way too much. She liked his masculine scent, the solid feel of his chest beneath her hand, the latent strength of his arm around her.

As if divining her thoughts, he turned onto his side. "I could get used to this. How about you?"

"Wolf..."

"I know, it's too soon. We agreed to take it slow." His fingers delved into the hair at her nape as he brushed a kiss across her lips. "Unless you want to change your mind?"

It was tempting, so tempting. She wondered what they used for birth control in the Old West. The thought of getting pregnant was like a splash of cold water.

With a sigh, he kissed her again, lightly, then rolled to his feet. "Since I can't seduce you, let's go get some breakfast."

Skye watched him go into the other room and close the door so she could have some privacy. She lingered in bed a few minutes longer, thinking she was far too tempted to let Wolf make love to her. She had never been one to indulge in casual sex. She had married the first man she had fallen in love with, Joseph Somers, and married him while they were still in college. A week later, he had been killed when a drunk driver plowed through a red light and broadsided him. She had only met two men she'd cared for since then, but she hadn't loved either of them enough to take them – or anyone else—to her bed. Until Wolf.

Throwing the covers aside, she washed her hands and face, pulled on her underwear, slipped the yellow dress over her head, and brushed her hair.

She had just stepped into her boots when Wolf knocked on the door. "You ready, woman?"

Grinning, she opened the door to the hallway. "Yes, cowboy, I am."

As soon as they were seated, the waitress who had served them once before hurried toward their table. "Hi, Wolf. Do you want the usual?"

"That'll be fine, Sylvie. Thanks."

Still looking at Wolf, Sylvie asked, "And for you, miss?"

"Pancakes, please. And a cup of coffee."

Sylvie wrote it down, winked at Wolf, and sashayed toward the kitchen.

"You seem to have charmed all the waitresses," Skye muttered.

Wolf shrugged. "What can I say? I have a way with women."

"You can say that again," Skye muttered, and glared at him when he laughed. It was annoying, the way the women fawned over him right in front of her, as if she wasn't even there. And even as she fought down a wave of jealousy, she couldn't really blame them. He was more attractive than any man had a right to be, with that roguish grin, beautiful dark eyes, and a smile worthy of a toothpaste ad. She had been smitten with him when he was nothing more to her than a cardboard cut-out.

Wolf frowned. Being a vampyre had its advantages, one of them being that he could read minds. He wished he had that ability now, because he would sure as hell love to know what Skye was thinking.

Their breakfast arrived a few minutes later.

"What would you like to do today?" he asked, between bites.

"I don't know. There really isn't a lot to do here, is there?" She supposed that wasn't true if you had a job. Or if you were a farm wife. No doubt they were busy from sun-up to sundown, raising kids, doing chores, washing clothes by hand, hanging then on a line to dry, mending, baking.

Wolf shrugged. "I usually spend my days at the poker table, but I guess you're right."

It occurred to her that if she stayed in the past with Wolf, they didn't have to stay here. They could live in the east.

There were theaters in New York and Boston where popular singers and dancers and actors performed. Parties and cotillions, fashionable stores to shop in, luxurious homes. "Wolf, when you come here, do you ever go back east?

"I did once."

"Did you like it?"

"Not much. People either looked at me like I was going to take their scalp, or they treated me like some sort of oddity – a man who looked like a man but was some kind of civilized savage."

"Oh." So much for living in the east, she thought glumly.

"You were thinking we could live there."

"I was."

They finished the rest of the meal in silence.

Leaving the restaurant, they strolled to the outskirts of town.

"Do you want to go home?" he asked.

"I don't know. I want to be with you, but I miss my own time. I thought I'd love it here, and I do, but it's not home. I don't think I'd be happy staying here, and you wouldn't be happy in the east…" She looked up at him, her expression troubled. "I don't know what I want."

"I know what I want." Taking her in his arms, he brushed a kiss across the top of her head. "I want you to be happy. I'll take you home in the morning."

Skye looked up at him. She had two choices – stay in the past with Wolf, or return to the future and live without him. Future or past? Man or vampyre? How could she make a decision like that?

She wrapped her arms around his waist and rested her cheek on his chest. How could she tie her life to that of a vampyre? How could she watch him stay the same while she grew older every day? How could she accept the fact that he lived on the blood of others? Or ever have a moment's peace, knowing there would always be men hunting him?

How could she live without him? Blinking back her tears, she said, "I don't want to go home."

"Skye!" Putting his finger beneath her chin, he tilted her head up. "Are you sure?"

She nodded. "I love you, Wolf, whatever you are, wherever we are."

"There are bigger towns than this," he said, lightly stroking her hair. "More civilized."

"But?"

"I need to stay close to the cave."

"Why?"

"Because I need blood from time to time."

"I don't understand. If you're human here—"

"I'm still a vampyre and even though it lies dormant within me while I'm here, every now and then I need to feed that part of myself. And my vampyre self has to be dominant for me to do it."

She mulled that over, thinking it was the most bizarre thing she had ever heard.

"There's a small farming town a day's ride to the south. The population is small, but the people are friendly. There's not much to do there, either, I'm afraid, but it's not as wild as this place. Or we could go visit my people. A handful of them left the reservation. They're camped a day's ride to the north."

Skye's love of the Old West had really been a love for Indians. She had always preferred the Indians to the cowboys, rooted for them in the movies. This might be her only chance to live in a real Indian village, to experience life as it had once been. She had to admit, she didn't care for the town they were in. A bigger town might be more civilized, certainly Boston and New York would be more like what she was used to, but Wolf had to be close to the cave.

And they could always go home.

"Let's go visit your people."

That afternoon, after lunch, they went shopping at the General Store. Skye trailed behind Wolf as he picked up a dozen blankets, two dozen sacks of tobacco, assorted blue-speckled pots and pans, a couple of coffee pots, bags of coffee, flour and sugar, three dozen bars of soap, some sharp knives, two dozen boxes of ammunition, and a Winchester rifle. He had the clerk fill several sacks with hard candy while he stacked the blankets and everything else on the counter.

Next, he bought three bolts of calico cloth, several packs of needles and spools of thread.

"Can you think of anything else?" he asked, glancing over his shoulder at Skye.

"Bonnets and hair brushes for the women? Maybe some mirrors?"

"Good thinking."

The counter was piled high with their goods when they finished. The clerk found several empty burlap bags to hold everything. Wolf paid the bill, then asked the clerk to hang onto their goods, saying he would be back to pick them up first thing in the morning.

"Now what?" Skye asked as they left the store.

"I need you to go back to the hotel and collect our things while I find a pack mule. We'll get cleaned up, take a walk around the town, then have an early dinner, and leave first thing in the morning."

"Sounds good."

He pulled her into his arms, right there on the street, and kissed her. "Keep your door locked," he said. "I won't be gone long."

It took less than half an hour to pack their few belongings. Skye washed her hands and face and brushed out her hair. She left her shirt and jeans on the foot of the bed, deciding she'd be more comfortable riding in them than in a dress and petticoats.

When she was done, she sat in the chair by the window, camera in hand. She had a whole new perspective of the town from the second floor and she snapped several pictures of a beer wagon lumbering down the street, a few of the Butterfield Stage as it pulled up in front of the station. She captured two soiled doves drumming up business on the boardwalk in front of Maud's Pleasure Place. She tried to imagine what it would be like to earn her living in a brothel, but she just couldn't imagine taking strangers to bed. Not for all the money in the world, she thought, as she watched one of the girls lock arms with a grubby cowboy who looked like he hadn't had a bath in a month.

She glanced up and down the street, wondering what was taking Wolf so long.

Wolf had intended to find a pack mule and return to the hotel, but as he passed by the Ten Spot Saloon, he ran into one of the few men in town he counted a friend. They talked for a few minutes and then Old Ned Foster insisted on buying him a drink before he left town. A drink led to a hand of poker and the next thing Wolf knew, an hour had turned into two and he'd won better than three hundred dollars.

Muttering under his breath, he shoved the greenbacks into his pants' pocket and headed for the hotel.

Skye was dozing in the chair by the window when she heard a knock at the door. A moment later, Wolf peeked inside. "You ready to go?"

"I've been ready for over two hours," she retorted. "Where have you been?"

Stepping inside, he closed the door. "I ran into an old friend. He insisted on buying me a drink and..." He shrugged. "Time got away from me. I'm sorry."

"Did you find a pack mule?"

"Yeah." Lifting her to her feet, he pulled her into his arms. "Don't be mad, love. I won three hundred dollars while I was at it. Good thing, too. After that trip to the general store, my bank account was running a little low."

She glared at him, determined to hang onto her anger. How could he just go off and leave her alone like that after what had happened last night?

"Skye?" He brushed a kiss across her lips, then kissed her again, his tongue sliding in to duel with hers while his hands slid up and down her back.

She stood stiff in his arms for as long as she could and then she leaned into him and kissed him back. Life was too short to stay mad, she decided. And his kisses were much too sweet to ignore. And she *had* gotten some really good pictures while he was gone.

"Maybe we could skip dinner," he murmured against her lips. And then he was kissing her again, his mouth hot on hers.

As always, the touch of his hands, the heat of his kisses, tempted her to throw caution to the winds. Everything feminine within her urged her to surrender, and she might have, if the sound of gun shots hadn't erupted on the street below. Mingled with the sound of gunfire were feminine screams accompanied by shouting and cursing and the sound of running feet.

Muttering, "What the hell?" Wolf went to the window and peered outside.

Skye followed him. Looking over his shoulder, she saw that the saloon across the street was in flames. Several of the ladies of the evening were running outside, a few of them wearing nothing but their underwear, while a crude bucket brigade threw water on the flames, but it was a losing battle.

"I hope everyone got out," Skye murmured.

Wolf nodded. Here in the past, he was vulnerable to everything ordinary mortals were. In the future, one of the few things that could destroy him was fire.

Driven back by the flames, the men forming the bucket line fell back and watched as the roof collapsed, sending sparks exploding through the air.

At a shout from one of the men, the others turned their attention to the building next to the saloon, and began dousing the roof and walls with water.

Eventually, the fire died down and the street cleared, though the bucket brigade remained close by, just in case.

Skye turned away from the window, and into Wolf's arms. She wasn't used to seeing violence close up, but she'd seen it in living color the last two nights. And would likely see again as long as they were here, in the past, where men often took the law into their own hands.

CHAPTER EIGHTEEN

They left town soon after breakfast the next morning. Wolf had gone down to load the pack mule while she bathed and packed the last of her things, and now they were heading north to find his people. They had a beautiful day for their journey – a vast, blue sky overhead, a carpet of green before them, the majesty of the mountains in the distance.

"We'll be there by nightfall," Wolf said, in answer to her question.

"Is your grandfather still alive?"

"As far as I know."

"I can't wait to meet him."

"He was a hell of a warrior in his day," Wolf said, his voice tinged with love and respect. "And a hell of a medicine man. I saw him heal people who should have died, heard him make predictions about the future of our people that, sadly, have come to pass."

"Is he psychic?"

"I don't know if he's psychic, exactly, but he has mystical powers of some kind."

"Does he know what you are?"

"I've never asked and he's never said. But it wouldn't surprise me if does."

Skye shifted in the saddle. "Did he fight in many battles?"

"Dozens. We fought in some of them side-by-side," Wolf recalled with a grin. "The man doesn't know the meaning of fear."

"I suspect that you don't, either," Skye said dryly.

"Yeah, well... I've always loved a good fight."

An image of Wolf shooting the two men in the hotel flashed through her mind.

"There's a stream just ahead," he remarked. "We'll stop there and rest the horses."

"And my backside," Skye muttered, rising in her stirrups.

The shallow stream meandered between a stand of cottonwoods and bunch grass.

Dismounting, Wolf lifted Skye from the saddle.

She stretched her back and shoulders while he let the horses and the mule drink, then tethered the animals to a low-hanging branch.

When he dropped cross-legged to the ground, she sat beside him, glad she had worn jeans instead of a dress.

"It's so quiet out here. It's hard to believe so many battles were fought here."

"Yeah. A lot of Sioux and Cheyenne went to Canada after the massacre at the Little Big Horn."

"Did your grandfather go?"

"No. He said this was his land and he wouldn't be driven out by the *wasichu*."

"By the what?"

"The white man. He hid out in the Black Hills with some of the others who refused to surrender."

"Do you look like him?"

"Pretty much, although his hair had gone gray the last time I saw him."

That morning, Wolf had given Skye some money and she had bought a dozen sugar cookies before they left town.

Rising, she pulled the sack from one of her saddlebags. She handed a couple to Wolf and took one for herself before sitting down again.

"Thanks."

"I bought a few apples, too," she said, "but I was in the mood for something sweet."

"So am I." Leaning forward, he licked a bit of sugar from her lips, then covered her mouth with his.

She sighed as he deepened the kiss, put the sack aside as he stretched out on the grass and pulled her down beside him. His fingers delved into the hair at her nape, lightly massaging her neck as he kissed her again and yet again, each more intimate, more arousing, than the last.

"Wolf…" She gasped his name, not knowing if she wanted him to stop or make love to her there, in the sun-warmed grass beside the stream.

"Damn, girl," he muttered. "You're hotter than a fourth of July firecracker."

"And you're the match that sets me off. But it's not July," she reminded him, twisting out of his arms.

"We can pretend," he said, his voice whisky-rough with desire. Sitting up, he blew out a breath.

Murmuring, "I'm sorry," she plucked a leaf and a blade of grass from her hair. "It's just that…"

"What?"

"We don't have any birth control, and…I know when you're a vampyre, you can't father a child, but what about here and now?"

"I don't know. I seem to be human here, but even while I'm here, I still have a need for blood, so there's still a part of me that's vampyre." He caressed her cheek with his finger-tips. "I understand where you're coming from, but, damn, woman, it's impossible to keep my hands off you."

A rush of warmth flooded her cheeks. It pleased her on some deep, feminine level, to know he found her desirable, even irresistible. After all, a man like Jason Wolf could probably have any woman he wanted. And probably had. But he wanted her. And heaven help her, she wanted him just as badly. How much longer she could resist his undeniable charm and her own desire was anybody's guess. She'd had no idea that insisting they take it slow would be so darn hard!

They had been in the saddle for a couple of hours when they passed within a few yards of a herd of buffalo grazing on the short grass. Skye reined her horse to a halt, fascinated by the huge, shaggy beasts. She had never seen a live buffalo and they were impressive. The animals paid little attention to them.

Wolf grinned as he reined in beside her. "They're something to see, aren't they?

"Incredible. I knew they were big, but…" She shook her head as she removed the camera from the case and snapped half a dozen photos. "They're enormous. They look so calm."

Wolf nodded. He had seen hunters take down several buffalo while the herd continued to graze, indifferent to the sound of gunfire. "The Lakota depend on the buffalo for just about everything," he remarked. "They use his hair for rope, his hide for robes and clothing and lodge covers, for moccasins, and drumheads, his meat for food. Horns are fashioned into spoons and decorations. The paunch makes a good kettle. Nothing goes to waste."

"They're beautiful," Skye murmured, thinking she would have been happy to sit and watch them the rest of the day. They didn't, of course. They still had miles to go. She managed to snap another half-dozen photos before they rode on.

She took pictures of Wolf, too, from every angle possible. She never tired of looking at him. She loved the determined set of his jaw, the sensual curve of his mouth, the way the sunlight danced in his long, black hair, the way he rode easy in the saddle. He looked like the statue of a Greek god come to life, his skin like bronze, every muscle well-defined.

Flattered and amused, Wolf grinned when he caught her taking another photo. "What are you going to do with all those?"

Flushing with embarrassment, she looked away. But it didn't stop her from taking more photos – of Wolf, the distant mountains, a small herd of deer, an eagle on the wing, their horses as they grazed beside a shallow stream, the pack mule.

They rode all that day, pausing once to rest the animals, another time to eat the bread and sliced roast beef she had packed. They munched on the rest of the cookies for dessert, washing them down with water from Wolf's canteen.

Skye was bone weary by the time they arrived at the Lakota camp. It looked like a smaller version of villages she had seen in the movies, she thought, as she snapped several photos. Instead of hundreds of lodges, there were only a dozen or so in a loose circle near a slow-moving river. Perhaps thirty horses grazed on the banks.

She put her camera away as men and women emerged from their lodges, apparently drawn by the sound of their approach. Suddenly apprehensive, Skye stared at them. Only a few years ago, these people had been at war with her people. There had been bloodshed and carnage on both sides. She imagined that hadn't changed much. Why had she thought coming here would be a good idea? She was the enemy.

Her apprehension slowly faded when she realized they didn't look ominous or savage, only curious. The men wore breechclouts and moccasins. Some wore leather vests. The women wore long tunics she thought were made from some kind of hide, though they looked soft and pliable. Little girls were dressed like their mothers; the boys wore breechclouts and little else.

The men gathered around Wolf when he dismounted, all talking at once.

The chatter ceased when a man with long, gray braids stepped into the middle. Skye knew immediately that it was Wolf's grandfather. The resemblance was uncanny.

Wolf stepped forward to embrace the older man. She listened to their rapid exchange, wishing she could understand what they were saying.

After a few minutes, Wolf lifted her from the saddle. "Skye, this is my grandfather, Chetáŋ."

She smiled at him, not knowing what was expected of her.

"I am pleased to meet you," the old man said, smiling. "My grandson has chosen wisely."

"Thank you," she said, surprised that he spoke English. "I'm happy to meet you, too." In spite of his years and the gray in his hair, Wolf's grandfather remained a handsome man who looked to be in good physical shape.

Chetáŋ's smile widened. "Come, let us go to my lodge." He spoke a few words in Lakota to the people gathered around, then dismissed the crowd with a wave of his hand.

Wolf took up the reins of their horses and the pack mule and they followed his grandfather to a lodge near the center of the circle.

Skye fell in behind them, glancing left and right. She saw strips of meat drying on long wooden racks. Horses grazed in the distance. Children ran through the camp, playing some kind of game. Two women were scraping flesh from a deer hide. Others stood stirring pots suspended on poles over firepits. They all looked up at her as she passed by, their dark eyes filled with curiosity. A few smiled uncertainly.

Chetán's tipi was quite large. A buffalo robe covered the floor. She spied what she guessed was a bedroll in the back. There was a small firepit, a backrest made of wood, a few pots and bowls.

"Please, sit," Chetán invited.

Thinking it would be rude to take the only thing that looked like a chair, Skye sank down on the buffalo robe. Wolf sat cross-legged beside her.

"How have you been, *tunkasila?*" Wolf asked.

"As well as can be expected for a man my age," his grandfather replied with a rueful smile.

Wolf grinned at him. "Is the hunting good?"

"*Ai.* Our hunts have been successful," he said, sitting across from them. "I want to hear about you." Glancing at Skye, he said, "And the woman. She comes from the future?"

"Yes."

Chetán nodded. "I thought so. She has that look about her."

Skye lifted one brow, wondering what "that" look was.

"Have you been to the future lately?" Wolf asked.

Chetán shook his head. "Not for several years. It is a scary place for an old man."

"Sometimes for a young one, too," Wolf said ruefully. "Your English is much improved since last I saw you."

"Blue Otter captured a white man not long ago. The *wasichu* was a teacher. I offered him his freedom if he would teach me the *wasichu* tongue."

"Blue Otter didn't object?"

Chetáŋ shrugged. "I gave him two good ponies for the teacher. It was a good trade."

"And the white man?"

"I let him go after a while. He was not much use. Do you want to eat?"

"Not right now. Skye?"

"No, thank you." She had read the Indians ate deer and buffalo. But also dogs and horses when the hunting was bad and food was scarce.

"How long will you stay?" Chetáŋ asked.

"I'm not sure." Wolf smiled at Skye. "It is up to my woman."

His woman. The two words went through Sky like warm honey.

"We have an empty lodge," Chetáŋ said. "It belonged to the *wasichu* teacher. I think you will be comfortable there."

Wolf nodded.

"It has a white man's house painted on the side," Chetáŋ said, with a grin. "He had trouble telling one lodge from another."

Wolf laughed as he reached for Skye's hand. "We'll go have a look, *tunkasila.*"

Chetáŋ nodded. "There will be a feast and dancing tonight in honor of your return to us."

"*Tunkasila…*"

The old man raised a hand to silence his protest. "I have spoken."

Wolf grunted his reluctant approval as he lifted the lodge flap for Skye and followed her outside.

"Don't you like dancing?" Skye asked as they went in search of the teacher's lodge.

"Only when you're in my arms. Here we are."

The teacher's lodge was not as big as Chetáŋ's, but was similarly furnished.

"Make yourself at home," Wolf said. "I'll go get our gear."

Skye made a slow circle, wondering how long they would stay and what they would do while they were here. Going into the past had seemed like a great idea in the comfort of her own home, but now she wasn't so sure. At least back in the town, she had been among people who spoke the same language, had somewhat similar backgrounds. Now, she was in a totally alien land surrounded by people with vastly different customs and beliefs. She had never cooked over an open fire, didn't know how to skin a deer, or make a dress from scratch. She didn't speak the Lakota language, which would make it difficult to make friends, assuming the women would be agreeable.

She peeked out of the lodge when she heard a commotion outside. Wolf had started unpacking the gifts they had brought with them and the people gathered around, oohing and aahing over the wealth of white man's goods. She smiled when she saw a little girl looking in a mirror, thinking it was probably the first time the child had seen her reflection in anything but a pool of standing water. The women ran their hands over the cloth, laughing and talking as they tried on the hats.

"This is for you, *tunkasila*," Wolf said, handing the rifle and a box of ammunition to his grandfather, who had also stepped out of his lodge.

Skye felt a moment of dismay when she saw the delight on the faces of the men as Wolf passed out boxes of ammunition. Would those weapons one day be used against her people?

Finally, everyone had at least one present and the crowd broke up.

"I'd say the gifts were a big hit," Wolf remarked as he stepped into the lodge.

"I'd say you were right." She smiled as he took her in his arms. "What does *tunkasila* mean?"

"Grandfather." His knuckles caressed her cheek. "Do you think you'll be happy here for a while?"

"I hope so."

"I thought you wanted to see how my people really lived?"

"I did. I do. But I just realized I'm not going to be able to communicate with anyone except you and your grandfather."

"I think a few of the younger women speak English pretty well. Chetáŋ told me just now that some of them sat in on the lessons with him."

Her relief was evident on her face.

"We can leave whenever you want," Wolf reminded her. Which was true, up to a point. But sooner or later, he had to return to the future to feed. It was a fact of life that could not be ignored, though it made no sense. He felt wholly human here in the past and yet, after a while, he experienced a need for blood that couldn't be denied, a hunger that could only be satisfied in the future.

As soon as the sun went down, the people gathered outside. The men and women were dressed in their best, Skye thought, the women wearing doeskin dresses intricately beaded across the bodice, some with tiny bells sewn into the hems of their dresses. The men wore fancy vests, their long black hair adorned with feathers.

Skye sat beside Wolf, feeling totally out of place in her jeans, her eyes wide as the women moved through the crowd handing out food – mostly meat. When she looked at Wolf askance, he grinned at her. "It's venison and buffalo."

There was some kind of soup, blackberries and plums, a kind of bread. And coffee.

When everyone had eaten their fill, three warriors sat around a large drum and began to play and Skye was soon lost in the rhythmic beat. "Do the dances mean anything?"

"I guess you could say that many of the dances have a spiritual meaning for my people. Some dances are to honor the spirits and the relationship of all living things one to another. Some dances honor fallen warriors, some honor the generosity of a man or a woman. Others are worship dances to pay homage to *Wakan Tanka*, the Great Spirit. And some are just for fun. Like this one."

Taking Skye's hand, he lifted her to her feet and led her toward the circle that was forming. "This is the round dance," he explained as the drumming began. "Also known as the friendship dance. It is one of the few dances where men and women come together, where we all join as one people to celebrate the hoop of the Lakota Nation. It is related to the sacred circle of life."

The steps were relatively easy to follow and Skye soon forgot that she was an outsider as they circled first one way and then the other.

The dancing went on for hours and she loved every minute of it. She had been fascinated while watching Indians dance at POW WOWs, but this was a hundred times better. These men weren't attired in brightly colored outfits, but the earthy hues of deerskin and rawhide. They moved with a kind of strength and power that was barely tamed, their bodies twisting and turning to the throbbing beat of the drum. The heartbeat of the people, Wolf said.

The women didn't wear hot pink and orange and bright blue or hold fancy embroidered shawls. The beads on their tunics were red and yellow. Their movements were graceful, delicate. Her only regret was that she couldn't take photos, certain that the flash of her camera would be considered rude and invasive.

Wolf danced several times with the men. He was magnificent. He wore only a breechclout and moccasins, gifts from his grandfather, and on this night, he was all Lakota. The firelight caressed the bronze of his skin, cast highlights in his inky-black hair. His steps were strong and sure as his feet pounded the earth, and she thought she had never seen anything as beautiful or as sensual as Wolf Who Walks on the Wild Wind dancing in the flickering firelight beneath a blanket of stars and a bright yellow moon.

It was late when she followed him into their lodge. They had been alone together in the hotel and on the prairie but, somehow, this seemed far more intimate. Tension arced between them when she met his gaze.

"Skye."

Just her name, but he didn't have to say more. The husky tremor in his voice, the desire blazing in his dark eyes, said it all. She swallowed hard. Was tonight the night she surrendered to the longing in his eyes, to the desire that even now made her blood run hot? He wasn't a vampyre here, just a man who wanted her.

And she wanted him. Oh, Lord, how she wanted him.

She hesitated for the space of a heartbeat.

He turned away.

And the moment was gone.

Skye lay curled up under a buffalo robe, silent tears tracking her cheeks. She had been in bed for hours, unable to sleep. She wanted Wolf desperately and yet she was hesitant to let him make love to her. Why? True, they hadn't known each other very long, but she was in love with him, there was no doubt of that. He'd known she had doubts about being with him when he was a vampyre, and he had brought her here so she could get to know him better, and still she hesitated. He was everything she had hoped he would be. Everything she had ever wanted. Maybe it was the possibility of getting pregnant, no matter how slim it might be, that made her hesitate.

And maybe, whispered a little voice in the back of her mind, she just missed the vampyre. She told herself that was ridiculous. Who would want to live with a vampyre? In many ways, he was the same man here that he had been as a vampyre, and yet she felt the difference in him. In her time, he was invincible. Powerful. A little intimidating. Here, he was also strong and powerful, but not in the same way.

She rolled over onto her stomach and wiped away her tears. What was she crying for, anyway? Because he hadn't made love to her? Whose fault was that? Was it because she didn't have the courage to take what she wanted and damn the consequences? Because he wasn't a vampyre here? That didn't even make sense. They had come here because she wanted to be with the man, *not* the vampyre.

She started when he touched her shoulder.

"What's wrong, love?"

"Nothing," she said, sniffling.

"You're crying. Why?"

"I don't know," she wailed softly.

Sliding under the buffalo robe, he took her in his arms. She noted he was still clad in his breechclout and nothing more. His skin was warm and inviting against her own.

"I'm here," he said, lightly stroking her hair. "Go to sleep. Everything will look better in the morning."

Somehow, she doubted it. Yet his very nearness filled her with a sense of peace. She felt safe in his arms, felt all her doubts and fears melt away as he continued to stroke her hair, his breath soft as a sigh against her cheek as he whispered that he loved her.

CHAPTER NINETEEN

Skye woke to the sound of a barking dog and childish laughter. Confused, she bolted upright, her gaze quickly taking in her surroundings. It took her a moment to remember where she was. And then she frowned. Where was Wolf?

Rising, she smoothed a hand over her hair before she stepped out of the lodge. Ordinarily, she would have showered, or at least washed her face and brushed her teeth, but at the moment, she didn't see any way to do either one.

The village was humming with activity. Children ran through the camp. Women stood over cookfires, fed their children. Across the river, several teenage boys were having a foot race. A small group of men were gathered together off to the side, watching. Wolf was easy to find. Taller than most of the others, he stood in the middle of the group. Although she couldn't understand what they were saying, she had the feeling he was answering questions. About what, she had no idea.

He left the group when he glanced over his shoulder and saw her standing outside, no doubt looking as out of place as she felt.

He splashed across the river and took her in his arms. "Did you sleep well?"

"Well enough."

"Are you hungry?"

"Starved."

"Me, too."

She had the distinct feeling he wasn't talking about food.

After breakfast, Wolf escorted her down to the river and stood guard while she bathed and brushed her teeth, glad she'd had the foresight to bring soap, a toothbrush and toothpaste with her into the past. Wolf had grinned when she handed him a toothbrush of his own.

She spent most of the afternoon people-watching. Movies usually depicted Native Americans as a wild, ferocious people who thought of nothing but making war and taking scalps, but she saw a whole new side to them here. She watched young mothers cuddling their babies, others playing with their children, skinning game, erecting a new lodge. One man was teaching his young son how to use a bow and arrow, while several other men cheered for a bunch of boys in a horse race. Near the river, a handful of older boys were having a mock battle. A couple of elderly warriors dozed in the sun. She smiled when she recognized Chetáŋ was one of them. She saw men repairing weapons and fashioning new ones.

Wolf had told her only a small group had followed his grandfather when he left the reservation. Judging by the number of people she saw milling about, she guessed more had joined their number since then.

Wolf looked at home here, among his own people. He wore a breechclout and moccasins, his copper-hued skin glistening in the sun's light, his long hair loose around his shoulders. He looked just like the cut-out figure in the museum, she mused, only better. His muscles rippled as he arm-wrestled another warrior. She felt a rush of pride when he won three times in a row.

A few minutes later, he dropped down beside her. "How you doing, sweetness?"

"I feel like I'm in the middle of a Western movie set," she replied with a grin. "I keep waiting for the director to call, 'cut'."

Wolf grunted softly. In some ways, it was true. But few movies had accurately portrayed the day-to-day life of his people.

"Tell me about the Lakota," Skye said, glancing at the activity around her. "What do they believe in?"

"The Lakota believe in many gods. *Wakan Tanka*, the Great Spirit, is the most powerful. But there are other gods below him. *Inyan*, the Rock, *Maka*, the Earth, *Skan*, the Sky, and *Wi*, the Sun. These four are connected to another four – *Wakinyan*, the thunder spirit, *Whope*, the spirit of peace and family, *Tate*, the wind, and *Hanwi*, the moon.

"Of course, you can't have benevolent gods without evil ones," he said with a grin. "There are water sprites and goblins and monsters, like *Waziya*, the Old Man, and his wife, *Wakanaka*, the Witch, and their daughter, *Anog-Ite*, the Double-faced Woman.

"The Lakota believe that all things are alive, with a spirit of their own—rocks, trees, mountains, water. The *Paha Sapa*, the Black Hills, are sacred to us, the heart and soul of the Lakota people.

"There are no clocks here. The People eat when they're hungry, sleep when they're tired. Four is a sacred number. There are four seasons in a year, four directions, four elements – earth, wind, fire and water. The circle is also sacred. The earth is round. Our lodges are round. The sun and the moon are round."

Skye nodded, intrigued by the thought that trees and rocks and mountains were alive, that the Lakota believed in many gods instead of one. "What about heaven? Do your people belief in an Afterlife?"

Wolf nodded. "I've heard two different theories about that. Some think that, after death, the soul follows the Sky-Road, the Milky Way, to heaven, which is a lot like this world, but the weather is better and the animals are easier to hunt than in the world of the living. Others think that the Sky-Road is the final destination and that every soul must pass by *Hihankara,* the Owl Woman. She will only allow those who have the right tattoos to enter. All others will be pushed off the Sky-Road back to earth where they wander as ghosts."

"I think I like the first version better," Skye said.

The Lakota way of life seemed peaceful enough, if rather dull, Skye mused as the days went by. Other than dancing and games, what did they do for entertainment? Of course, since they had to hunt their food and make everything from scratch, they didn't really have a lot of free time, although the women seemed far more busy than the men. What was *she* going to do here? She had no children to look after, didn't know how to skin a deer or a buffalo, or how to make clothes from animal hides. She had no idea how to cook venison or buffalo, jerk meat, or make pemmican. If they stayed, she would have a lot to learn.

She was surprised to discover that the women owned the lodge and everything in it, save for a warrior's clothing and weapons. It was the mother's responsibility to raise the children. She looked after her daughters until they wed, and over her sons until their voices changed and they were considered men. At that time, the father or another male relative took over the boy's education.

She learned a few Lakota words. *Waste* meant good. *Skuya* meant sweet. *Cocola* was the word for soft. *Pilamaya* meant thank you, *hohahe* meant welcome, *le mita cola* meant my friend, *lila washtay* meant very good.

She noticed that naughty children were never spanked, nor were they ordered to do anything. Rather, they were asked and expected to obey. When they did something wrong, they were asked to stop and then given the reason why such behavior was unacceptable. Babies were not allowed to cry. She thought that odd until Wolf explained the reason behind it.

"In wartime, the women are often hidden away from camp. A crying baby can alert the enemy to your whereabouts. For that reason, babies aren't allowed to cry."

She supposed it made sense. But she had always believed that a crying infant should be picked up and cuddled.

She noticed that the boys were taught at a very early age how to fight and how to handle a bow and arrow. She spent one whole morning watching a father instruct his son. Another time, she watched, wide-eyed, as a child barely old enough to walk was taught how to ride a horse. She had seen other boys only a little older ride like they were part of the animal itself. Now she knew why.

They had been in camp for over a week when a middle-aged woman approached Skye, a cloth-wrapped bundle in her arms. The woman smiled tentatively. "Wolf Who Walks on the Wild Wind asked me to teach you our ways, if you would like to learn."

Skye blinked at the woman, who was not Lakota, but white. "Yes, I'd like that."

"You are surprised that I am not Indian."

"Well, yes." Skye gestured at the place beside her. "Please, sit."

"I am called Macha," she said, "but my mother named me Carolyn. I was captured eight years ago by the Crow. When the Lakota raided their camp, one of the warriors rescued me."

"Rescued?" Skye asked, frowning. How was being kidnapped from one tribe to another being rescued?

Carolyn laughed softly. "I know what you are thinking. But the Crow warrior who captured me was cruel and unkind. He beat me and ..." She lowered her gaze. "Abused me. Takoda brought me here. He did not treat me like a slave and, in time, I learned to care for him. And then to love him. I am happy to be here, with him."

Skye nodded, not knowing what to say.

"I brought you this," Carolyn said, handing Skye the bundle in her arms.

It was a dress made of soft doeskin bleached almost white, with fringe along the hem. "It's lovely," Skye murmured. "*Pilamaya.*"

⚜ ⚜ ⚜

In the days that followed, Skye and Carolyn became good friends. Skye learned how to cook in a kettle made from a buffalo paunch, how to make moccasins, how to skin the deer and rabbits Wolf brought her – a task she was sure she would never look on with anything but distaste.

One day, while Wolf was hunting with the men, Carolyn asked Skye if she'd like to go listen to a Lakota story. "It's about White Buffalo Calf Woman," Carolyn said. "I think you'll like it."

After a moment's consideration, Skye agreed and they sat on the outside of a circle of children. An old woman with long gray braids sat on a blanket in the middle of the circle.

Carolyn translated the story. "Once, long ago, during a time of warfare and famine, two warriors were riding across the plains looking for game, when they saw a woman surrounded by a misty light. A white buffalo walked beside her. She carried sage in one hand, and wore a feather in her hair. She was incredibly beautiful. One of the warriors approached her, with lust in his eyes. But before he could touch her, he was frozen by a bolt of lightning. The other warrior fell to his knees, afraid he would meet the same fate, but the woman touched his head. She told him she was *wakan* – holy—and that she had come to help the People.

"The Lakota welcomed her and gave her a lodge. As soon as she entered, the morning turned to twilight and the land was enveloped in a rosy glow. White Buffalo Calf Woman taught the people how to smoke the pipe and gave them tobacco made from willow bark. She taught them many spiritual things/ She taught them to revere Mother Nature and corrected ancient rites and ceremonies. She asked them to sing with her to please Mother Earth and to offer incantations to the Four Directions.

"She told the Lakota she would protect them as long as they performed the ceremonies she had taught them, and then she conjured a herd of black buffalo from the horizon. The buffalo brought new life to the People. Before the holy woman left, she promised to return. The Lakota are waiting for her to return and bring back harmony and peace to the earth."

"What a wonderful story," Skye remarked as they walked back to her lodge. She smiled inwardly, thinking the Lakota had some lovely beliefs. Once her misgivings had subsided, she found the women to be warm and friendly, the men respectful, the children delightful.

They had been at the Lakota camp for almost a month the night Wolf took her in his arms. "Are you happy here?" His gaze moved over her face. She was so lovely and he wanted her so desperately, needed her more than his next breath. How had he lived so long without her?

"I'd be happy wherever you are." She felt herself melting from the heat in his eyes. She loved the way he looked at her, the way he made her feel, as if she was something extraordinary. She loved the sound of his voice, low and husky and filled with longing. The way the mere touch of his hands filled her with warmth. And desire.

"Marry me, Skye."

She blinked at him. "Marry?"

He nodded. "It won't be legal in your time. For that matter, it wouldn't be considered legal in this time, either. It would be just for now, while we are here."

She looked at him, one brow raised. "Is this just to ease your conscience before you ravish me?"

"Have mercy on me, woman," he said, his voice a low groan. "I can't wait any longer. I ache deep inside with wanting you."

It seemed like the perfect solution, she thought. But what about when they went back to her time? She bit down on her lower lip. If they made love here, how could she refuse him when they returned to the twenty-first century? How could she make love to the man he was here but refuse the vampyre he was in the future?

Seeing the doubt in her eyes, he pulled her body against his, letting her feel the hard evidence of his desire as he covered her mouth with his in a long, searing kiss that left her breathless and aching with need. His hands moved over her, skimming the sides of her breasts, sliding over her hips, down her thighs. His kisses deepened, grew longer and more intense. His tongue ravished hers, until she writhed against him, the heat in his eyes burning away the last of her resistance. He was here and she wanted him. The future could take care of itself.

"Yes," she gasped, feeling as though she might explode with need. "I'll marry you!"

"Tomorrow?"

"Yes, oh, yes."

There was no formal marriage ceremony in the traditional sense among the Lakota. When a warrior wished to take a woman as his wife, he presented her father with a number of horses. If the father accepted the offering, an announcement was made and the warrior took the woman to his lodge.

Skye frowned as Wolf explained that to her. "That doesn't sound like a marriage to me. And I don't have a father to give me away."

"My grandfather is the chief of our tribe. He has agreed to marry us in a modified ceremony."

That afternoon, dressed in her doeskin dress, and carrying a bouquet of wildflowers that Carolyn had given her, Skye stood beside Wolf. Hand-in-hand, they faced his grandfather. The entire tribe encircled them, all dressed in their best.

"Be it known that on this day, Wolf Who Walks on the Wild Wind wishes to join his life with Skye. Wolf, do you wish to have this woman as your wife?"

Gazing deep into her eyes, Wolf said, "I do."

"Skye, do you wish to spend your life with Wolf Who Walks on the Wild Wind?"

She looked at Wolf, resplendent in a fringed buckskin shirt, pants, and moccasins. A single eagle feather adorned his hair. Heart pounding, she whispered, "I do."

"Then, in the white man's way, I say you are now man and wife." Chetáŋ smiled. "You are no more two, but one. One heart. One flesh. May *Wakan Tanka* bless you with long life and many children."

At his words, the tribe cheered.

Wolf took Skye in his arms. "I love you, wife," he said. "The Lakota rarely show affection in public, but I'll show you how much I love you later, when we're alone."

His words, the love and desire in his eyes, brought a flush to her cheeks.

Tonight, she thought, tonight she would be his.

And he would be hers.

CHAPTER TWENTY

There was a feast and dancing after the brief ceremony. As soon as it got dark, Wolf tugged on Skye's arm and they walked hand-in-hand into the shadows, then hurried to their lodge.

Skye had been waiting impatiently for this moment, but now that it was here, she felt suddenly shy and uncertain.

Wolf whispered her name as he drew her gently into his embrace. Cupping the back of her head in one hand, he kissed her lightly, and with that single kiss, all her doubts melted away. Locking her hands behind his head, she went up on her tiptoes and ran her tongue across his lips.

With a low groan, he pulled her body flush with his. "I thought we'd never be alone."

"We're alone now," she said, her voice tinged with laughter. "What would you like to do?"

Grinding his hips against hers, he growled, "Does that give you any ideas?"

In answer, she pulled his shirt over his head, tossed it aside, then ran her palms over his chest and shoulders, across his flat belly.

He unfastened the shoulder ties that held her dress, letting it puddle around her feet as he lifted her into his arms, carried her to the back of the lodge, and placed her gently on the furry robe that served as their bed. Skye removed her moccasins while he removed his buckskin pants and moccasins to stand naked before her, tall, dark, gorgeous, and fully aroused.

Whispering her name, he stretched out beside her and drew her into his arms. Her skin was like warm satin, her hair like fine silk. He rained kissed on her eyelids, her cheeks, the curve of her neck. She smelled of woman and desire and it aroused him even more. He had wanted her for so long.

Determined to make the moment last, he kissed and caressed her. "I feel like I've waited a lifetime to make you mine," he murmured, his hands gliding over her breasts and belly.

"The wait is over," she said, her whole body throbbing with desire. "Love me, Wolf."

His lips claimed hers, hot and hungry, as he rose over her.

Skye lifted her hips to receive him, her fingers tangling in the thick fall of his hair as he thrust into her. The intensity of his gaze warmed her blood even as his caresses scorched her flesh.

She let out a soft cry of delight as they came together, their bodies joined in a timeless dance of mating. Two hearts beating as one, she thought, as she reveled in the erotic sensation of his bare skin against her own, the wonder of his touch, the strength of his arms, the husky sound of his voice as he groaned her name, vowing that he loved her, would always love her.

She clung to him, quivering with pleasure as he brought her to fulfillment, sighed as he poured his life into her. And then there was only a sense of peace, of belonging, as they lay wrapped in each other's arms while their bodies cooled and their breathing returned to normal.

Wolf brushed a kiss across her lips. "Did I hurt you?"

"No." She smiled a dreamy smile. She was truly his now. And he was hers.

"Skye."

She heard the wanting in his voice, surprised that he wanted her again so soon. But she had no complaints, because she wanted him just as desperately.

It was, she thought, even better the second time.

Skye woke slowly, a smile on her face when she saw Wolf lying beside her. So, it hadn't been a dream. She hadn't been able to see him clearly last night. Now, her gaze caressed him, admiring the width of his chest and shoulders, the corded muscles in his arms, his hard, flat belly and long, long legs. He was so beautiful, she thought she would be content to spend the rest of the day just looking at him.

Eyes still closed, he murmured, "Good morning, wife."

"Good morning, husband."

Turning onto his side, Wolf propped himself on one elbow, his heated gaze slowly moving over her from head to heel before he lowered his head and claimed her lips with his. With a wicked gleam in his eye, he asked, "What do you want to do first? Make love, or have breakfast?"

"I don't have to ask what *you* want," she said dryly. "I can see it."

"I'm trying to be a thoughtful husband," he said, running his hand along her thigh.

Stifling a laugh, Skye muttered, "Shut up, husband," as she pushed him onto his back and then straddled his hips. "You talk too much."

It was hours later before he left the lodge.

The warriors all grinned at him, a knowing look in their eyes when Wolf joined them later that morning. He took their teasing good-naturedly, all the while looking forward to the time when he would be alone with Skye again. Making love to her had been incredible. She had been like silken fire in his arms, her body smooth and hot. She had teased him mercilessly, bold one moment, shy the next, until the last moment when she had given herself to him without restraint. He had never know anything like it. Like her.

Having possessed her, he knew nothing but death would part them. Nothing, he thought, save her rejection of him if and when they returned to the future.

The future. If she stayed with him when they returned to her time, their love-making would be even better, he mused. With his vampyre senses, making love would be even more intimate. He would feel what she felt, know what she was thinking, so that he could satisfy her every desire, her every wish. And if they shared blood, it would be an even more intimate act. It would allow her to know what he was thinking, feeling.

Skye felt as if everyone in camp was looking at her when she emerged from the lodge. She supposed it was normal, no matter who you were, to wonder how a newlywed couple had come together. It had certainly been more wonderful than she had ever dreamed. Wolf had been a tender, thoughtful lover. He had taken his time, loving her as if they had all the time in the world, seeing to her pleasure before his own.

She tried not to think of all the women he had known before, although she couldn't help wondering how many there had been in the last three hundred years. Her only consolation was that he had never loved any of them enough to marry them. She remembered asking him if he had ever been married. He'd answered that he had made love to many women, but that he had never loved any of them until he met her. Thinking of that now brought a warm glow to her heart. He loved her. And she loved him.

Her heart skipped a beat when she saw him striding toward her, tall, dark and handsome in breechclout and moccasins, a pair of eagle feathers in his hair, the exact image of the cardboard figure in the museum.

A thrill ran down her spine when he took her hand in his and led her into their lodge and secured the door flap – a sign that visitors were not welcome.

She went into his arms gladly, anticipation dancing in the pit of her stomach as he undressed her and then shucked his own clothing. The buffalo robe was soft beneath her bare skin, Wolf's hands hot and eager as they caressed her. He was here, he was real, and nothing else mattered. Not the past, not the future. Only this moment, his voice husky with desire as he whispered that he loved her, would always love her...

Sometime later, they strolled down to the river. Wolf found a secluded place, sheltered from view. After undressing, they slipped into the slow-moving current to bathe with a bar of soap that Skye had brought with her.

Skye thought she had never felt anything more erotic than the touch of Wolf's soapy hands on her skin. The air was warm, the water cool, but his hands were hotter than the afternoon sun shining on her shoulders as his hands moved slowly over her. She basked in his touch, then took the soap from his hands and discovered, to her delight, that washing him was even more delightful. She reveled in the feel of his skin, the corded muscles in his arms and chest, his easy strength as he carried her out of the river, laid her down on the sweet-smelling grass and covered her body with his. Heaven, she thought, she had died and found heaven in his arms.

A week passed and Skye found herself growing accustomed to the Lakota way of life. Wolf spent time with his grandfather and the men during the day, doing those things expected of a Lakota warrior, like guarding the village, repairing their weapons, looking after their horses.

Skye was grateful for Carolyn's friendship, to know someone who came from a similar background and spoke the same language, who could answer her seemingly endless questions. It was Carolyn who taught her Lakota etiquette. If the lodge flap was open, you were welcome to enter. If it was closed, you were to make your presence known and wait for an invitation. When a man entered a lodge, he went to the right. Women went to the left. It was bad form to walk between a seated person and the fire. When the host started to clean his pipe, it was the signal for guests to leave. She also learned that when lodges were built, the entrance always faced the rising sun.

"The lodge is more than just a home," Carolyn said. "It is like a church, as well. The walls represent the sky, the floor represents the earth, the lodgepoles are reminders of the trails that leads from the earth to the world of spirits.

Most lodges have an altar behind the firepit. There isn't one here because the teacher had his own beliefs."

Skye nodded. Wolf had told her about the Lakota belief in the Afterlife, but what did he believe, she wondered. Did he believe in the Christian god? The Lakota gods? Or none at all?

Wolf came to sit beside her one afternoon. Noting her interest in watching a father teach his son to ride, he said, "As soon as a boy can walk, he is put on a horse. His father or another male relative teaches him how to care for the animal. When the boy is old enough, he'll be put in charge of his father's horses." Looking into her eyes, he asked, "Are you happy here, *mitawicu?*"

"Yes," she said. And then frowned. "What does *mita-wicu* mean?"

Caressing her cheek with his fingers, he said, "It means, my wife."

"How do I say 'my husband'?"

"*Mihingna,*"

Whispering, "*Mihingna,*" she leaned forward and kissed his cheek.

With desire blazing in his eyes, he took her hands in his and lifted her to her feet. Skye felt as though her whole body was smiling when he led her into their lodge and closed the door flap.

Days later, they were sitting by the river. Skye had lost track of time. There were no clocks here, no calendars, no dates to keep. "Your people don't keep holidays, the way mine do, do they?"

"No. My people live their lives by the seasons. In the spring, the people leave their winter camp and begin gathering food, and looking forward to the first buffalo hunt. Spring is known as the Moon of the Birth of Buffalo Calves.

"Summer is the Moon When Strawberries are Ripe. It is the time for vision quests. In the old days, before the tribes were sent to the reservation, all the Lakota tribes gathered together. For four days, the warriors purified themselves in preparation for the Sun Dance, which is our most sacred ceremony."

"I've heard of that. It sounds barbaric."

He nodded. "To the white mind, it is. But we believe every warrior needs a vision to guide him through life."

"Did you ever..."

"Yes."

She grimaced. "How did you stand it?"

Wolf shrugged. "It's part of becoming a man, a ritual of sacrifice for the good of the people."

Skye nodded. There were, she thought, some things about the Lakota and their way of life that she would never understand. Just as she would never understand how he could be both vampyre and human.

"Fall is known as the Time of the Harvest Moon." His fingers sifted through a lock of her hair. "Many buffalo hunts are done in the fall in order to obtain enough meat to see the people through the winter.

"November brings the Winter Moon. It is a hard time. Our men and boys repair tools and weapons or fashion new ones. The women make new clothing. Little girls make dolls. Many stories are told by the old ones around the campfires at night."

"So much to learn," Skye remarked.

"So much to learn about you," he murmured as he pulled her down on the grass, his mouth covering hers, driving every other thought from her mind but her need for this man and this man alone.

CHAPTER TWENTY-ONE

It was mid-afternoon a few days later when one of the war-riors rode into camp, shouting that two of the boys watching the horse herd had been killed and a part of the herd stolen.

"It was the Crow," the warrior exclaimed. "Their tracks are everywhere!"

There was an immediate call for a war party to avenge the boys' deaths and recover their horses.

Wolf muttered an oath as the warriors collected their weapons and caught up their horses.

"Are you coming with us, Wolf Who Walks on the Wild Wind?" Anoki asked. "Or has living with the *wasichu* made you soft?"

Wolf snorted. "Don't worry about me, Anoki." Heaving a sigh, he went to tell Skye he was leaving.

"You're going to war?" Skye stared at him, her eyes wide and afraid.

"I won't be gone long," he said, taking her into his arms.

"Please don't go." What if he was hurt? Or worse, killed? She couldn't imagine her life without him. If anything happened to Wolf, how would she ever find her way home again?

He gazed into her eyes. "Would you have me stay behind with the women?" he asked quietly.

She wanted to say yes, but how could she? He was a man, a warrior. She could not ask him to be less than he was, could not shame him in front of his people.

It amazed her how quickly the war party assembled. She watched in silent, fearful fascination as Wolf tied a pair of black eagle feathers into his hair, then dipped his fingers into a pot of yellow war paint and drew a zigzag design on his cheeks and a long, zigzag line on his horse's left flank.

"What do the symbols means?" Skye asked, as she watched the other warriors paint their horses.

He gestured at Enapay's grulla. "A circle around the horse's eyes and nostrils are for keener sight and smell. The stripes on the legs of Takoda's mare are called thunder stripes. They're to please the god of war. The red circle drawn around the scar on Ogaleesha's buckskin means the horse was wounded in battle. The zigzag on my horse's flank symbolizes lightning to give him added speed and power."

Skye glanced around as the warriors swung onto their ponies' backs.

Taking her in his arms, Wolf said, "It's time to go."

"Come back to me."

"You know I will." He kissed her again, quickly, then vaulted onto his horse's back.

The warriors rode out of the village amid shouted war cries and a cloud of dust.

Feeling lost and alone, Skye stared after them. Were the other women as worried as she? Did their hearts pound with fear for the lives of their husbands and sons? She glanced at the solemn expressions on the faces of the children. There was sadness there, along with resignation. But it was the looks on the faces of the boys not yet men, the excitement in their eyes, as they visualized themselves riding off to war, the disappointment because they were not yet old enough to ride with the men.

"He will return."

Skye turned to see Wolf's grandfather standing behind her.

"I hope so," she whispered.

He placed a reassuring hand on her shoulder. "Do not worry. Wolf Who Walks on the Wild Wind has always had strong medicine. It has never failed him."

"If he doesn't come back…" She bit off her words.

"If he does not come back," Chetáŋ said quietly. "I will take you home."

Skye stared at the old man. She remembered asking Wolf if his grandfather knew what he was and Wolf's reply that he didn't know, but it wouldn't surprise him. "How did you know that I'm not from this time?"

A slow smile spread across his face. "The Spirits told me," he said, his black eyes twinkling. "They have told me many things. And shown me far-off times and places in vision." He gave her a gentle hug. "I am an old man. I have walked many paths."

Once, she would have scoffed at such a notion, Skye mused, as she made her way back to her lodge. But no more. She had the distinct feeling that Chetáŋ was talking about time-traveling, and not just from here to her future, but to other times and other places.

Carolyn was waiting for Skye when she reached her lodge. "I thought you might like some company," she said. "I know how hard the waiting can be."

Skye nodded. "I'm so afraid for him."

"Men go to war and women stay behind and worry. It has always been so," Carolyn said with a wisdom beyond her years. "It never gets any easier."

Never had time passed so slowly. Skye tried to keep up her end of the conversation as Carolyn helped her cut out a pattern for a new pair of moccasins, but her mind kept drifting toward Wolf and the war party. Had they found the Crow? Had there been a battle? Had Wolf been hurt? Killed? How much longer would they be gone?

"Worrying will not make the hours go by any faster," Carolyn remarked with a sympathetic smile.

"I know." Skye laid the pattern aside. "I can't concentrate on what I'm doing. Maybe we'd better finish this another time."

"Very well." Carolyn laid a hand on Skye's shoulder. "You love him very much, don't you?"

"I guess it shows."

"A blind man could see it."

"I've never known anyone like him. I think I loved Wolf the moment we met." She must have, Skye thought, to go traipsing off into the past with a man she'd known a relatively short time. A man who was also a vampyre. Here, in the past, she went days without thinking about that. But she was thinking about it now. If he was badly hurt, there would be no supernatural power to heal him.

It was a frightening thought and it chilled her to the marrow of her bones.

Wolf rode near the head of the war party. A dozen warriors armed and painted for war were strung out single-file behind him. It felt good to be riding with his Lakota brothers again, to feel the blood pounding in his veins as he contemplated the upcoming conflict.

He had fought many battles in years past – against the Crow, against the whites. As promised in his vision quest, his medicine had always been strong. It had been a strange vision, he mused. He hadn't realized what it meant until he became a vampyre. In his vision, a large, black wolf had come to him and led him into a world of darkness, a world he had come to realize represented death, and the dark side of his nature. The vampyre side. A thunderbird had flown above the wolf's head, representing his Lakota heritage.

They found the Crow resting their horses in a shallow draw. Wolf counted a half-dozen warriors milling about below. He glanced at Anoki, who was leading the Lakota warriors. At his signal, the air rang with their war cries as the Lakota charged into the draw.

The Crow sprang for their horses and the battle was on.

Arrows whistled through the air. Other warriors fought hand-to-hand with knives and clubs. The Crow were out-numbered two-to-one and when they realized they were losing the battle, they picked up their dead and lit out for home, leaving the Lakota ponies behind.

Wolf was in favor of giving chase, but Anoki shook his head.

"The Crow ran like cowards. Let them go. We have what we came for."

Shrugging, Wolf fell back to bring up the tail-end of the herd as the stolen horses splashed across a shallow river and raced for home.

Wolf felt the slam of the bullet in his back before he heard the report of the gunshot, the sound all but lost in the thunder of pounding hooves and the victorious shouts of the Lakota. Glancing over his shoulder, he saw a lone Crow warrior racing away. Wolf stared after him. For a moment, he was numb and then the pain came, stealing his breath.

He reeled in the saddle as the world spun out of focus and when it righted itself again, he was lying face down on the ground. He had been hurt often enough to know that he was badly injured, perhaps fatally. As a vampyre, the wound would have been insignificant. He would have healed in a matter of moments, with nothing left to show for it. But in this time and place, he was vulnerable. He could feel the blood coursing down his back, soaking into his clout. It hurt to breathe, to move, and he closed his eyes, wondering if anyone would come looking for him before it was too late, if he would ever see Skye again, or if he would die here, his life's blood watering Mother Earth.

As his vision dimmed, he saw a large black wolf stalking toward him out of darkness.

He whispered Skye's name before the blackness carried him away.

Skye ran out of the lodge when she heard the exultant shouts of the war party.

Standing on her tiptoes, she searched for Wolf. Where was he?

His grandfather came to stand beside her, his dark eyes mirroring the worry she felt.

"He's not there," she wailed.

"Anoki!" Chetáŋ called. "Where is my grandson? Where is Wolf Who Walks on the Wild Wind?"

Anoki glanced at the warriors behind him. Making a vague gesture, he said, "Wolf was riding behind the herd. He must have stopped for something."

Chetáŋ's eyes narrowed. "Why did you not go back to make sure he was not hurt? Or captured?"

Ashamed, Anoki looked away. As war leader, it had been his duty to look after those who followed him. He had failed. If something had happened to Wolf Who Walks on the Wild Wind, he would be forever disgraced in the eyes of the people.

Skye pressed a hand to her heart. Captured! She knew enough about Indians to know that the Crow would likely torture their captive before they killed him.

Chetáŋ strode to his lodge, took up the reins of his horse, swung onto the animal's back, and rode out of the village.

Skye stared after him. The very thing she had feared had happened. Wanting to be alone, she returned to the lodge.

Sinking down on the buffalo robes, she stared blankly at the small slice of darkening sky visible through the smoke hole. He couldn't be dead. *Please, please, don't let him be dead.* She sent the prayer, unspoken, toward heaven, repeated it over and over in her heart until the numbness passed and the tears came.

He was dying, something he had never seriously contemplated since becoming a vampyre. He had been practically invincible then, able to survive almost anything. Poison, knife wounds, gunshots, he had survived them all. He had known coming here would be a risk, but for Skye's sake, he had brushed it aside. She didn't want a vampyre, she wanted a man and he had been willing to do anything to please her.

Foolish man, he thought, to tempt the fates.

The pain in his back had eased and now he felt nothing at all.

It was not a good sign.

Closing his eyes, he fell into the everlasting darkness that hovered around him.

Unable to sit still, Skye paced back and forth in front of their lodge. The Lakota seemed to sense she wanted to be alone, though from time to time she saw pity in their eyes.

He couldn't be dead. *Please, please, don't let him be dead.* The same prayer, over and over again.

Her heart seemed to stop when she saw Chetáŋ riding through the darkness toward her. Wolf lay limp across the horse's withers.

She looked up at the old man, her gaze searching his. "Is he …?"

"Not yet."

Two warriors came forward. One of them held Chetáŋ's horse, the other lifted Wolf from the back of the mare, carried him into the lodge, and lowered him onto the floor, and then left the lodge.

Skye fell to her knees beside Wolf. His breathing was slow and irregular, his face deadly pale and sheened with perspiration. She took his hand in hers as tears dripped down her cheeks.

Looking up at Chetáŋ, she said, "Wolf told me he's seen you work miracles, that you've saved those who should have died."

"I cannot help him. He has stayed with us too long. I cannot give him what he needs."

"You know, don't you? You know what he is."

Chetáŋ nodded. "I have always known."

Skye glanced at Wolf, felt a flicker of hope when she saw that he was awake.

"Skye."

"Wolf! Oh, Wolf," she sobbed. "Thank God!"

"There is no time for tears," Chetáŋ said. "We must get him to the cave before it is too late. He is badly wounded and has lost much blood. The bullet is lodged against his spine. So close I dare not try to remove it."

Her heart sank at his words. She looked down at Wolf, fear striking her very soul when she saw that he was unconscious again.

Chetáŋ laid a hand on her shoulder. "I have a travois to carry him. We must hurry. Gather some blankets and a waterskin while I get your horse."

Skye quickly did as bidden, her gaze constantly drawn to Wolf. He lay so still, so silent, his eyes closed, his breathing growing labored. He couldn't die, she thought, as she grabbed her camera case and slung it over her shoulder. She would not let him die.

Minutes later, they were ready. Covered by a buffalo robe, Wolf lay on a travois pulled by Chetáŋ's horse. Skye rode Wolf's pinto.

It would take two days, at least, to reach the cave.

Would they make it in time?

CHAPTER TWENTY-TWO

They rode through that night and the next day, stopping only briefly to water and rest the horses, to choke down a few bites of pemmican. Wolf drifted in and out of consciousness. Occasionally he mumbled a few nonsensical words. Once, he cried out, his face twisted with pain. Skye watched him constantly, certain every cry would be his last. He was in pain and she couldn't help wondering if it was from his wounds or his desperate need for blood.

It would be all her fault if he died, she thought. She hadn't wanted to be with a vampyre so she had convinced him to come here. She had known it might be dangerous, but he had always seemed so strong, so invincible, she had convinced herself nothing could go wrong.

She prayed day and night, begging heaven to let him live, knowing she couldn't carry the guilt of his death for the rest of her life.

She was hungry and bone-weary as they climbed the last ridge to the cave in the hills.

Chetáŋ lifted Wolf into his arms and carried him inside. Amazed at the old man's strength, Skye followed him into the unnatural darkness, a blackness so thick it seemed to have a life of its own. Why hadn't she noticed that before? And then she wondered if it was death waiting to wrap Wolf in its dark embrace.

A moment later, she heard Chetáŋ begin to chant. She recognized the same haunting notes Wolf had used.

When he finished, he said, "Skye, take hold of my arm."

She reached for him blindly, relieved when her fingers brushed his arm.

A dozen steps and they emerged from the cave into the night.

Chetáŋ gently lowered Wolf to the ground.

"What do we do now?" Skye asked anxiously.

"You need to leave."

"Leave?"

"He will not be himself when he wakes. You will not be safe here."

"What are you going to do?"

"He will need blood. I will give him mine."

Skye stared at the old man. "If he's not himself, It won't be safe for you, either."

"I am an old man. He is my grandson. Blood of my blood. Go, Skye."

Torn by the need to run yet needing to stay, Skye stared at Wolf. She couldn't believe he would hurt her, but what if Chetáŋ was right? If he didn't recognize her, what chance would she have to fight him off? Yet she couldn't let Wolf kill his grandfather. It would haunt him the rest of his life.

For better or worse, she thought. The words hadn't been spoken when they wed, but she felt bound by them just the same.

"You should go back to your people," Skye said. "They need you. Wolf is my husband. He won't hurt me."

Chetáŋ's gaze met hers. "You are a brave woman. My grandson has chosen well. I will pray to the Great Spirit for you both." He rested his hand on her shoulder for a moment, then ducked back into the cave.

A moment later, Wolf shuddered convulsively. His eyes flew open – eyes as red as blood, and glowing with a fierce, hungry light.

She took an instinctive step back as he jackknifed into a sitting position, afraid her bravado was about to cost her her life.

Wolf stared up at her through those fiendish red eyes. A low growl, like that of a hungry wolf, rose in his throat as he bared his fangs.

Skye stared at the cave, wishing she had gone back into the past with Chetáŋ, wishing she was anywhere but here, staring into the blazing red eyes of a hungry vampyre.

"Wolf." She whispered his name as he rose slowly to his feet. "Please don't hurt me."

She froze when he reached for her, his hands rough when he yanked her body up against his. He pressed his face against her neck and took a deep breath.

I'm a dead woman, she thought, and closed her eyes.

He sniffed her again.

She cringed when she felt his teeth at her throat.

Abruptly, he lifted his head. "Skye?"

"Yes, it's me."

A deep, shuddering sigh wracked his body. He was on fire with the need for blood. Every cell in his body screamed for relief from the agony clawing at his vitals. His hands tightened on her shoulders, his fingers digging into her flesh. Relief was only a bite away. Just one bite, he thought, to ease the excruciating pain burning through him like hellfire.

"Skye ..."

"You promised you wouldn't drink from me without asking."

"I'm asking." His voice was low, angry and impatient.

"One drink," she said, a quiver in her voice. "One drink from my wrist."

"Two?"

"One!" Oh, Lord, what would she do if he didn't stop? If only she had a weapon!

"One." He snarled the word at her.

She stared at him. In the faint light of the midnight moon, he looked truly frightening, his fangs extended, eyes red, the skin of his face stretched taut. His fingers felt like claws where they held her fast against him. "Let me go."

"Don't run." He forced the words through clenched teeth. "Please, Skye, don't run." He was barely holding it together, knew if she ran now, when he was hungry and desperate for relief, he wouldn't be able to resist the urge to chase her down. He didn't want to think what would happen when he caught her. For catch her, he would.

"I won't," she whispered, more frightened of him than she had ever been. "I promise."

He lowered one hand, then the other.

She longed to turn and run away as fast as she could, but every instinct she possessed told her doing so would be fatal. He was in predator mode and she was prey. Taking a deep breath, she held out her left arm, palm up.

He was shaking as he took hold of her wrist. Eyes blazing, he sank his fangs into her flesh and drank.

It was, she thought, a very long drink.

Sweet relief washed through her when he lifted his head. "You damn fool, why didn't you run when I was unconscious?"

She glared at him. "Because I'm a damn fool."

"Skye." Some of the red faded from his eyes.

She flinched when he reached for her.

"Relax. I'm going to take you home."

She closed her eyes as his arm went around her waist. When she opened them again, they were standing on the front porch of her house.

She huffed a sigh as the world righted itself again. "Are you all right now?" she asked. He didn't look all right. There was still a faint red glow in his eyes. When his gaze moved to her throat, she took a wary step back.

"I need more."

She wished she had the courage to let him drink from her again, knew he would never deliberately hurt her. But what if he couldn't stop?

"Not from you."

She knew a moment of relief, quickly followed by concern for whoever he preyed upon. "You can't go hunting!" she exclaimed. "Not now, when you're not in control. What if you kill someone?"

"Better someone else than you."

"Wolf..."

"I won't kill anyone. I promise."

She held out her arm. "Just take it from..."

He pressed his fingertips to her lips. "Don't tempt me, love. I know you're frightened by what you've seen tonight, and you should be. This is what I am." He took a deep breath. "You won't see me for a while." He shook his head when he saw the protest rising in her eyes. "It isn't safe for you or anyone else to be around me right now. In a way, I died again. I have the same, almost overpowering urge to drink you dry." He caressed her cheek with his knuckles. "Think about us while I'm gone."

"Wolf, I..."

But she was talking to empty air.

He fled from her presence, his preternatural speed carrying him into the next city, afraid if he stayed anywhere near her, he would do the unthinkable. He was tortured by the same insatiable hunger he had known as a new vampyre, the urge to hunt, to sink his fangs into his prey and drink and drink until he was glutted with their blood.

He mesmerized the first unfortunate mortal to cross his path, a nurse leaving a hospital. He buried his fangs in her neck, there, in the parking lot, and lost himself in the euphoria of her life's blood. Reveled in it.

He would have taken it all if a couple of men hadn't exited the hospital. Cursing under his breath, he quickly released the woman from his thrall and fled the scene.

A drunk passed out in an alley was his second victim. High on fresh hot blood, he drank his way through the city until a prickling in his skin warned him that the sun was rising.

He willed himself to his lair and surrendered to the darkness of oblivion, his last conscious thought for Skye. He loved her more than his life. And because he did, he was never going to see her again.

Skye woke late after a long and restless night. She had slept for a few hours but had awakened several times through the night, haunted by horrible nightmares of Wolf prowling the city like a rabid animal, killing every living thing in his path.

She turned on the morning news, afraid she'd hear about a rash of midnight killings, but there had only been two, and they were the result of gang violence, not a blood-hungry vampyre.

Relieved, she took a long, hot shower, then went downstairs to fix breakfast, only to remember that she had cleaned out her fridge before they left. She heated a can of soup she really didn't want and after several swallows, she poured the remainder down the sink and settled for a cup of hot chocolate.

Hoping to take her mind off Wolf, she booted up her computer and uploaded the photos she'd taken. Pictures of the town and its people. She grinned at the one of the women leaning over the balcony of Maud's Pleasure Palace. There were numerous photos of the Lakota people, the animals, the land. And Wolf. Scores of pictures of Wolf. The ones in the Indian village were her favorite. Wolf on his horse, talking with his grandfather, standing beside the river, sitting with some of the warriors. There were a couple of pictures of Carolyn and the other women, of bright-eyed children, and seasoned warriors dozing in the sun.

She sorted them by date. She usually kept her photos on her computer, but later that afternoon, she went out to look for a photo album, deciding she needed hard copies of her favorites in case her computer crashed or she lost the SD cards. Some photos could never be replaced.

She stopped at the grocery store on the way home and picked up the essentials – bread, milk, eggs, lunch meat, a roasted chicken for dinner, a couple of bags of dark chocolate candy for consolation, a six-pack of soda.

At home again, she fixed a sandwich and washed it down with a glass of iced tea.

A glance at the clock showed it was a little after four. The rest of the day yawned before her. Needing to be busy, she dusted the furniture, vacuumed the carpets upstairs and down, and all the while, she thought of Wolf, of what he had told her the night before. She knew she would never forget the hellish red glow in his eyes, the sight of his fangs, the feral growl in his voice. He'd told her he had the same urge to kill he'd had when he was first turned, and that frightened her more than anything. He had killed people back then. Had he succumbed to that urge last night? Just because there was nothing on the news about mysterious deaths didn't mean there hadn't been any, only that if there were bodies drained of blood somewhere in the city, they hadn't yet been found.

How long would it take him to overcome the urge to kill his prey, to gain control of his hunger? He'd told her it had taken a year or so when he'd first been turned. Would it take that long again?

After putting the vacuum away, she dropped into the easy chair in the living room and stared out the large picture window. He was her husband in the past, among the Lakota people.

What was he to her now?

Late that night, Wolf lingered in the shadows outside Skye's house. She had drawn all the curtains, but he could hear her moving around downstairs, fixing a cup of hot chocolate in the kitchen, carrying it into the living room where she turned on the ten o'clock news. He grinned into the darkness, knowing she was wondering if the police had stumbled on any bodies drained of blood.

He had sworn never to see her again, but he couldn't stay away. She would never know he'd been there, but he needed to be near her. Closing his eyes, he inhaled the warm, sweet, womanly scent that was hers and hers alone. He listened to the steady beat of her heart, the whisper of the blood flowing through her veins, and felt the hunger rise up within him, and with it the memory of drinking from her, the taste of her life's blood on his tongue, the warmth that had flowed through him.

Cursing under his breath, he turned away from the window before his desire got out of hand, before he forced his way into her house and made love to her there, on the living room floor, his body sheathed in hers, his fangs buried in the curve of her neck...

A vile oath rose in his throat as he felt his eyes go red, the brush of his fangs against his tongue.

He was a monster. No fit company for the woman he loved or anyone else.

He raced into the night, knowing he had to get away from her before it was too late, before he succumbed to the lust, the terrible, insatiable hunger that pounded inside him like a Lakota war drum.

Before he threw himself at her feet and begged her to love him.

Chapter Twenty-Three

A fraid he wouldn't be able to stay away from Skye, Wolf
went to the cave the following night. He'd bought a
new pair of jeans, boots, and a Western-style shirt to replace
those that had been ruined.

His pinto waited for him outside the cave.

Knowing his grandfather would be wondering whether
he had lived or died, Wolf swung onto the mare's back and
rode hard for the Lakota village. For the first time, returning to the past did not ease his thirst for blood, leaving him
to wonder why.

It was midafternoon a couple of days later when he
reached the village. The people looked at him in awe as he
rode into camp and he realized that most of them thought
he had died. A few made the ancient sign to ward off witches.

He dismounted in front of his grandfather's lodge and
stepped inside.

Chetáŋ looked up, a slow smile spreading over his weath-
ered face. "*Wicatakoza*," he murmured. "I am glad to see
you."

Wolf embraced his grandfather. "And I am glad to see
you, *tunkasila*. I came to thank you for saving my life. I would
have died had you not taken me to the cave. But you know
that, don't you?"

"*Ai.* I sensed the change in you. At first, I thought you had been stricken with the curse of the witch, but the spirits told me that was not it."

Chetáŋ lowered himself to the floor and Wolf dropped down across from him. "Are you well, *tunkasila?*"

"My years are catching up with me." The old man's gaze moved slowly over his grandson. "How are you? Where is your woman?"

"I'm different," Wolf said. "Whatever happened to me when I was wounded has changed me. I have always been human here, but I no longer feel that way. Do you understand?"

Chetáŋ frowned and then shook his head. "Perhaps you were closer to death than we thought."

"I don't know. All I know is I can't stay here long." Riding toward the village had been almost painful. The sun, which had never bothered him here before, had made his flesh tingle as though it was on fire. And the hunger – it had never bothered him here before. Even when he knew he'd to go back to the future to feed from time to time, there had been no real discomfort.

"I am sorry for that," his grandfather said, his voice heavy with sadness.

"I just came to let you know I survived, and to thank you for ... for everything."

"The woman?" Chetáŋ asked again. "What of her?"

"I'm afraid to be with her."

Chetáŋ nodded. "Perhaps, in time ...?"

"I hope so."

"Will you stay the night?"

"No. I have to go back. My life is there now."

"Then let us ride together one last time."

"Will you go with me all the way to the cave? I will not be needing my horse again. There is no need for her to wait for me."

Sadness filled his grandfather's eyes as he nodded.

They rode out of the village a short time later. Knowing in his heart that he would never be able to return, Wolf took a last glance at the village as they rode away. He felt a sense of loss, of regret, as he realized that Wolf Who Walks on the Wild Wind had died in the cave. Never again would he hunt the buffalo with the Lakota, or hear the old stories of his people. Never again would he see the land of his birth as it was now. Whatever had let him live in two worlds had also died in the cave.

His gaze lingered on the land he knew and loved so well—the rolling prairie, the distant mountains, the cottonwoods that lined the rivers and streams, the beauty of a sky untouched by the pollution of the future. Fat white clouds dotted the sky. He watched a red-tailed hawk soar effortlessly overhead, wings spread wide as it searched the land for prey. Prey. He grimaced as he felt the urge to feed rise within him. It was constant now, a never-ending hunger.

They rode until nightfall, then made camp alongside a shallow stream. They had jerky and pemmican for dinner, then hunkered down around a small fire.

"Do not give in to despair, *wicatakoza*," Chetáŋ said, placing his hand on Wolf's shoulder. "I know all seems dark now, but you must not give up hope. The woman loves you. You love her."

"Is love enough for two people as different as we are?"

"Yes," Chetáŋ said solemnly. "I believe so."

Wolf grunted softly, wondering how long Skye would wait for him, if, indeed, she was waiting. Or if she thought herself better off without him, now that she had seen him at his worst. Now that she knew the monster that lurked within him.

"I have faith that everything will work out for you, *wicata-koza,* if you do not give up hope."

"Pilamaya, tunkasila."

Chetáŋ smiled at him. "The spirits have never been wrong."

They were in the saddle again at sunup, stopping only once to rest the horses and let them drink. It was mid-day when they reached the cave.

Dismounting, the two men stood there for a moment, reluctant to part. "Be well, *tunkasila,*" Wolf murmured. "Say a prayer for me now and then."

With tears in his eyes, the old man murmured, "Every day and every night."

Heart aching, Wolf embraced his grandfather one last time before ducking into the cave. His voice was thick with unshed tears as he chanted the words he knew so well and would never use again.

As always, it was night when he stepped out of the cave.

And the hunger was upon him, driving every other thought from his mind but the urgent need for blood.

CHAPTER TWENTY-FOUR

After five weeks of hoping to see Wolf again, Skye admitted it was over. Wolf was gone and there was nothing she could do about it. She had driven past his house on numerous occasions, pausing to stare at the closed door, the dark windows. Was he even staying there now, she wondered, or had he left town, never to return?

She had gone to the museum one Saturday night and felt a sense of loss, of finality, when she saw that the Native American exhibit had been replaced with a science exhibit about global warming and melting icebergs. She wished fleetingly that she had thought to ask the museum if she could have the cardboard figure of Wolf Who Walks on the Wild Wind when they were done with it.

The Sunday morning after that, she pulled up in front of his house, walked up the porch stairs and sat on the top step. She didn't know what had brought her there, she only knew sitting there made her feel closer to him. She pulled her cell phone out of her pocket and stared at the screen. His image stared back at her. It was a picture she had taken of Wolf astride his pinto mare. It was her favorite photo. Shirtless, an eagle feather in his long, black hair, he looked every inch the Lakota warrior.

She sat there for a long while. Cars drove past. Three teenage boys in hoodies strolled by. She grinned when one of them whistled at her. In the distance, church bells chimed the hour. How long since she had been to church? she wondered. Two years? Three?

Feeling a sudden need to pour out the feelings churning in her heart and soul, she checked her phone for the hours of Sunday worship, then hurried down the steps. If she broke the speed limit just a little, she would just make it on time.

Deep in the bowels of his lair, Wolf came awake as a familiar scent was borne to him. Skye! What the devil was she doing here?

Struggling through the darkness of the Dark Sleep that held him fast, he gained his feet and made his way to the first floor. He squinted against the sun as he opened the door and peered out in time to see her driving away.

Closing his eyes, he took a deep breath, filling his nostrils with the remembered fragrance of her hair and skin. The tantalizing scent of her blood. Always her blood. It called to him like no other.

He yearned to go after her, but the sun was too bright, the lethargy that held him in its grasp too strong to resist. He closed and locked the door, then staggered back down the stairs to the safety of his lair. And all the while, his heart ached for the woman he loved and longed to see. But he dared not, he thought as the dark sleep ensnared him in its grasp again. Not until he was in control of the terrible hunger that plagued him.

Another week passed. Looking back, Skye remembered little of it save for going to church. She had listened to the words of the hymns, words of peace and love, and for a time, she had known a sense of peace, of hope. The sermon had been on love and forgiveness, and though she loved Wolf with all her heart, she wasn't sure she could ever forgive him for leaving her the way he had. She knew he had done it because he was afraid of what he might do. And Heaven knew she was afraid of him now as never before. She told herself she hated him and yet she was angry because he hadn't at least called to see how she was doing, to let her know how he was getting along. She told herself she was better off without him, that she never wanted to see hm again…Lies, she thought, all lies. She missed him dreadfully, worried about him constantly.

That night, her dreams were filled with images of death, of bloody fangs and hell-red eyes, of being chased through an endless darkness by a man clad in a long, black cloak that billowed behind him like the wings of death. She let out a horrified scream when he caught her. Helpless to fight him off, she whispered that she loved him, missed him, needed him, but her words fell on deaf ears as he buried his fangs deep into her throat and drank and drank until there was nothing left…

She woke to the sound of her own cries. Lurching to her feet, she ran into the bathroom, dropped to her knees, and retched until her stomach was empty.

She sat there a moment before she stood and moved to the sink where she rinsed her mouth, washed her face, and then staggered back to bed.

She was sick every morning after that. With mounting horror, she bought a pregnancy test, held her breath as she waited for the results to be revealed.

Just as she'd feared, she was pregnant with Wolf's child.

She told herself it was impossible. Vampyres couldn't have children.

But he hadn't been a vampyre in the past...

A second test the next day produced the same results.

She was pregnant and Wolf Who Walks on the Wild Wind was the father.

Filled with apprehension, Skye made a doctor's appointment for the next day and when he confirmed what she already knew, she called her parents. Needless to say, they were distressed when she told them she was pregnant and that the father was no longer in the picture. When they asked for details, she told them she didn't want to talk about it, and they graciously dropped the subject after she assured them that she had been married to the father.

That night, she wrote an email to Wolf, read it over three times, and deleted it.

She started a text, and deleted it.

She picked up the phone only to put it down again.

He didn't want her. Why would he want her child? Would he even believe it was his? As her anger grew stronger, she told herself he didn't deserve to know.

That night, she cried herself to sleep and in the morning, she vowed to put him out of her mind once and for all. She had a child to think about now. Fresh tears burned her eyes. How would she ever be able to forget Wolf when his child would be a constant reminder?

Days turned into weeks and weeks into months. She spent her time redecorating one of the upstairs bedrooms – new paint, cute new curtains for the window. She donated the old furniture to the Goodwill and replaced it with a white crib, a padded rocking chair, a changing table, and diaper pail.

She bought a colorful mobile for the crib, a cute little stuffed bear, crib sheets and blankets, diapers and bath towels, bibs with cute baby animals on them, a music box that played lullabies. She bought sleepers and rompers and booties and anything else that caught her eye, determined that her child would never want for anything.

Except a father.

When her jeans grew tight and uncomfortable, she went shopping for maternity clothes. She bought a dozen outfits and a couple of nursing bras, a roomy nightgown, a new robe.

Skye was sitting on the front porch late one night when she felt the baby move for the first time. Startled, she pressed her hand to her belly. She had known for months that she was pregnant but feeling the baby move made it more real.

She was about to go into the house when she felt a strange stirring in the air and Wolf suddenly appeared at the foot of the porch steps.

Skye stared at him, unable to believe he was there. That he was real. As always, just looking at him filled her with a soul-deep yearning to be in his arms, a hunger for his kisses, the sound of his voice whispering her name ...

She banished those thoughts from her mind. He was no longer a part of her life.

He climbed the stairs until he was standing in front of her, his eyes blazing with anger. "Why?" he growled. "Why didn't you let me know you were pregnant?"

Her own outrage rushed to the fore. "Why?" she demanded, her voice rising. "Why? Because you have no right to know, that's why! You gave up that right when you left me. Left us." She folded her arms over her breasts. "We don't want you."

The anger faded from his eyes. "Skye, you must know why I couldn't be with you," he said quietly. "I've been through hell since we returned here. You have no idea what it's been like. I've thought of you every damn day. It took every ounce of my self-control to stay away. Even now…" His voice trailed off and he closed his eyes. When he spoke again, his voice was an anguished whisper. "Even now it's all I can do not to… to take you in my arms and ease the pain. I've come so close to killing so many."

"How did you know I was pregnant?"

"I felt it. Whether you like it or not, the child is blood of my blood, as well as yours." His gaze moved to her swollen belly. She was carrying his child. How was that even possible?

Blood of his blood, Skye mused. Human blood? Or vampyre? She looked up at him, a touch of panic in her eyes. "It won't be a…?"

"I don't see how it could be anything but human," he assured her, though he had doubts of his own. "I would appreciate it if you would let me know when it's born," he murmured, and vanished from her sight.

Skye was pregnant with his child. It was, he thought, a miracle. Since being turned, he had never considered the possibility of fatherhood, not in the future, not in the past. He had assumed that being turned had permanently nullified that option whether he was human or vampyre. Now the woman he loved was pregnant and she hated him. Not that he could blame her. Selfishly, he had refused to call her. It was hard enough not to see her, he couldn't torture himself by hearing her voice when the very sound of it reminded him that she was out of reach.

Vampyres didn't dream, yet visions of Skye had haunted the dark sleep, as did the memory of holding her in his arms, making love to her, being loved in return. Her blood called to him, the taste of it so warm, so sweet, binding them together in a way he had never known before. He loved every inch of her, the silk of her hair, the warmth of her smile, the sound of her laughter. She had loved him as no one else ever had and because he loved her more than his life, he had let her go.

And now he had lost her forever.

But she would never forget him, he thought. Their child would be a constant reminder of the love they had once shared.

She would never forget.

And neither would he.

Lying in her lonely bed that night, Skye wept for the pain she had heard in Wolf's voice. She had heard the loneliness, the regret, and for the first time, she understood why he had left her, why he hadn't called. The hunger that had once been under control was now a constant torment and he was afraid that in a moment of weakness, he would lose control. She knew, deep in her heart, that hurting her would destroy him.

And yet, seeing the pain in his eyes, hearing it in his voice, she thought that living in solitude was also destroying him.

And her, as well.

How long, she wondered, how long until he was in control again? Until they could be together?

She tossed and turned all that night, and in the morning, she knew what she had to do.

Chapter Twenty-Five

Wolf rose with the setting of the sun. He showered and dressed, then stood staring into the distance, wondering why the hell he didn't just let the hunters who had been following him destroy him once and for all. The more he thought about it, the better it sounded. Perhaps he would find relief in death. It was cowardly, true, but it would put an end to his relentless hunger, his loneliness, his constant yearning for Skye, for the memories of the short time they had lived together as husband and wife.

He was about to will himself to Night's End, figuring it would be the best place to find the hunters, when he caught Skye's scent.

She was here, on the front porch.

Hope flared in his heart as he flew up the stairs and opened the front door. "Skye! What are you doing here? Is something wrong?"

"No. I came to remind you that we're married," she said sternly. "As my husband, you have certain responsibilities and I intend to hold you to them. I expect you to support me and our child, to be there with me when it's born, if possible, and to ..."

"Skye!" He pulled her into his arms and into the house. Kicking the door shut, he held her close, unable to believe she was there, in his arms.

"Wolf, I've missed you so. Please don't send me away."

"I don't want to."

"Then don't."

He closed his eyes as the scent of her blood teased his senses. This was never going to work.

But he didn't let her go.

"Maybe if you drink from me before you go hunting, it will help. I know you're afraid of losing control, but I'm willing to take that chance."

"I'm not." Taking a step away from her, he raked his fingers through his hair. "You don't know what you're saying."

"It's worth a try. I don't want to live without you. I can't bear it any longer. I tried to hate you, to forget you, but…" She rested her hand over her swollen abdomen. "How can I"

He stared at the tears shining in the depths of her eyes. How could he send her away? Maybe she was right. Her blood had always eased his hunger, calmed the urge to kill. He wasn't sure why, but it had strengthened him like no other.

Turning on his heel, he went to the closet and pulled out a silver-bladed knife with a wooden handle that he had taken off of a hunter.

Skye looked at him, one brow raised, when he handed it to her. "What am I supposed to do with this?"

"I'm going to test your theory. If you're wrong, if I don't stop after a moment or two, I want you to drive that into my back."

She stared at him in horror. "No way!"

"Not into my heart," he said with a faint smile. "Unless you want to. The pain of it will stop me."

Skye stared at the wicked-looking knife, wondering if she would be able to stab him to save her own life and that of their child.

"What do you say?"

She blew out a deep breath, then nodded. "All right."

"No matter what happens, remember that I love you," he murmured as he swept her hair out of the way and lowered his head to her neck.

She froze as she felt his tongue brush her skin, the prick of his fangs as he bit her ever so gently. Pleasure unfurled within her as he drank from her. One swallow. Two. Three. "Wolf…"

A low growl rose in his throat as he lifted his head. "Sweet," he muttered. "So damn sweet."

Her gaze searched his. "Are you all right?"

"More than all right, love. You?"

She smiled up at him, a dreamy look in her eyes. "I'd forgotten how pleasurable that can be."

"So, have you forgiven me?"

She looked thoughtful a moment, sighed dramatically, and said, "I guess so."

"Have you seen a doctor?"

"Yes."

"And everything's all right?"

"As far as I know."

He ran his hand lightly over her belly. "I can't believe it's true." His eyes grew wide. "Did you feel that?"

"Of course. Isn't it amazing?"

Drawing her into his arms, he buried his face in the wealth of her hair, too choked up for words. With his preternatural powers, he could smell the blood in the child's veins, hear the rapid beating of the baby's heart. It was the sweetest sound he had ever heard. "Skye?"

"Yes?"

"Never mind."

"Is something wrong?" she asked and then she knew what he wanted. Because she wanted it, too. Taking him by the hand, she asked, "Which way is the bedroom?"

Sweeping her into his arms, he carried her up the stairs and into a large room with a king-sized bed and a large fireplace. "Are you sure it's safe?" he asked, as he laid her gently on the mattress. "I don't want to hurt you. Or the baby."

"The doctor said it would be okay for another month or two."

A glance started a fire in the hearth. As if by magic, their clothing disappeared and they were wrapped in each other's arms, getting to know each other as if it were the first time. His hands were gentle as he caressed her, whispering that he loved her as he rained kisses on her brow, her cheeks, her eyelids, her breasts.

The passion between them burned hotter than the flames in the hearth as he sheathed himself within her velvet softness and fulfilled her every fantasy.

Wolf gazed at the woman sleeping in his arms. After making love, he had taken her out for dinner and dancing and then they had come back here. They had talked for hours and then they had made love again.

He couldn't stop looking at her, couldn't believe she was here. She had always been beautiful, but never more so than now, when she was carrying a new life beneath her heart. It humbled him to think that she had forgiven him, that she had trusted him enough to come here to confront him. That she had forgiven him for his callous behavior. But he'd done it for her, surely she understood that, knew that the only reason he had stayed away was because he'd been so afraid of hurting her, when her blood had been the answer the whole time.

Perhaps it was more than her blood, he thought with a smile. Perhaps it was her love that made the difference.

He stayed by her side until his senses warned him the sun was rising. Brushing a kiss across her lips, he covered her before leaving the room. Using his preternatural power, he strengthened the protective wards around the house before he sought the safety of his lair.

As the darkness dragged him down into oblivion, he wondered if she would still be there when he woke that night.

CHAPTER TWENTY-SIX

When Skye woke, it was mid-afternoon and she was famished. While collecting her scattered clothing, she wondered where Wolf had gone. She had hoped to wake in his arms.

After dressing, she grabbed her shoes and padded barefooted down the stairs. The living room was empty, as was the rest of the house. Surely he hadn't gone out. So where was he?

The house had a kitchen, complete with all the necessary appliances. They all looked brand new, untouched and unused. Of course, there was no food in the house, only a bottle of very old red wine and a couple of crystal goblets.

Stepping into her shoes, she wondered if her car was still outside. When she'd come here last night, she hadn't intended to stay longer than a few minutes and she had left her handbag and her keys in the car.

She would have left Wolf a note, but she couldn't find paper or pen. With a shrug, she left the house, relieved to see her car still parked at the curb, her handbag still on the floor.

Sliding behind the wheel, she drove home, smiling all the way.

"Should we follow her?"

The man in the passenger seat nodded. "The vampyre's house is warded against intruders. We'll never get in there. Damn, Ryan, this might be the break we've been waiting for. She spent the night with him, after all."

"She can't be his woman, Macklin. She's pregnant."

"A housekeeper, maybe?"

"A sheep?"

Macklin laughed. Sheep was a term the hunters used for humans who willingly let vampyres feed on them.

"He's not going to surrender to save a housekeeper's life," Ryan muttered. "Or a sheep's."

Macklin shrugged. "Follow her anyway. We've got nothing better to do."

"Did you hear about what happened to the hunters who killed Gray?"

"Yeah. Nasty bit of work, that."

"They never knew what hit 'em. Do you think it was Wolf?"

"I don't doubt it for a minute. Don't lose her. She turned down the next street."

"I saw her," Ryan said irritably. "Dammit, man, I'm not sure I want to tangle with Jason Wolf."

Skye hadn't paid any attention to the black SUV behind her until it turned down her street and stopped at the corner.

Thinking she was getting paranoid, she pulled into the driveway and made her way to the front door. Glancing over her shoulder, she saw the SUV coming down the street. It slowed as it came abreast of her house. There were two men inside.

She felt a sudden chill when she met the passenger's gaze. She quickly unlocked the front door and hurried inside. After engaging the deadbolt, she stood there, wondering if they had been following her. It certainly seemed that way. But if so, why? Oh, Lord, were they hunters? The cold hand of fear knotted around her insides. Were they looking for Wolf? Had they followed her to his house?

She paced the living room floor for several minutes, her thoughts chaotic. What should she do?

Grabbing her phone, she called Wolf, praying that he would answer.

The ringing of his phone pierced the darkness that engulfed him. Clawing his way to consciousness, he growled "What's wrong?"

"I'm sorry to bother you but I think someone is following me."

"I'll be right there." He didn't bother to change clothes. It took him a moment to shake off the dark sleep. Moments later, he materialized in Skye's living room.

She let a little gasp of surprise when Wolf appeared, seemingly out of nowhere, wearing only a pair of dark gray sweatpants, his hair uncombed. For a moment, she forgot why she had called him. All she could do was stare. Rumbled and sleepy-eyed, his feet and chest bare, he exuded the very essence of virile masculinity.

"Skye?"

"What? Oh. Two men in a black SUV followed me from your house. I'm probably over-reacting, but..." She shrugged. "It scared me."

"You were right to call me." Taking her in his arms, he threaded his fingers through her hair, then pressed a kiss to the top of her head. "Do you want me stay here?"

"Can you?"

He nodded. All he needed was a dark room. "Sit down and rest. I'm going to reinforce the wards around your house."

"Wards?"

"Vampyre protection. Sort of like vampyre witchcraft."

Skye sat on the sofa, watching curiously as he walked around the room, murmuring words in a foreign language. She felt an odd shift in the air as he moved from room to room, then went up the stairs.

Wolf paused in the nursery doorway. She had been busy while they were apart, he thought, as he noted the changes she had made. He was going to be father. It was hard to wrap his mind around the idea.

When he finished warding the rest of the rooms, he went to the second floor landing and peered over the rail. "Skye? I'm finished. If it's all right with you, I'm going to rest in the closet in the guestroom."

"Do you need anything?"

"No." He blew her a kiss before taking refuge in the dark.

Skye crossed her arms protectively over her belly. She told herself there was nothing to be afraid of as long as Wolf was in the house. He would protect her and their child.

But she couldn't forget the speculative way the man in the SUV had looked at her.

❖ ❖ ❖

Wolf came awake with the setting of the sun. For a moment, he stayed where he was, listening to the sounds of the house. The TV was on. Skye was in the kitchen fixing dinner. The smell of tomato sauce and basil stung his nostrils.

Rising, he raked his fingers through his hair before padding down the stairs.

He found her standing at the stove, stirring a pot of spaghetti sauce. Moving up behind her, he slid he arms around her waist and nuzzled her neck. "Good evening, wife."

Her lips twitched in a smile as she turned in his arms. "Good evening, my husband."

His gaze drifted to her lips, lingered on the pulse throbbing in the hollow of her throat. "Let me?"

She tilted her head to the side, giving him access to her throat, closed her eyes as she felt his fangs gently pierce the skin. Warmth engulfed her, that amazing sensual heat that made her forget everything else.

He ran his tongue over the tiny wounds before raining kisses along the length of her neck as his hands skimmed over her breasts, her belly. "Skye?"

"Yes," she whispered.

Reaching around her, he turned off the burner, swung her into his arms and carried her swiftly up the stairs. A moment later, they were lying naked in each other's arms.

She ran her hands over him, reacquainting herself with the hard planes of his chest, the way his muscles bunches and flexed when she touched him. When he caressed her, his hands were gentle as they aroused her.

"Taste me, Skye," he whispered.

"What?"

"Drink from me."

She reared back, eyes wide with shock. "Now? You want me to drink your blood now? Why?"

"Will you do it? For me?"

She stared at him, her whole body throbbing for release. And then, overcome with curiosity, she nodded.

Sitting up, he bit into his wrist.

Curiosity turned to revulsion and then alarm when she saw the dark-red blood oozing from the twin punctures. Was he going to turn her into a vampyre?

"It will bind us closer together," he said, his gaze intense. "That's all."

One taste, she thought. What could it hurt? She licked a bit of blood from his skin, felt it burn through her, disgusting at first, and then strangely pleasant when he urged her to taste a little more.

And then he was pressing her down on the mattress again, his body rising over hers, his tongue and his lips teasing and tempting.

Skye let out a muffled cry of wonder as she aroused him in turn. It was like making love for the first time, she thought incredulously. She felt everything he felt, knew that he was equally aware of her every thought, her every desire. It took their love-making to a whole new level, until they no longer seemed like two, but one.

She cried out as he brought her to the edge of fulfillment again and yet again until, at last, his love poured into her and she closed her eyes, sated and complete as never before.

Later, lying in his arms, she asked, "How is it possible?" Her fingers trailed over his chest. "I could feel what you were feeling. I knew what you were thinking as clearly as I knew my own thoughts."

"It's because we've shared blood." He rested his hand on her rounded belly, felt his heart swell as the baby moved beneath his palm.

"Will it always be this way from now on?"

He nodded. "We are truly bound to one another now." He chuckled when her stomach growled. "Why don't you go have your dinner while I dress and go search for mine?"

They had never been closer than they had been while making love, Skye mused as she sat at the kitchen table. And yet, at this moment, with both of them satisfying their hunger in vastly different ways, they had never seemed farther apart.

She stared at the small pool of spaghetti sauce on her plate. It reminded her of blood. How would she explain Wolf to their child? He would wonder why his father never shared a meal with them, why he was absent during the day, even on weekends. A young child couldn't be trusted with the truth. Maybe it would be wiser to never reveal Wolf's secret.

She told herself to stop worrying. They had years to figure it out.

Where had Wolf gone hunting? Had he found … prey? No sooner had the thought crossed her mind than she knew. He was in the neighboring city, with a woman in his arms.

It was necessary. She knew that. He had to have blood to survive, especially now, when he needed it more than ever. She would just have to get used to it. Accept it. But she couldn't stop the wave of jealousy that swept through her at the thought of his drinking from another woman.

She had just finished cleaning up after dinner when he appeared in the kitchen.

"Skye. There's nothing for you to be jealous of."

"I know. I just can't help it."

"Maybe it's a good thing," he said with a wicked grin. And then he grew serious. "If it will make you feel better, your blood is helping much more than I expected. I'm already needing to feed less often."

"I love you, Wolf."

"No more than I love you."

She sighed as he wrapped her in his embrace. She had to believe that, somehow, it would all work out.

Skye was on edge for the next few days. She tensed every time a strange car drove down the street, started at every loud noise. She stayed inside the house, not going out even in daylight unless Wolf was with her.

She knew she was over-reacting, that her fears were making everything worse, but she couldn't forget what it had been like to be held by those hunters. She had never felt so helpless or so frightened, not only for herself, but for Wolf. And soon they would have an infant to think about.

Skye wasn't the only one on edge, although that was little comfort. She was mortal, weak, unaccustomed to being in danger. The fact that Wolf was visibly worried, as well, only intensified her own anxiety.

And yet, a week passed, two, and there were no further incidents, no strange cars cruising slowly past the house.

Gradually, she relaxed. When the weather was nice, she often sat out in the backyard, book in hand, enjoying the last of the warm weather, and a glass of lemonade, dreaming of the day when she would hold their baby in her arms.

Was it a boy or girl? Not that it mattered. This child was likely to be the only one she would ever have.

The days grew colder, the nights longer, which meant more time with Wolf.

Winter came in a flurry of storms. She felt like she grew bigger every day. The baby's movements came more often and grew stronger.

Wolf rarely left Skye's side except to feed. He hadn't detected any sign of the hunters, and yet he knew they were out there, waiting. But waiting for what?

He glanced at Skye, sitting before the fire. She was big with child now. The thought of being a father filled him with excitement one minute, and dread the next. He didn't know a darn thing about babies.

His gaze moved over her. They hadn't gone anywhere in the last two weeks and he felt a sudden urge to get out of the house. "Skye?"

"Hmm?

"What do you say we go to a movie?"

He saw the hesitation in her eyes, watched her gather her courage. With a smile, she said, "I'd like that."

By the time they were ready, it was raining. "If you don't want to go out in the rain, I can transport us there."

"Good idea." No one could follow them that way.

Wolf put his arm around her and the next thing she knew, they were at the theater.

He paid for their tickets, bought her a bag of popcorn, a candy bar, and a drink.

Skye laughed when he insisted they sit in the back row.

"What's so funny?" he asked

"It reminds me of when we were in South Dakota. You always sat with your back to the wall."

"Always a smart move when you're a wanted man." He swore under his breath, wishing he could call the words back, knowing they would remind her that he was being hunted.

He transported the two of them home when the movie was over. He was tired of waiting for whoever was hunting him to make their move.

Maybe it was time he went hunting them.

CHAPTER TWENTY-SEVEN

Starting the next night, Wolf prowled the city after he fed. He visited every goth club, every vampyre hangout, every nightclub frequented by the hunter-slayers, to no avail. Thinking they might be holed up in one of the nearby towns, he spent several nights searching them as well, and found nothing.

And then, late one night, a hunter found him. The scent of the man's aftershave was Wolf's only warning. He managed to block the man's thrust, so that the knife missed his heart and plunged low into his left side. The hunter had dipped the tip of the blade in silver and it burned its way through skin and flesh as it skidded along his ribs.

Cursing, Wolf yanked the blade free and drove it into the hunter's chest. The man dropped to the ground, dead before he hit the pavement.

Wolf searched the hunter's pockets for identification, but all he found was a crumbled sheet of paper. Unfolding it, he read the words and read them again.

CALLING ALL HUNTER-SLAYERS.
A PARTY WHO WISHES TO REMAIN
ANONYMOUS HAS OFFERED A
ONE HUNDRED AND FIFTY THOUSAND DOL-
LAR REWARD

FOR THE HEAD OF THE VAMPYRE KNOWN AS WOLF.
TO CLAIM THE REWARD SEND
AN EMAIL TO THE ADDRESS BELOW

Wolf cursed as he pressed a hand against his side, which was bleeding profusely thanks to the silver. Jaw clenched against the pain, he willed himself to his lair to get cleaned up. His side ached like the very devil as he bandaged it up. If not for the silver, the wound would have healed in a matter of minutes, but it would take a day or two for the silver to work its way out of his system. He was about to throw the flyer away when he thought better of it and shoved it into the pocket of his jeans, thinking he might send an email to Anonymous and find out who was willing to offer such a hefty reward for his head.

Once he'd changed his clothes and washed the blood from his hands, he willed himself back to Skye's, praying she would have gone up to bed when he got there.

He found her asleep on the sofa, her cheek resting on her hand. Pregnancy agreed with her, he thought, as he brushed the hair away from her face. She looked more beautiful than ever. Even asleep, there was a glow about her. Her breasts were fuller, heavier, her belly swollen with their child.

He was debating whether to carry her to bed or cover her with a blanket when her eyelids fluttered open. She smiled when she saw him. "You're late."

"Yeah. Sorry."

"Did something happen?"

"Why would you think that?"

Skye sat up, fully awake now, and he realized she had cried herself to sleep.

"Did you need me for something while I was gone?" he asked, troubled by her tears.

"No, I'm fine." Her gaze moved over him, eyes narrowing when she noticed he wasn't wearing the same shirt he'd had on when he left. "How about you?"

He dropped into the chair across from the sofa, hands dangling between his knees. "I ran into a little trouble."

"I know. Are you all right?"

"What do you mean, you know?" And even as he asked the question, he knew the answer. He had neglected to block the blood link between them when he left the house.

"Wolf. How badly are you hurt?"

He swore softly.

"Wolf?"

"A hunter took me by surprise." He shrugged. "It's not serious. Just painful."

"I know. " Reaching out, she touched his side. "I felt it."

"I'm sorry, love."

"Is that why you were so late?"

He nodded. "I went to my place to get cleaned up. I didn't want you to know what happened."

"Please don't shut me out of your life, Wolf. We're in this together now, no matter what."

Dropping to his knees in front of her, he took her hands in his. "What did I ever do to deserve you?" He kissed the backs of her hands, turned them over and kissed her palms.

The touch of his lips sent a shiver of delight through her. When she yawned, he lifted her into his arms and carried her up the stairs to bed. He undressed her as if she were a child, tucked her under the covers, then shucked his own clothing and slid in beside her.

"Go to sleep, love," he murmured. "You're sleeping for two now."

Skye was surprised to wake in the morning and find Wolf sleeping beside her. Always before, he had left her before sunrise, seeking the darkness of the closet in the guestroom.

In the bright light of day, the gauze bandage around his middle looked very white against his copper-hued skin. She stared at the dried blood that stained the cloth and thanked the Good Lord that it wasn't worse.

She stayed there a long time, content to look at him, admiring the strong line of his jaw, the sensual curve of his lips. His hair was long and straight, as black as night. She longed to run her hands over the width of his shoulders, down his muscular arms, to follow the dark line of hair that disappeared under the sheet. Instead, she curled her hands into fists to keep from touching him, afraid she might wake him.

A faint smile curved his lips. "Feel free to touch me, sweetness. Anytime, anywhere, any place."

"I thought you were asleep!" she exclaimed.

"Your lustful thoughts roused me," he said, his voice a sexy growl. "Now, what are you going to do about it?"

"What would you like me to do?"

Turning onto his side, his gaze met hers. "Read my mind, love," he whispered, his voice low and whiskey-rough. "Read my mind."

It was much later when Wolf sought his rest in the guestroom closet.

Skye made the bed, took a shower, dressed in a pair of comfy old sweat pants and an over-large tee shirt, and decided to do the laundry. She added Wolf's clothes to the pile and carried the load downstairs. Soon, it wouldn't be safe for them to make love, she thought sadly.

She was about to drop his jeans into the washer when she heard a rustling noise. She searched his pockets and pulled out a wrinkled sheet of paper. Curious, she unfolded it, let out a gasp when she read the message. Someone had put a bounty on Wolf's head! And what a bounty it was. One hundred and fifty thousand dollars.

Good Lord, every slayer in the country must be looking for him.

The flyer was the first thing Skye mentioned when Wolf rose that evening. Waving it in the air, she said, "What are we going to do about this?"

He looked at her, one brow raised. "We?"

"We're in this together, remember? What affects you, affects me, too."

"Yeah. I've been thinking about that."

Skye glared at him. "If you're thinking of leaving me again, you can just forget it."

Laughing softly, he took her in his arms. "Leave my pregnant wife? What kind of monster do you think I am?"

"You're not a monster."

"Right. Listen, I have a vampyre friend who lives in a small castle in England. What would you think about going there for a while?"

"A castle? Seriously?"

"It's been modernized with heat and electricity, flush toilets, the Internet, TV, all the modern conveniences. My friend's been out of the country for a while, so we'll have the place all to ourselves."

"Is there a city nearby? A doctor?"

"There's a small town not far away. And I can always transport us anywhere you want to go."

Skye grimaced at the thought of packing for another trip and closing up the house again, but if it would get them away from the hunters, it seemed a small price to pay.

It wasn't until they were ready to leave three nights later that it occurred to her that there were probably vampyre hunters in England, too.

It was raining the night Wolf transported them to the English countryside. The first thing he tried to do was set protective wards around the castle and the grounds to keep intruders out, but the vampyre who owned the castle had already done so, making his of no effect.

Skye was immediately enchanted by the castle. It reminded her of something out a fairy tale. Smaller than she had expected, it was made of native stone, with turrets at the corners and double doors intricately carved with a coat of arms. As Wolf had said, the interior had been renovated so that it was modern and yet managed to keep the feeling of the Old World. There was an up-to-date kitchen downstairs, a living room, dining room, family room and bathroom on the first floor. The second floor held four large bedrooms, all with walk-in closets and their own bathrooms. The master bedroom was enormous. It was the only one that was furnished.

"It was originally two rooms," Wolf explained. "They knocked down the wall between two of the bedrooms."

It was lovely, with a large, four-poster bed, an antique dresser and matching bedside tables, and a walk-in closet big enough to be another bedroom. A small, round table and two chairs stood in the corner near a leaded window that overlooked a rose garden. Adjoining the bedroom was a bathroom and a sitting room. A thick, gray carpet covered the floor.

Coming up behind her, Wolf slid his arms around her waist. "What do you think?"

"I love it. Is it for sale?"

He chuckled. "I'll ask my friend the next time we talk."

Turning in his arms, she asked, "How do you happen to be pals with someone in England?"

Wolf shrugged. "I've done a bit of traveling in my time. I met Braelyn eighty or ninety years ago in London. She was being chased by a couple of hunters and I helped her out."

"She?"

Uh-oh. "Did you think there weren't any female vampyres?"

"I never gave it any thought. Just how friendly are the two of you?"

Well, damn, he thought, maybe coming here hadn't been such a good idea.

"Wolf?"

"Don't go there, Skye. It was a long time ago. I saved her life and she was grateful. Last I heard, she was happily married. End of story."

She glanced pointedly at the bed.

Cupping her chin in his hand, he turned her head toward him. "She didn't own the castle back then. We were never here together, but if being here is going to bother you, we can go back home."

"I'm sorry, but I can't help being jealous of every other woman you've ever known."

"I told you, I've never loved any other woman the way I love you. Nothing will ever change that, sweet Skye. Believe that if you believe nothing else."

While Wolf rested the next day, Skye explored the castle. The living room was beautiful, the walls white, the carpets a dusty rose. Leather couches, flanked by glass-topped coffee and end tables, faced each other in front of a red brick fireplace. A half-wall separated the living room from a family room, which held a large, wall-mounted TV over a long, low bookcase crammed with books, CDs and DVDs. A large, black leather sectional faced the TV. The tables in here were English Oak.

The kitchen was ultra-modern, which she thought was odd, considering the owner was a vampyre, and then she shrugged. Maybe a previous owner had modernized things. Maybe the vampyre was married to a mortal. She was surprised when she peeked into the side-by-side refrigerator and found it stocked with food. The freezer held meat, frozen vegetables, and ice cream. Now that really was odd.

She wondered if Wolf had stocked the kitchen as she fixed a fried egg sandwich and a cup of coffee for breakfast.

She sat at the table for a long while after breakfast, one hand resting on her swollen belly as she considered names for the baby.

Later, after loading the dishes into the dishwasher, she started upstairs to unpack, and then changed her mind. Wolf was asleep and she didn't want to disturb him.

Padding into the family room, she searched the bookshelves. Wolf's friend had a varied taste in reading, everything from philosophy and religions of the world to the most popular fiction of the day – romance, mystery, dystopian, fantasy, time travel, and historical novels—to poetry, mythology, folklore, and witchcraft.

She found a romance novel by one of her favorite authors and settled onto the sofa to read.

It started to rain in the afternoon and the sound soon lulled her to sleep.

Wolf woke a little before sundown. Eager to see Skye, he didn't bother to dress, but padded barefooted down the stairs to the living room where he found her sleeping on the sofa, the novel she had been reading lying on the floor beside the couch. He grinned when he picked it up and saw the title – *Vampyres Among Us, A Love Story*.

Setting the book on the end table, he brushed a kiss across her lips. "Hey, sleeping beauty, wake up."

She stirred, a smile curving her lips as she reached for him. "There really are vampyres among us," she murmured as she drew him down beside her.

"Indeed." Wrapping her in his arms, he said, "I'd think you'd have enough of the real thing without needing to read fiction."

"It's a sweet story," she said, her hands stroking over his broad back and shoulders. "I hope it has a happy ending."

She rained kisses on his chest, his neck, claimed his mouth with her own, her desire for him rising as he caressed her in turn. Desire burned in his eyes as her hands grew bolder.

"I'll have a happy ending if you keep that up," he said, his voice low and husky as her hands continued their exploration.

She laughed softly, gasped as he turned the tables on her, his tongue like a flame as it dueled with hers. A thought dispatched her clothing and then he was rising over her, his eyes hot as he carried them both over the edge.

⚜ ⚜ ⚜

They showered together, then Wolf dressed and went hunting while Skye prepared something for dinner.

Wolf returned a few minutes after she finished and they sat together on the sofa, his arm around her, her head pillowed on his shoulder.

"This is nice," she said. "I'm glad we came."

"Yeah, me, too."

"So, how do you like English food?"

Wolf stared at her. English food? And then he grinned. "Since you asked, English blood tastes pretty much the same as anybody else's."

"So, all blood tastes the same?"

"More or less. Although yours is sweeter and infinitely more satisfying."

"In most of the books I've read, vampyres have no reflection. But you do."

"It's an old myth. In ancient times, people believed vampyres had no soul, and since they were dead, they couldn't cast a reflection."

"You must have a soul," she said adamantly. "You're not dead!"

He shrugged. "Some people would disagree."

"The dead don't walk and talk. Or make mad, passionate love," she said with a seductive smile. "They don't breathe." She placed her hand over her belly. "Or create life."

"Ah, sweetness, I wasn't a vampyre when you conceived."

That brought her up short. "You're not really dead, are you?" she asked in a small voice.

"No, love. Only alive in a different way." Drawing her closer, he whispered to her mind, assuring her that he was, indeed, very much alive, even though he had often wondered if it was true.

Chapter Twenty-Eight

Wolf went hunting late that night after Skye had gone to bed. He hadn't been to England in a century. He prowled the streets of Snowshill, which was the closest village to the castle. Snowshill Manor, a sixteenth century house had once been owned by Charles Paget Wade, a collector of unusual furniture, as well as musical instruments, toys, bicycles, clocks, and samurai armor. These days it was a favorite tourist spot, along with the Snowshill Lavender Farm.

But tonight he was interested only in prey and it was damn scarce. Deciding the hunting was sure to be better in London, he transported himself to The Coach and Horse, a Tudor-style pub. Built in the 1770s, it was thought to be one of the oldest surviving taverns. He arrived just before closing. Standing at the end of the bar, he surveyed the room and chose his prey – a middle-aged couple. A word shielded the three of them from the sight of the other patrons as he moved up beside the pair. He mesmerized them with a look and quickly took what he needed. When he finished, he wiped the memory of what had happened from their minds, strolled out of the pub, and into the foggy night.

A light rain was falling when he reached the castle.

He had thought to find Skye asleep, but she was sitting up in bed, looking worried.

Sitting on the edge of the mattress, he asked, "What is it?"

"I woke up and you were gone."

He toed off his boots, stood and peeled off his shirt. "I needed to ... to go out."

"Oh." There was no need to ask why. "Where did you go?"

"To London."

Her eyes widened. "London?"

Removing his trousers, he slid under the covers and drew her into his arms. "Would you like to go there?"

"Do you mean it?"

"Sure."

London. She could hardly wait.

Wolf rose shortly after noon. The day was overcast and cloudy, which suited him perfectly. With his preternatural power, he transported the two of them to London. As always, traveling from place to place took no more than a thought.

Skye decided traveling by vampyre was the perfect mode of transportation. It was quick and saved her from walking long distances or having to rent a car.

They made a trip to Tower Bridge, wandered through the Tower of London, visited Hyde Park, and then went to Westminster Abbey. It was an amazing place. And so old. Built by Henny III in 1245, it had a long, long history. It had once been the home of Benedictine monks. Known as the coronation church since 1066, it was the final resting place for seventeen monarchs, including Mary, Queen of Scots.

They viewed paintings and breath-taking stained glass, textiles and books and sculptures. It would have taken hours to see it all. After two hours, Skye was ready to sit down, so Wolf whisked her to a café where she indulged in fish and chips and sticky toffee pudding while Wolf enjoyed a glass of red wine.

Sighing, she pushed her plate away. "I can't eat another bite."

"I could use a bite," Wolf said, stifling a grin.

"Of pudding?" she asked, stifling a grin of her own.

He scowled at her, his gaze moving to her throat. "Don't I get any lunch?"

"Later," she said, glancing at the people strolling past the outdoor café. "When we're alone."

They wandered through the city for another hour and then Skye was ready to go home. "Can we come back another day? I still want to see St. Paul's Cathedral and Buckingham Palace."

"Sure, love. Whatever you want."

"You're spoiling me," she said as he wrapped her in his arms. "You know that,

don't you?"

"It is my pleasure to do so," he murmured, and transported the two of them back to the living room in Braelyn Castle.

Still holding her close, he murmured, "Now?"

With a nod, Skye brushed the hair away from her neck, closed her eyes as he gently bit her. She sighed as a wave of sensual warmth spread through her. Did he have any idea how pleasurable his bite was? And even as the thought crossed her mind, she wondered if those he preyed on thought so, too.

❧ ❧ ❧

Two nights later, Wolf surprised her with front-row tickets to *The Phantom of the Opera* for the following evening.

"How did you get these on such short notice?" Skye exclaimed. "I've always wanted to see this play! I went on the website for Her Majesty's Theater this morning and it said tickets were sold out for all performances for the next six weeks."

"A little vampyre magic," he said, pleased by her reaction.

"You really are amazing!" Throwing her arms around him, Skye kissed him soundly "Thank you!"

"You're welcome, love."

"It's a perfect excuse to wear my new dress!" She'd bought it a few weeks earlier but hadn't yet had occasion to show it off. Of course, considering she had bought it at a maternity shop, it wasn't what you'd call sexy. But it was a beautiful shade of blue. She just hoped it still fit.

Wolf grunted softly. Usually, it was the woman who said she had nothing to wear, but in this case, he was the one in need of something suitable. All he'd brought with him were jeans and shirts.

He grinned when Skye's stomach rumbled. "Dinnertime, love?"

"I think so." She knew a moment of regret that they couldn't enjoy a meal together, but he made up for that in so many other ways. Like tickets to Phantom!

"Listen, I'm going to the city to pick up a jacket and a pair of slacks while you have dinner. I won't be gone long."

"All right." She lifted her face for his kiss and then he was gone.

❧ ❧ ❧

After feeding, Wolf went to Harrod's, credited with being the most famous menswear store in the world. Strolling through the aisles, he didn't doubt it. They carried all the major brands – Gucci, Tom Ford, Armani, Burberry. He finally settled on a suit by Tom Ford and a shirt by Armani. As long as he was spending a small fortune on clothes, he decided to treat himself to a new pair of boots, as well.

Leaving the store, he strolled down the street, looking for a quiet place where his sudden disappearance wouldn't be noticed, when he sensed he was being followed.

He paused in front of a store window, his gaze darting left and right. The hunter had stopped a few yards away. He was a tall man, in his thirties.

Muttering an oath, Wolf turned down the next street, dropped his garment bag behind a car and dissolved into mist.

The hunter followed him, walked halfway down the block and stopped, glancing right and left, obviously wondering where his quarry had gone.

Moving up behind him, Wolf resumed his form and wrapped his arm around the man's neck. "Looking for me?" he growled.

The hunter froze.

"Who are you?"

"Nobody."

Wolf's arm tightened around the man's throat. "You can do better than that."

"You know who I am."

"Are you hunting vampyres in general? Or me in particular?"

"Just hunting."

"You're lying. I can smell it on your skin."

"All right, I recognized you from an old photo."

Wolf frowned. A photo? What the hell? "Hoping to claim that hundred and fifty grand?"

"I was."

"Have you got that photo on you?"

The man nodded as best he could.

"I want it."

The hunter reached into his coat pocket, pulled out a wrinkled sheet of paper, and held it up.

Wolf took it from his hand and swore again. It was a flyer from the museum. What the hell was it doing in England? He might be dressed in contemporary clothing, but his hair and face looked the same.

Damn. Someone had put two and two together, he thought, as he stared at the flyer before tucking it into his pocket. "Are there any other hunters in the city?"

"Not that I know of." The man swallowed hard. "What now?"

Leaning forward, Wolf hissed, "How would you like to be a vampyre?"

The man shuddered when he felt Wolf's fangs graze his throat. "I've got a wife! A family."

"If you ever want to see them again, you'll give up hunting and get the hell out of England, If you come after me again, I'll turn you and you can find out what hunting is like from the other side."

Grabbing the garment bag with his free hand, Wolf gave the man a shove, then disappeared from sight.

Skye was loading the dishwasher when Wolf appeared in the kitchen. "Did you have any luck?"

He held up the garment bag. "I'm going to go put this away," he said, then frowned when he saw her expression. "What's wrong?"

She tapped the corner of her mouth with her finger.

Lifting his hand, he wiped the smear of blood from his lips. "Sorry." Muttering an oath, he headed for the bedroom.

Skye stared after him. She didn't know why the sight of blood on his mouth upset her so. She knew he was a vampyre. The knowledge was always there, in the back of her mind, no matter how hard she tried to forget it.

She pressed a hand to her belly when she felt the baby move. She wondered again what life would be like for their child, having a vampyre for a father. Would Wolf try to hide what he was from their son or daughter? Or explain it to them when they were old enough to understand? Would they be able to have anything resembling a normal life? It seemed impossible. There would always be hunters eager to take his head. And if he decided not to reveal his true nature, how would they explain it when she and their child grew older and Wolf did not?

Sinking down on one of the kitchen chairs, she blinked back her tears as she stared out the window and wondered what was to become of them.

Upstairs, Wolf cursed the vampyre who had turned him as he listened to the doubts and fears flooding Skye's mind. Yet, even as he cursed the one who'd made him, he knew that if she hadn't turned him, he would have died long ago. He never would have met Skye, and for that, he owed his maker a debt of thanks, should he ever meet her again. Was his sire still alive? he wondered. Odd, that she had never

SECRETS IN THE NIGHT

come looking for him. Did she ever wonder about the man she had turned and abandoned? Ever wonder what had become of him, if he still lived?

He had never turned anyone. Having been turned against his will, he couldn't imagine doing the same to anyone else, yet even as the thought crossed his mind, a little voice in the back of his head asked what he was going to do when Skye started to age. Would he simply let her grow old and die when he had the power to keep her forever young? He thrust the thought aside, then wondered if she had ever thought about it. She seemed impressed with his preternatural powers. Had she ever thought of what it would be like to have them for herself?

With a shake of his head, he made his way downstairs to see if he could banish her doubts.

Skye looked up when she felt Wolf's hands on her shoulders.

"Are you all right?" he asked.

She shrugged.

Taking the chair across from hers, he reached for her hands. "Don't give up on us, love," he said quietly. "Don't give up on me."

She gazed into his eyes, those beautiful, midnight-blue eyes that could sometimes be as hard as flint but were now filled with love and tenderness.

"I love you, Skye. I know it's not easy for you, being with me. and I can't promise it will get any easier." His gaze searched hers. "If you want to end things between us, I'll understand."

She had been thinking of that very thing, but seeing the love in his eyes, hearing it in his voice, she knew she couldn't leave him. "It can't be easy for you, being with me," she said matter-of-factly. "I must seem weak and cowardly."

Wolf shook his head. "Darlin', you've the bravest woman I've ever known."

Rising, he lifted her to her feet and drew her into his arms. One kiss banished her fears and her doubts. There was no telling what tomorrow would bring. But for now, there was nowhere she would rather be than here, in Wolf's arms, his voice whispering that he loved her as he caressed her, arousing her until all thought was gone and there was only Wolf taking her to bed, covering her body with his... proving his love with every touch, every kiss...

CHAPTER TWENTY-NINE

Skye woke with a smile on her face as she remembered the ecstasy of the night past, felt her smile grow even wider when she saw Wolf lying beside her. Was there ever a more handsome man? Her gaze moved over his bare chest, down his washboard abs, to where the sheet covered the rest of him.

She studied his profile, his fine, straight nose, his sensual mouth, his dark brows. He had hair any woman would envy—thick and straight and black as ink. Just looking at him made her heart skip a beat. Lordy, he was the sexiest man she had ever seen and he was all hers.

With a sigh, she slid out of bed. For a moment, she stood there, her hands spread over her ever-growing belly. Closing her eyes, she tried to imagine what the baby would look like. Would it have Wolf's black hair, deep blue eyes and coppery skin? Or would it take after her? Boy or girl? She had always hoped for a daughter, but now, looking at Wolf, she hoped for a son that looked just like his father.

Scuffing into the bathroom, she took a long hot shower, wishing Wolf was there to wash her back.

The thought had no sooner crossed her mind than he was standing behind her, taking the soap from her hand.

It was the longest, most wonderful shower of her life as his soapy hands aroused her to fever pitch. Somehow, the running water made it even more sensual. Her legs were weak by the time he brought her to fulfillment. He turned off the water, toweled her dry, helped her into her robe.

"Go get some breakfast, love, and take your sexy thoughts with you so I can get some rest."

He winked at her, gave her an affectionate swat on the rump, and gallantly bowed her out of the door.

Skye found herself smiling every time she thought about their lovemaking. She had never made love standing up before. Never made love in a shower. It was like making love in the rain, she thought, with a grin. Maybe next time it rained, she would drag him out into the backyard.

After breakfast, she read for a while, watched a little TV, and took a nap.

When she woke, Wolf was sprawled at the far end of the sofa, watching her.

"Wake up, sleeping beauty. We don't want to be late for the play."

In spite of her new dress, Skye felt frumpy when she saw Wolf. He wore a black suit that looked like it had been made for him. It clearly emphasized his broad shoulders and long legs. He looked like a matinee idol, or maybe a rock star, she thought, while she just looked fat.

"Stop that," he scolded. "You're not fat, you're pregnant with my child and you've never looked more beautiful."

She knew it wasn't true, but she loved him the more for saying it.

A thought whisked them to Her Majesty's Theater in London. Skye stared at it in awe.

"The theater opened in 1897," Wolf remarked. "The name of the theater changes with the gender of the monarch. It was His Majesty's Theater until 1952, when Queen Elizabeth took the throne. The Phantom opened here in 1986."

It was an impressive building, Skye thought as they made their way through the crowd to their seats.

Excitement thrummed in the air as the curtain went up and the auctioneer offered one item after another – a poster, three human skulls, a musical box with the figure of a monkey in Persian robes. Chills ran down her spine as the orchestra began playing the Overture. The anticipation grew palpable when the chandelier began its slow assent.

Skye soon lost herself in the story, in the haunting strains of the music of the night. Her heart ached for the phantom, so in love with a woman he could never have, being forced to live in the shadows, hated and feared by one and all. She understood his anger, his jealousy, wept when he sent Christine away with the man she loved. Skye thought it cruel of Christine to return. How his heart must have leapt with hope that she had come back to stay when it was only to return his ring. Tears filled Skye's eyes as he declared his love for Christine one last heartbreaking time.

They remained in their seats for a short while after the final curtain call, waiting for the crowd to disperse.

Wolf wiped away her tears with the pads of his thumbs. "Did you enjoy the play?"

"I loved it and I'd love to see it again. But it was so sad." Tilting her head to the side, she regarded Wolf. "You remind me of the phantom."

"Oh? How so?"

"You hide your real face in the dark, too, and your true nature from the world."

"Perhaps I should buy a mask and a long black cloak and carry you away to my underground lair."

"Do you have an underground lair?" she asked, intrigued by the idea.

"I did once, long ago."

"Really?"

"Really. I rested there by day and hunted by night."

"Such a lonely life."

His hand cupped her cheek. "I was lonely for centuries, my sweet, until you walked into my life."

The next day, Skye ordered the soundtrack for the "Phantom of the Opera" and for days after that, the music of the night filled the castle.

Her dreams were often filled with images of Wolf as the phantom, carrying her down, down, down to his underground lair where he ravished her time and again. Sometimes the dreams were so real, she woke certain that they hadn't been dreams at all.

As her pregnancy advanced, it seemed she was either hungry or tired all the time. Wolf treated her as if she were made of spun glass. He fulfilled her every whim, her every wish, no matter how foolish.

As she neared the end of her eighth month, Skye started to worry about the baby's birth. She read book after book about labor and delivery, which did nothing to ease her fears. What if the baby came during the day, when Wolf was asleep, and she couldn't wake him up? She told herself she'd never had trouble waking him before, that he had often roused during the day when she was thinking of him.

She had been seeing a doctor in the town regularly, but he wasn't an obstetrician. He assured her that the town midwife, Margaret Mary Lee, had years of experience and would be more than happy to deliver the baby. And Wolf assured her that if anything went wrong, he could have her at the hospital in London in the blink of an eye.

Wolf took her to meet Margaret Mary a few days later. After talking to the midwife for almost an hour, and after Wolf's repeated reassurance that he could have her at the hospital in nothing flat, she told herself to stop worrying. But she couldn't help it. This was her first child, and likely the only one she would ever have.

It was a bitterly cold night when her labor began. At first, there was only a slight discomfort, which rapidly grew stronger and more intense.

Wolf sat beside her until her contractions were regular and getting closer together and then he went to pick up the mid-wife. He had liked the woman the first time he met her. She was a few years past middle-age, with dark-gray hair and twinkling blue eyes.

"Don't you be worrying," Margaret Mary said as she put on her coat and grabbed her umbrella. "I've never lost a mother or a babe. Or a father," she assured him with a smile. "And I don't intend to start now."

Wolf nodded. Capturing her gaze with his, he said, "You're not going to remember how we get to the castle.

Instead, you will remember that we drove there. Just as you will forget how I bring you home again. Do you understand?"

She nodded, her gaze slightly unfocused.

Wrapping his arm around her waist, he transported them to the castle's entrance. "Here we are," he said, opening the door for her.

He took her umbrella and her coat and put them aside, then led her up the stairs to the bedroom.

Skye smiled faintly when the mid-wife bustled toward her. "How far apart are your contractions, dearie?"

"About four minutes."

"Excellent." Turning to Wolf, she said, "We'll need some hot water, clean towels, a diaper and a blanket for the baby." Pausing, she frowned. "And a clean sheet."

With a nod, Wolf went to gather the things she'd asked for.

He flinched when he heard Skye cry out as the contractions came harder and faster.

Returning to the bedroom, he stood beside her and took her hand. "Look at me, sweetness," he said. "Listen to the sound of my voice."

Face twisted with pain, she looked into Wolf's eyes, felt the hurt fade as she listened to his voice speaking to her mind, taking away the discomfort, the fear. Lost in his thrall, she heard only the mid-wife speaking to her, telling her when to push, until she heard the welcome sound of her baby's first cry.

With a word, he released her from his thrall.

"Tis a healthy little lad," Margaret Mary said, swaddling the child in a blanket. "Have a look-see and then I'll clean him up."

Skye stared at her son, surely the most beautiful child ever born, with a thatch of thick black hair and dark-blue eyes she knew would stay that color. "He looks just like you," she murmured. "What shall we name him?"

"Anything you want."

"Adam," she said, with a faint smile.

"Any particular reason?"

"It's a good, strong name."

"Adam." Bending down, he brushed a kiss across her lips. "I love you, wife

A short time later, with mother and baby cleaned up, Margaret Mary laid the baby in Wolf's arms.

He stared down at his son, felt his heart swell with an emotion he had never experienced before, a sense of love and wonder stronger than anything he had ever known. He gazed at Skye, sleeping now, and knew he could never repay her for the gift of her love, or for the miracle of his son.

CHAPTER THIRTY

Skye sat in the easy chair in the living room, her son at her breast. She stroked his hair, his cheek. Hard to believe he was already a week old. She had called her parents the day after his birth to let them know they were grandparents, and yes, Mom, I married the father.

She glanced out the window. Wolf had gone hunting about an hour ago and she was beginning to worry. He wasn't usually gone so long. When she felt a shift in the air, she smiled, thinking he had returned.

But instead of her husband, a tall, dark-haired woman clad in a pair of tight-fitting jeans and a gauzy red shirt materialized in the room.

"Well, hello," the woman drawled. "You must be Wolf's woman."

"Yes, I must be," Skye said, holding the baby closer. "And you'd be …?"

"Braelyn."

She was lovely, Skye noted, with honey-brown hair, light brown eyes, and a figure that looked just about perfect. She looked to have been in her late twenties when she was turned, but with vampyres, you couldn't always tell.

"Where is Wolf?" the vampyre asked.

"He's … out."

"Ah," Braelyn said, a knowing look in her eyes. "We haven't hunted together for a long time, Wolf and I," she remarked wistfully. And then she smiled. "Perhaps I can find him."

And so saying, she vanished from the room.

Skye muttered a very unladylike oath at the thought of her husband and that woman hunting – or doing anything else – together.

Wolf had just sealed the wounds in his prey's throat when there was a shimmer in the air and Braelyn materialized at his side.

"Hey," he said, "what are you doing here? I thought you were spending the winter in Bavaria."

"I got bored." She gestured at the woman standing between them. "Mind if I have a bite?"

Wolf shrugged. "Just don't take too much. Unlike you, I like my prey to walk away."

"Spoil sport." She drank quickly, sealed the wounds in the woman's neck, and stepped back as Wolf released the woman from his thrall and sent her on her way.

"Where's Rothchild?" he asked.

A shadow passed behind her eyes. "He's dead. Killed by a hunter last week. They seem to be everywhere these days. I barely escaped with *my* life."

"I'm sorry."

"Charles and I were together a long time." Linking her arm with Wolf's, Braelyn glanced up at him. "Your woman is lovely. Is she prey?"

"No." He fixed her with a hard stare. "She's my wife and off limits. And that goes for the baby, too. Are we clear?"

"Very. But...a baby, Wolf? Did you steal it?"

"It's mine."

"Yours!" She stared at him incredulously. "How can that be possible?"

"I took her into the past with me and..." He shrugged. "Nature took its course."

"A baby," she murmured. "Do you think she'll let me hold it?"

"Only if I'm in the room." He liked Braelyn well enough, but she had no scruples about who she preyed on. She had often told him the blood of babies was the sweetest of all. There were few things he hadn't done as a vampyre, but drinking from a child was one of them.

"You won't mind if I stay in the castle for a few days, will you?" she asked. "It's the only lair I have in England."

"It's your place. I can hardly throw you out."

"I was only asking to be polite," she said with a laugh.

"I'm going home," he said. "I've been gone too long. Are you coming?"

"I don't think so." She grinned at him, displaying a flash of fang. "I'm still hungry."

Skye was pacing the floor when Wolf returned to the castle. He had the feeling they were about to have a heated discussion he would rather avoid.

"Did she find you?" Skye asked, her voice icy.

Here it comes, he thought, as he nodded.

"She's very pretty."

"Yes, she is."

"You used to hunt together."

He nodded again.

Skye perched on the edge of the sofa, her hands clasped tightly in her lap. "When you told me about her, you made it sound like you saved her life and that was the end of it."

"We saw each other a couple of times after that. We hunted together because it was safer to hunt in pairs back then."

"You said she was happily married. Where's her husband?"

"He was killed last week."

"Oh. I'm ... I'm sorry." Very sorry, she thought. But not for the usual reason. It meant Braelyn was single. And perhaps hunting a new husband.

Wolf blew out a sigh, thinking he might as well get the worst of it out in the open. "She'll be staying here for a few days."

Flabbergasted, Skye stared at him. If there was one thing she didn't need, it was an unattached, sexy, female vampyre parading around the house.

"She asked if it was all right," Wolf said. "I couldn't very well tell her no. It's her place, after all." Taking Skye's hands in his, he lifted her to her feet and into his arms. "She doesn't mean anything to me, sweetness. I've never loved anyone but you and I never will. You're my whole life."

With a sigh, Skye laid her head against his chest. She had to stop feeling jealous. Wolf had done nothing to give her cause to worry.

But as soon as she felt stronger, they were going home.

Skye sat in the family room the following night, rocking the baby to sleep. She could hear Wolf and Braelyn talking in the living room, their voices too quiet for her to catch what they were saying.

It was late, she thought, yawning. The vampyres had returned from hunting a couple of hours ago. She wished Braelyn would go out again or go to bed. Or leave the country. The woman made her uncomfortable. Every time Braelyn glanced her way, Skye couldn't shake the feeling the vampyre was wondering what she tasted like. Nor did Skye like the way the woman looked at Adam. Earlier, she had held her breath when Braelyn asked to hold the baby, praying Wolf would refuse. He hadn't, but he had stayed within arm's length the whole time Braelyn held Adam.

Smothering another yawn, Skye eased out of the chair. She hated to leave Wolf and Braelyn downstairs alone, but she could barely keep her eyes open. She didn't bother saying goodnight, just made her way up the stairs to the bedroom. Laid the baby in the cradle.

And slammed the door.

Wolf materialized inside the room seconds later. "Something tells me you're unhappy here," he said dryly.

"Did you read my mind to find that out?" she snapped, unable to hide her irritation.

"No need. The slamming door pretty much said it all."

"I want to go home, and I want to go now."

"Why don't we leave tomorrow afternoon? You look like you're about to fall asleep on your feet. And we need to pack our belongings."

Skye glanced around the room. They had bought a lot of things for the baby, not just clothes, but a lovely, hand-carved cradle, blankets, clothing, a few stuffed toys, bottles, a changing table.

He was right, darn it. Nodding, she checked to make sure Adam was covered, kissed his downy cheek, and climbed into bed, clothes and all. She was asleep as soon as her head hit the pillow.

Wolf removed her shoes, eased her out of her jeans, sweater and underwear, and slipped a nightgown over her head, then pulled the blankets over her. He wasn't much help with the baby and he was sorry for that. Maybe when they got back home, he would hire someone to look after the house and do the laundry so Skye would have more time to rest.

When he went downstairs, Braelyn was gone. He opened his senses, but she was nowhere in the house. She had always had an insatiable appetite. No doubt she'd gone out for a midnight snack.

Leaving the house, he went into the backyard, sighed as the night wrapped him in her arms. He loved the night, the darkness, the silence, although with his preternatural hearing, it was never totally quiet. The sound of a falling leaf, the slither of a night creature across damp earth, a bird stirring in its nest, he heard them all, a midnight lullaby.

He was about to go back inside when a scream rent the stillness.

A thought took him into the bedroom. For a moment, he stood frozen at the sight that met his eyes – a splash of blood on his son's neck, Skye pinned to the bed under Braelyn's weight, the vampyre's fangs at her throat, Skye's face as pale as the ivory pillowcase beneath her head.

With a war cry that would have made his Lakota ancestors proud, Wolf sprang forward, trapped the vampyre's head in his hands and broke her neck. And because there was always a chance she would rise again, he reached into her chest, ripped out her heart, and tossed it into the hearth.

A word, and a fire sprang to life. It devoured the heart immediately.

"Skye!" He pulled her into his arms, dread replacing his rage. She was pale, so pale, her breathing shallow, labored. "Skye, dammit, don't you dare die on me."

Her eyelids fluttered open. "The ... baby ..."

Wolf glanced at his son. He wasn't badly hurt. Apparently, Skye had stopped Braelyn before she did any real damage. "Don't worry, love, he's fine."

But she wasn't. He was losing her. Her heartbeat was so faint he could scarcely detect it, her lips were turning blue.

"Skye, can you hear me?"

She tried to speak, but couldn't form the words.

Skye, I'm going to turn you.

No ...

I can't lose you. Forgive me, love.

And if she wouldn't forgive him, what then? He brushed the thought aside as he robbed her of the last of her life's blood, then bit into his wrist and held it to her lips, willing her to drink.

If she wouldn't forgive him, he would live with her hatred.

He wiped the blood from Adam's neck, licked the tiny wound Braelyn had made, ensuring that it would heal without a trace. Cursing himself for leaving Skye and the baby alone even for a short time, he cradled his son in his arms, and sent a heartfelt prayer of gratitude heavenward, thankful that he had been nearby. Damn Braelyn. She had managed to block her presence in the house. Thank heaven Skye had awakened before it was too late, he thought bitterly. He should have taken Skye and the baby back home the minute Braelyn showed up.

He held his son all through the night, fed him a bottle when he cried, awkwardly changed his diaper.

First thing in the morning, wearing a broad-brimmed hat and sunglasses, he went to see the midwife.

"Why, Mr. Wolf," Margaret Mary said, wiping the sleep from her eyes. "What brings you here so early in the day?"

"Skye's taken ill and can't look after the baby. I need to take her to London for treatment and I was hoping you might look after Adam for a few days."

"I don't know..."

"I'll make it worth your while."

"Only for a few days, you say?"

He nodded, thinking he would compel her to do so if necessary.

"Will you be wanting me to watch him up at the castle?"

"No. You'll probably be more comfortable staying in your own home."

"Yes."

"I'll bring his things by in a little while, if that's all right?"

Back at home, Wolf packed up all the baby's things – bottles, formula, diapers, his cradle, and transported everything to the midwife's home before returning to the castle for Adam.

"Take good care of him," he said, placing the infant in the midwife's arms.

"Sure and he'll be fine. Don't you worry. I hope your missus feels better soon."

"Thanks." He kissed his son's forehead, then walked away.

Returning to the castle, he picked up the vampyre's body, willed himself to the coast, and hurled her corpse into the sea.

Back at the castle, he removed his hat and sunglasses, locked all the doors, then warded the place against intruders, since Braelyn's wards had died when she did. Lastly, he found some clean blankets in a closet and carried Skye and the bedding into one of the guestrooms. After spreading the blankets on the floor, he lowered her gently onto them, then stretched out beside her and surrendered to the dark sleep, wondering if she would despise him when she woke.

Wolf woke as the sun was setting. Propped up on one arm, his gaze moved over Skye. The changes in her appearance were subtle, but there. Her skin was a little more pale than it had been, her hair thicker and more lustrous. Her eyelids fluttered and then she was fully awake.

She frowned when she saw him lying beside her. "What are you looking at?"

"You."

Her gaze moved around the room. "What are we doing in here?" She bolted upright. "Where's Adam? Is he ...?"

"He's with Margaret Mary."

"Why?"

Wolf placed his hand on her arm. "Calm down, love. He's fine."

"I want to see my baby. Now." She rose effortlessly to her feet. And frowned. "It's dark outside."

He nodded.

"Why can I see everything so clearly when there's no light in here?"

"What do you remember of last night?"

"Last night?" Her eyes narrowed. "Braelyn attacked the baby!" She lifted a hand to her neck "And when I tried to stop her, she attacked me. She bit me! I...I don't remember anything after that."

"I destroyed her," he said quietly. "You were dying. I couldn't let that happen."

She stared at him, waiting for him to go on. Afraid for him to go on.

"I couldn't let you go. I tried to speak to your mind, but you were too far gone."

Her gaze probed his, a cry of denial rising in her throat as she read the truth in his eyes. "You turned me." Her voice was flat, filled with accusation.

Wolf didn't move. Her anger filled the room, a palpable presence so thick he could feel it pummeling him like invisible fists.

"I'll hate you for this," she hissed. "Hate you as long as I draw breath."

He nodded.

"I want to go home."

"Not yet. Not until you can control yourself."

She opened her mouth to argue, only to double over, gasping in agony as pain ripped through her, worse than anything she had ever known. "What's...happening?"

"You need to feed."

She glared at him through eyes tinged with crimson. "No!"

"It's the only thing that will ease the pain." He bit into his wrist and held it out to her, knowing his blood would make the pain stop, that after she drank a little of it, the hunger wouldn't torment her as badly.

She tried to ignore the sight of it, the tantalizing smell of it, but it was impossible. Lunging forward, she grabbed his arm. One taste and the dreadful ache in her gut disappeared. And still she drank, reveling in the taste of it, the way it slid smoothly down her throat and filled her with a heady sense of strength and contentment.

Vampyre.

She jerked her head back as the word whispered through her mind.

Vampyre. Nosferatu. Undead creature of the night.

She met Wolf's eyes and burst into tears.

He longed to go to her, to take her in his arms and tell her everything would be all right, but he wasn't sure his touch would be welcome. When he could no longer stand to see her so unhappy, he drew her into his embrace. "Skye, please don't cry. It's won't be as bad as you think."

Not bad? she thought. Never to see or bask in the warmth of the sun again? Never to taste her favorite foods again? Or photograph a sunrise? See a rainbow? Or do any of the hundred other things she had taken for granted?

She lifted a hand to her breast. It felt different, empty, and she realized that her milk had dried up. The thought brought a fresh wave of tears. "I want to see Adam. I want to see my baby."

"It's isn't safe for you to be around him or anyone else until you can control your hunger."

"Do you think I'd ... I'd hurt him?"

"I don't know. Are you willing to take that chance?"

She wiped the tears from her eyes, knew a moment of horror when she saw they were tinged with blood. "I despise you," she whispered.

"I know. And as soon as you can control your hunger, I'll get out of your life."

"It won't be soon enough for me." She should have felt a sense of satisfaction when she saw the pain her words had caused. Why didn't she? It was no more than he deserved. How could he have turned her without her permission?

Anger stirred within her again. She would never forgive him. Never!

She felt bereft when he vanished from the room.

For a moment, Skye stood there, trying to come to grips with what he'd done to her. Leaving the guestroom, she padded downstairs. She wanted to see Adam, had to know he was all right. She was his mother, she would never harm him. But when she tried to open the front door, a wave of supernatural power pushed her away.

She tried all the doors and the windows, but to no avail. She was trapped inside the castle until her lord and master decided to let her out.

Screaming her rage amid a growing sense of frustration, she flew up the stairs to the master bedroom. She stared at the bed – the bed she had shared with Wolf – and before she knew what she was doing, she had ripped the pillow he had slept on to shreds. White feathers drifted through the air like snow.

Laughing, she tore the sheets from the bed, her fingers shredding the material as if it were made of paper. Wandering into the sitting room, she hurled a damask-covered chair against the wall, an exultant cry rising in her throat as it broke in half. She tore the heavy drapes from the windows, slammed her hand on a mahogany table and grinned as it split in half.

Standing in the middle of the floor, hands fisted on her hips, she surveyed the destruction.

And wept.

CHAPTER THIRTY-ONE

Wolf stalked the darkness, Skye's words repeating themselves in his head, slicing into his heart like a knife. *I'll hate you for this. Hate you as long as I live.* How could he blame her? How could he have let her die when he had the power to save her? Even knowing she would be angry, knowing she would despise him for what he had done, he couldn't let her go. He couldn't have lived with himself if he had, but he could live with her hatred. He deserved it, after all. He'd had no right to steal her life. And yet he would do it again in a heartbeat. Better to endure her hatred than never see her again. And as long as she lived, he had hope that, one day, she would forgive him.

Caught up in his own outrage, it took him a moment to sense the unbridled fury radiating from Skye. He let his mind brush hers, felt her anger and frustration as she stormed through the house. He thought briefly of confronting her, but decided it might do more harm than good. At the moment, he was the last person she wanted to see. Knowing that, he decided it was better for both of them to let her vent her frustration alone.

When his temper cooled, he went to see Margaret Mary. "Is everything okay?"

"He's a fine boy," she said, leading the way into a small bedroom where Adam slept in his cradle. "How's the missus?"

"The same. I'm afraid it might be a week or two before she's no longer contagious. Will that be a problem?"

"Goodness, no. My babes are all grown and gone. Tis a pleasure to have a wee one in the house again."

"I don't know how I'll ever repay you for your kindness," Wolf said fervently.

She dismissed his thanks with a wave of her hand. "Just take good care of your missus and don't fret about the lad. He's a fine, healthy boy and no trouble a'tall."

With a nod, Wolf took his leave. His blood was old and strong, his power would be passed on to Skye. With luck, she would soon be in control of her hunger. It had taken him a long time to come to terms with what he was, but he'd had no one to guide him, to help him understand what he was. Skye might hate him, but she was too smart to think she could adjust to her new reality on her own. And she loved their son too much to risk losing control and putting Adam's life in danger.

Wolf raked his fingers through his hair. She would put up with him as long as necessary, and he would savor every minute he spent with her.

He stayed away from the castle the rest of the night, giving her time to adjust to her new world, and hopefully burn through the worst of her anger. She wasn't a fool. He figured once she'd made peace with what she was, once she adjusted to the changes in her life, she would accept it and move on. She might not be happy to be a vampyre, but it had its compensations. She would never grow old, never be sick. In time, she would be able to fight her way through the dark sleep and be awake when the sun was up, though that might take a good long while. It wouldn't happen overnight.

The biggest problem was their son. Young blood was like catnip to vampyres old and young alike, and damn hard to resist. But he was counting on the age and strength of his blood to help Skye over the rough spots. She wouldn't be able to care for the baby during the day, but he could hire a full-time nanny to look after Adam when he couldn't be there. Whether Skye liked it or not, Wolf intended to be part of his son's life. She could hardly object when she was at rest, and that would give him plenty of time to get to know his child.

He told himself it would all work out, that sooner or later she would forgive him. Maybe in a century or two.

Skye wandered through the castle, her mind in turmoil until, gradually, she calmed down. She was a vampyre. She had to face it, accept it, and move on. Wolf could do a number of amazing things – move from place to place so fast as to be invisible. He was strong, invincible. He might live for a thousand years. He could start a fire with no more than a thought, read her mind, enflame her senses with little more than a kiss … She quickly closed the door on that thought.

How long would it take her to learn to use her vampyre powers? To control her hunger?

Where was Adam? Was he all right? Did he miss her? He was still so young. Had he already forgotten her?

What would Wolf say when he saw the wreckage she had caused upstairs? And then she shrugged. Would he care? Braelyn was beyond caring what happened to the place.

Dropping down on the sofa, she put her head in her hands and wept because she missed her son, because her whole life had turned upside down. Because the man she had once loved had turned her into a monster who couldn't be trusted to be near her own child.

The hours and minutes dragged. Shuffling to the window, she pulled back the drapes and stared into the darkness. Gradually, the sky grew lighter and she was overcome with a strange lethargy. Sinking down on the floor, she felt herself falling, falling, into nothingness.

As she had the night before, she woke to find Wolf beside her. And, as had happened the night before, pain engulfed her.

Face impassive, Wolf said, "Go get cleaned up. You need to feed. I'll wait for you here."

For a moment, she stared at him, confused, and then she realized he meant blood, not steak and eggs.

She went into the bedroom – the one where the vampyre had died. The one she had trashed. Trying not to look at the dried blood splattered over the headboard and the floor, she changed into a pair of jeans and a sweater, washed her face and hands, stomped into a pair of boots, and went downstairs.

Wolf stood in front of the fireplace, staring into the hearth. He turned as she stepped into the room. "Are you ready?"

She shrugged.

He regarded her for a moment, then strode toward the door.

With a sigh of resignation, she followed him outside. She didn't want to be a vampyre. She didn't want to hunt or drink blood. But learning how to be a vampyre, to control the hunger raging through her, was the only way to see her son again.

She flinched when Wolf reached for her hand.

"I'm going to transport us to the city," he said.

She knew what he meant but not how it was done. "How do I do that?"

"There's nothing to it. You just concentrate on where you want to go."

Skye nodded. That sounded easy enough. His hand wrapped around hers, strong and familiar.

A moment later they were on a dark street in a rather questionable part of London.

Skye pressed closer to Wolf, her gaze darting left and right. She had never been in such a disreputable place in her life.

He took her into a tavern and led her toward an empty booth. She slid in and he took the opposite seat.

Skye glanced at the other patrons. To her surprise, they were all well-dressed, mostly in black. The women seemed pale. The music was subdued, the lighting dim. A man in a white shirt and black vest stood behind the bar.

"What is this place?" she whispered.

"It's a vampyre bar."

Her eyes widened. Was he kidding?

Wolf beckoned a tall, good-looking man clad in black slacks and a blue silk shirt.

"How may I be of service?" the man asked in a well-modulated voice.

"I have a fledgling who needs to feed."

The man glanced briefly at Skye. "I'm willing, if the price is right."

Wolf pulled a handful of cash from his pocket. The man took it without counting it, shoved it into his pants' pocket, and slid into the booth beside Skye.

"Now what?" she asked.

"He's for you," Wolf said.

Skye frowned, not understanding, and then her brows shot up. "You expect me to bite him?" Except for tasting Wolf, she hadn't bitten anyone since she was five years old and Billy Huston had tried to kiss her at a friend's birthday party.

Wolf shrugged. "It's how Dion makes his living."

This couldn't be real, Skye thought. She had to be dreaming.

"Neck or wrist?" the man asked.

"What?"

"Where do you prefer to feed?" he asked patiently. "Neck or wrist?"

Skye looked at Wolf. "I can't do this." It was one thing to drink from Wolf. She knew him. But this man was a stranger.

With a sigh, Wolf reached across the table, took hold of the man's arm, and bit into his wrist.

The scent of hot, fresh blood rose in the air. It called to Skye. She stared at the bright red blood oozing from the man's arm, felt her fangs brush her tongue. Fangs, she thought absently. I have fangs. And even as the thought crossed her mind, she was clutching the man's arm, drinking the crimson liquid that oozed from the twin punctures. It wasn't as good as Wolf's, but it was warm and satisfying and she drank until Dion said, "Enough!" and jerked his arm from her grasp.

Mortified, she licked her lips.

Leaning forward, Wolf sealed the wound in the man's wrist and gestured for him to take his leave.

Skye sat there, head lowered, embarrassed by what she had done.

And craving more.

Skye was still trying to come to grips with what she'd done and how much she had enjoyed it, when Wolf took her back to the castle. With a curt, "Good night," he vanished from the living room.

She blew out a sigh as she faced another long, lonely night. She didn't feel like reading or watching a movie or doing anything else.

Going upstairs, she gathered up the torn sheets, swept up the feathers as best she could and dumped them into a wastebasket, then carried everything into the sitting room. She piled the broken furniture into a corner with the ruined bedding, and closed the door.

She searched the linen closet in the hallway until she found a clean set of sheets and made the bed, glad she hadn't trashed the mattress, as well.

Returning to the living room, she drummed her fingers on the mantel. "So, all you have to do is think yourself where you want to go," she murmured. Closing her eyes, she pictured herself outside, but no matter how hard she tried, nothing happened. Of course she couldn't leave, she thought irritably. Whatever vampyre magic Wolf had worked to keep her inside was still in place. Oh, how she hated him!

Curling up on the sofa, she stared into the hearth and thought about fire, let out a startled gasp when flames licked at the logs. "I did it!" she exclaimed. "I made fire!"

She fell back against the sofa cushions, wishing she had someone to share it with.

Night after night, Wolf tutored her on how to be a vampyre, how to dissolve into mist, how to shield her presence from others, how to transport herself from one place to another. The first time she did it, she let out an exultant shout. She was free!

Seconds later, he was beside her. "You can't hide from me," he reminded her, his voice emotionless. "I've tasted your blood. You've tasted mine. No matter what form you're in, no matter where you are or how far you go, I will always be able to find you."

"Can I find you, too?" she sked, her voice arctic cold. "Not that I'd want to."

"Only if I want you to," he said, his voice equally cold. "Not that I'd want you to."

Skye recoiled as if he'd struck her. She hated him, she told herself. So why had his words hurt so much?

CHAPTER THIRTY-TWO

E very few days, while Skye was at rest, Wolf went to see
their son. He had never had anything to do with babies,
never even held one before Adam. He'd been unprepared
for the wave of love that had swept over him the first time
he held Adam. And equally unprepared for the overwhelming urge to protect the child from harm. And from the boy's
mother and father, if necessary.

Now, gazing into his son's eyes, he wondered how the
hell a pair of vampyres could raise a child. Sure, they could
hire a full-time nanny to look after Adam during the day
and when they needed to hunt, but what kind of life could
they give him? It would be especially hard on Skye. By the
time she had been a vampyre long enough to be awake during the day, their son would be a grown man, likely with
children of his own. She would miss school plays and awards
ceremonies, little league games and a dozen other activities
unless they were held after dark.

Wolf swore under his breath. The fact that he would be
able to attend these events would likely make her hate him
even more than she did now. Although he wasn't sure that
was possible.

The tension between them was almost unbearable.
Time and again, she had tried to elude him and the fact
that she couldn't only made matters worse.

Her hatred was like a wound that wouldn't heal. He had apologized, pleaded with her to understand why he couldn't let her die, but she refused to listen.

He looked up as Margaret Mary rapped on the nursery door, then stepped into the room.

"He's growing so fast," Wolf said, laying the baby in her arms.

"Aye, they have a way of doing that. He's a bonnie lad."

"You don't mind watching him?"

"Heavens, no! He's never any trouble during the day. Sleeps, mostly." She smiled down at the baby. "'Tis a regular night owl, he is."

"Is that unusual?"

"A little, perhaps. But he seems healthy enough."

Frowning, Wolf took his leave.

"You went to see Adam today, didn't you?" Skye asked, her voice thick with accusation. "You needn't deny it. I can smell him on you." She paused a moment. "Is he all right?"

"Margaret Mary says he is."

"What aren't you telling me?"

He shrugged. "I'm sure it's nothing."

"Nothing? Then tell me."

"She said he sleeps a lot during the day."

"All babies sleep a lot."

"I wouldn't know. Are you ever going to forgive me?"

"I don't know."

"Would you rather I had let you die?"

Her gaze slid away from his. She had asked herself that question a thousand times in the last four months. Most of the time, the answer was yes. She hated what she was, hated not being able to see Adam, hated the blood. Hated Wolf. And yet, no matter how angry she'd been because he kept her away from Adam, she knew he'd done the right thing.

"Skye?"

"Can we go back to your people?"

He shook his head. "Something changed in me when I was wounded. I don't know what it was or why it happened. All I know is I'm different now. I'm not even sure I could go through the cave again, or what I'd find if I did. Although I'm willing to try, if that's what you want."

"Would I be human if I went there?"

"I don't know. Do you want to try?"

"I'll think about it."

"It's time to hunt."

They hunted in a new city every night. It came easy to her now, she thought, as she called her prey to her and mesmerized him with a glance. She told herself she hated what she was doing, but the truth was, she loved it. More than that, she craved it as she had never craved anything else in her life. She had learned when to stop, discovered that not all blood tasted the same. She wasn't sure why. Blood type, perhaps? Or maybe it depended on what her prey had eaten recently. The reason didn't matter.

She loved the strength, the power, the fact that she was never tired. Some nights, she ran through the darkness for no other reason than it filled her with a kind of exhilaration she had never known before. Of course, Wolf trailed behind her, a silent, dark shadow in the night.

Her only regret was that Wolf wouldn't let her see her baby. It was a constant ache in her heart, the longing to hold him in her arms.

Later, lying in bed alone in her part of the castle, she thought about going into the past by herself, although she doubted it would be possible, since she didn't know the words that had carried Wolf from one time period to the other. Plus, he had told her the ability to do so passed from grandfather to grandson. And even if by some miracle she made it, how would she find her way around without Wolf to guide her? How would she earn a living? Who would care for the baby while she rested? How would she protect herself? The Old West was a dangerous place for a woman alone.

Did she really want to be human again? That was the real question.

Surprisingly, the answer was no.

Wolf was aware of Skye's inner turmoil, her every thought. She had learned everything he had to teach her in a remarkably short time. He had allowed her to drink from him on several occasions, knowing his blood would strengthen her. She had insisted she didn't want to drink from him, but he knew she was lying, knew the effect it had on her, deny it though she might.

And when he was certain she was able to control her hunger, at least for a short time, he took her to see Adam.

Anticipation filled Skye's heart as they transported themselves to Margaret Mary's home. The midwife smiled when she saw Skye. "How well you look!" she exclaimed. "No one would ever know you've been seriously ill, and for such a long time."

Skye smiled, careful not to show her fangs. "I feel wonderful."

"Well, don't just stand there, dearie. Come in, I know you must be anxious to see your wee one."

Skye felt an odd shimmer in the air when she crossed the threshold. Funny, the midwife didn't feel it. And then she heard Wolf's voice in her mind.

Some humans aren't sensitive to it.

I don't understand.

I guess I never told you. Thresholds repel vampyres. Her invitation negated it.

Imagine that, she thought, as she followed Margaret Mary into the nursery where Adam lay in his cradle, arms and legs waving as he cooed at the mobile overhead.

Rushing forward, Skye scooped him into her arms.

Margaret Mary beamed at her. "I'll just leave you alone," she said as she backed out of the room and closed the door.

"You've grown so big," Skye murmured, blinking back her tears. "Do you even remember me?" She kissed his cheeks, the top of his head, counted his fingers and toes. He was a handsome little fellow. She glanced over the baby's head to where Wolf stood by the door. No doubt Adam would look just like his father when he grew up.

Wolf met her gaze, his expression impassive. "I'll wait in the other room."

She watched him go, unable to believe he was leaving her alone with their son.

With a sigh, she sat in the rocking chair by the window and filled her eyes with the sight of her son. His eyes were still blue, his hair as black as a raven's wing, his skin a lovely shade of pale copper. He stared back at her, his fingers tangling in her hair, and she felt her heart break.

Standing outside the door, Wolf let his mind brush Skye's. She grieved for the time she had lost with her son, knew a sense of peace when he fisted his tiny fingers in her hair. She loved the baby-clean scent of him, the softness of his skin. A bottle waited on the table beside the rocker and she held it for him, wholly content for the first time since she'd been turned. He detected no sign that the baby's nearness had stirred her hunger or any other emotion save that of a mother's undying love for her child. Perhaps he'd been wrong to keep her from their son. Perhaps a mother's love was stronger than the urge to feed, even for a fledgling vampyre.

Tears stung his eyes and he blinked them away. If she could be trusted with the baby, he would take her home, hire a full-time nanny, and maybe a housekeeper, and get out of her life.

But not out of his son's life. He would visit Adam while Skye rested. And if she was ever tempted to feed on the boy, he could be there in time to stop it.

CHAPTER THIRTY-THREE

"Home?" Skye looked up at Wolf the following night, her eyes sparkling with excitement. "We're going home? Do you mean it?"

"I've taught you everything I can. Let me know when you're ready to leave. I'm going to go let Margaret Mary know."

Home. She couldn't believe it. To sleep in her own bed...Would that be safe? They hadn't run into any hunters here, but they were plentiful back home. She would need a secure lair, especially now, when she wouldn't have Wolf to protect her.

She bit down on her lower lip as tears burned her eyes.

Putting the thought from her mind, she went upstairs and began to pack her things.

"You're leaving?" Margaret Mary stared at Wolf. "So soon?"

"Skye wants to go back to America. She has a house there and she's homesick."

"But..." Tears welled in Margaret Mary's eyes and dripped, unchecked, down her cheeks. "I guess you'll be taking the wee one with you."

"I'm afraid so."

"I'll miss him so much."

Wolf grunted softly as an idea occurred to him. "Would you like to go with us?"

She looked up at him, eyes wide. "Do you mean it?"

"I think we could work something out."

She clasped her hands to her breast. "Bless you, Mr. Wolf. Sure and it would break my heart to have him gone so far away."

"How soon can you be ready?"

"As soon as you need me to be."

"Tomorrow around sundown," he said. "I'll come by for you."

"I'll be ready!"

Skye was ready to go the following night. He followed her upstairs to see if she needed help with anything, shook his head when he opened the door to the sitting room and saw the wreckage inside.

"I knew you trashed the place," he said, "but I had no idea you did such a thorough job. Good thing Braelyn isn't here to see it."

Skye shrugged. "I was angry."

"I can see that. Glad I wasn't in the room at the time," he said dryly.

Wolf locked up the house and warded it against intruders, then they transported themselves to Margaret Mary's.

The midwife opened the door with a smile.

"Are you ready?" Wolf asked.

When she nodded, he captured her gaze with his. "You will not remember what is about to happen," he said, his mind linking with hers.

"I won't remember."

"Nor will you think it odd when we return to America and Skye is gone all day and is only home at night. If anyone asks, you will tell them she works long hours, but you don't know where. I will also be gone much of the time."

"She works during the day and will only be home at night."

"You will look after Adam. You will not invite anyone into the house unless Skye's home, or I am. Is that clear?"

She nodded.

"Do you understand everything I've told you?"

"Yes, Mr. Wolf."

"You won't remember this conversation, or anything else, until we reach Skye's house. You will believe we arrived by airplane and took a cab to the house."

Margaret Mary nodded, her expression blank.

Wolf made a couple of trips back and forth from the castle to Skye's house, transferring their luggage and the rest of the baby's things.

When they were ready to go, Wolf wrapped one arm around Skye, who held the baby, and his other arm around Margaret Mary.

A thought took them through time and space to the living room in Skye's house.

Once there, Wolf released the midwife from his spell. "How did you enjoy the flight?"

"T'was amazing," Margaret Mary said, smiling. "I scarcely remember it."

Wolf caressed his son's cheek. "If you need me, just call."

Fighting the urge to cry, Skye nodded.

"Since our marriage isn't recognized here, there's no need to file for a divorce."

She nodded again, unable to speak past the lump rising in her throat.

Bending down, he dropped a kiss on the baby's head and then, conscious of Margaret Mary's presence in the room, he left the house by the front door.

Outside, Wolf warded the house against any and all strangers and intruders, then willed himself to his own house, praying that Skye's pride wouldn't keep her from calling for help if she needed it.

⚜ ⚜ ⚜

Skye glanced around the room. She had forgotten how big the house was. She gave Margaret Mary a tour, showed her the bedroom that would be hers, then showed her the nursery.

"Tis a lovely place," Margaret Mary murmured as they returned to the living room.

"I hope you'll be happy here with us," Skye said.

"I'm sure I will be."

"Well, make yourself at home. I mean that. Think of the house as yours, except for my bedroom. I'll get you a credit card so you can shop for groceries and whatever the baby might need, and you'll need to open a bank account. I'll be gone days. I was thinking I'd hire a housekeeper, too, so all you'll have to do is look after Adam when I'm not home."

"No need for that, missus," Margaret Mary said. "I'll be happy to do the cooking and the cleaning."

"That would be wonderful. Thank you so much. I think we'll get along fine."

Margaret Mary yawned. "'Tis late. I'll be turning in now if you don't mind."

"Not at all."

Holding the baby close, Skye watched Margaret Mary make her way upstairs. "We're home, baby mine," she murmured, sinking down on the sofa. "We're home."

So why wasn't she happier about it?

The next few days passed quickly and life gradually fell into a routine. Skye slept all day, woke at sundown, and materialized at the front door, as if she was just getting home from work. She played with Adam, gave him his dinner and his bath, and then played with him until he fell asleep sometime after eleven. Pretending to go to bed, she slipped out of the house and went hunting.

Soon after returning home from England, she uploaded all the photos she had taken in the Old West. Dozens and dozens of photos—of the prairie, of antelope and elk and buffalo, a deer and her twin fawns, a black bear scratching its backside against a tree, the rivers and mountains, the town and its inhabitants, the saloons and the whorehouse, the blacksmith, the stagecoaches, the Indian village and its people. And Wolf Who Walks on the Wild Wind. One of her favorite photos was of Wolf on his pinto mare, with the wind in his hair and the hills rising majestically behind him.

Someday, she thought, some day she would write a book about her adventures in the Old West.

She didn't like hunting alone. Always, in the back of her mind, was her fear that she would run into a hunter. But tonight, she was thinking about Wolf, wondering how to mend the rift between them. He had begged her to forgive him several times and she had always refused. How could she go to him now and admit she missed him, and that she loved him in spite of everything?

She didn't see the hunter until he was on her, and by then, it was too late. Moonlight glinted off the dagger in his hand as it plunged toward her heart with amazing speed and accuracy.

Before she could fight him off, Wolf was there. He grabbed hold of the hunter and tossed him aside as if he weighed no more than Adam, then wrapped her in his arms and transported the two of them to her bedroom.

Releasing her, he took a step back, his gaze running over her. "Are you all right?"

She drew in a shaky breath, then nodded. "I think so."

"You need to be more careful. Pay attention to your surroundings. Use your senses. You should have been able to scent his presence before he ever got close to you. Dammit, Skye, if you don't keep your head in the game, you'll lose it."

She looked at him, mute. *Read my mind,* she thought. *Please, read my mind.*

"Skye?" He stared at her, eyes narrowed.

"I love you," she whispered. "Even when I hated you, I loved you."

"Skye!" He pulled her into his arms, crushing her body against his.

If she'd still been human, she was certain he would have broken a rib or two, he held her so tightly. And she wouldn't have cared at all.

"I'm sorry," he said. "I ..."

Covering his mouth with her fingertips, she said, "Don't. Don't apologize. I was wrong for the way I behaved. If things had been reversed, and I could have saved you, I would have done so rather than let you die. I don't know why I was so angry." Going up on her tiptoes, she kissed him hungrily. "Say you forgive me."

"There's nothing to forgive. Do you still want to try going back to the past?"

She bit down on her lower lip as she gazed at her surroundings. And then she shook her head. She wanted Adam to grow up here, where he belonged, to get to know his grandparents, who would be coming back to the States next year. She wanted him to go to a good school, see a dentist regularly, have access to the best doctors. Maybe when he was older, they would go to the cave and see what happened. But for now, she was happy where she was.

Wolf glanced at the bed, then back at her, a question in his eyes.

At her nod, he swung her into his arms and carried her to bed. A thought removed their clothing and then he was touching her, his hands gliding over her while he rained kisses on every inch of her from her head to the tip of her toes. He explored every hill and valley, ran his tongue over her breasts and belly, murmuring that he loved her, adored her.

For a moment, she lay there, reveling in the touch of his hands, his lips, and then she reached for him, measuring the width of his shoulders, trailing her eager hands over his chest and flat belly, running her fingers through his hair, claiming his lips with her own until he rose over her, fully aroused, his eyes blazing with desire as he sheathed himself deep within her and carried her home.

EPILOGUE

Adam grew amazingly fast, the spitting image of his father. He was incredibly strong and fast. His teachers complained that he often fell asleep at his desk, though he was often wide awake at night.

He was eight years old when they received the first of many notes from his teachers saying that all the girls were complaining because he liked to nibble on their necks.

~finis~

ABOUT THE AUTHOR

Amanda Ashley started writing for the fun of it. Her first book, a historical romance written as Madeline Baker, was published in 1985. Since then, she has published numerous historical and paranormal romances and novellas, many of which have appeared on various bestseller lists, including the *New York Times* Bestseller List and *USA Today*.

Amanda makes her home in Southern California, where she and her husband share their house with a Pomeranian named Lady, a cat named Kitty, and a tortoise named Buddy.

For more information on her books, please visit her websites at:

www.amandaashley.net

and

www.madelinebaker.net

Email: darkwritr@aol.com

ABOUT THE PUBLISHER

This book is published on behalf of the author by the Ethan Ellenberg Literary Agency.
https://ethanellenberg.com
Email: agent@ethanellenberg.com
Facebook: https://www.facebook.com/EthanEllenberg LiteraryAgency/

Made in the USA
Monee, IL
31 March 2022

93886280R00164